THE ELEMENTALS

THE ELEMENTAL ORIGINS SERIES, BOOK 6

A.L. KNORR

INTELLECTUALLY PROMISCUOUS PRESS

"Nearly all can stand adversity, but if you want to test a (hu)man's character, give [them] power."
    Abe Lincoln

"Even the most intelligent people tend to seek out evidence that confirms what they already think, rather than new information that would give them a more robust view of reality."
    Think Like a Freak

"And now these three remain: faith, hope, and love. But the greatest of these is love."
    1 Corinthians 13:13

1

PETRA

The Van Allen belt.
    Radioactive electrons.
    Impenetrable barrier.
Plasmapause.

My mind was spinning with the strange terms and vocabulary that had come from Hiroki's mouth over the past two days. He'd also been showing me drawings and animations of radiation belts, particle movement, and...

"You're doing it."

Hiroki's whispered words broke through my reverie and I opened my eyes.

"A complete field," he went on, "and no emission of other radiation."

Holding my palms down and out, the tingling sensation of frequencies ran up my arms. A hot energy spun in the center of my being, connecting my tailbone with the top of my head. Power flowed through me.

Hiroki was barely visible behind a protective barrier, a booth similar to the kind the technician hides in just before they zap you with radiation for a CAT scan. Only Hiroki's head was visible behind the dark glass, and if I wasn't mistaken, his face was alight with surprise. His features were obscured not only by the dark glass, but by the waves of the force-field now encircling my form as I stood in the center of the lab.

The field was visible as a thick wall of shimmering air, the way heat bakes off desert sand at the height of a torrid midday. Hiroki had explained to me that the field was invisible to him, but visible to me due to the proteins in my body called cryptochromes which helped me detect magnetic fields. Whatever they were, learning to use them had been like trying to pin pudding to the wall. But as I got used to my powers, the control I had over them was increasing exponentially. They were getting easier and more natural to wield.

It had dawned on me slowly, like the first of the sun's rays on a crisp spring morning, that my powers increased as my understanding of them deepened. It had been like reaching into what I thought was a shallow pool for a sparkling gem, only to realize that the gem was far away, and it was not in a pool but a deep well. I was learning that my powers were unleashed and controlled not by my body, but by my thoughts and my will.

Still, old habits die hard and it was difficult not to use my hands and arms to make gestures while I executed the tasks Hiroki assigned. Hiroki had likened these hand-movements to a baby's pacifier, explaining that I needed them while I was learning but that I would cast them off as I gained confidence.

Hiroki moved and my eyes followed him. He came out from behind the protective barrier. My heart skittered up my throat and crouched in my mouth like a frightened bird. The old fear was diminishing but it was still there and at times reared its head with ferocity. What if I hurt him? What if it was the kind of hurt that didn't reveal itself right away, but years later showed up in the form of some horrible cancer?

"Hiroki, wait. Are you sure it's safe?"

"You'll just have to make sure it is." Hiroki's voice was cavalier as he closed the booth's door behind him and faced me. He was mere feet from the borders of my force-field. "I trust you, Petra."

He took a few steps closer.

"I hate it when you say that," I grumped, not relaxing my hands. I narrowed my eyes at his approach.

Hiroki reached a hand out.

"Don't!" I closed my fists.

He'd never left the safety of his booth and I had no idea what would happen if he did. The bubble vanished. I felt the energy dissipate. The spinning vortex running through my core stopped immediately.

"It's all right, Petra," Hiroki said softly. "If it wasn't safe, this would have gone crazy." He held up the small Geiger-counter which he'd held so often this past week that it had practically become part of him.

I frowned.

He continued, "But the needle wasn't jumping like before. You did it! I'm proud of you. Now let's try making one that stays intact, the same way you can orbit material and walk away from it, leaving it to rotate indefinitely."

"Are you going to tell me what we'll be using this force-field for at some point?" I tried to deliver my question casually, but it came across as sly. I'd been looking for chinks in Hiroki's armor ever since he'd started prepping me for a project mysteriously labeled Project Expansion.

He gave me a withering look which was not entirely devoid of humor. "You never give up, do you?"

I shrugged but didn't answer, because it wasn't a question.

Shaking his head, he said, "You know I can't tell you anything yet. Jody says you'll just have to wait until we have the Elemental girls. You'll learn the parameters of the project at the same time as them and not a moment before."

I let out a long sigh. It was futile to ask why. I'd tried that already. No dice.

"Ah." Hiroki held up both his index fingers in a comical display of 'Eureka.' "Shall we throw some projectiles? How do you feel about that?"

"At my barrier?"

He nodded and rubbed his hands together with no small amount of glee. "Aren't you curious to see what happens? Besides, the primary missiles are basically foam balls. They're not going to hurt you if they do penetrate."

"Yeah, we start with foam and we graduate to live ammunition."

"I already told you about that, did I?"

I nodded slowly, eyebrows raised. "Sometimes, you do let things slip." In the short time I had been developing and measuring my skills and abilities with Hiroki, I had discovered that inside the consummate professional lived a young boy who loved video games, laser tag, and obstacle courses. This young boy version of Hiroki made his appearance during breakthroughs and just before trying some dangerous new drill.

One of his index fingers returned. "I won't use anything harder than foam until you give me the go-ahead, all right? How's that?"

"I can't ask for better." I waited for Hiroki to disappear inside the booth. Six panels in the gleaming black metal walls of the lab slid open, revealing the stacked barrels of cartoonish-looking guns.

The technology of this lab—Hiroki had explained—had been licensed for millions of dollars to a high-tech gaming and virtual reality park in Japan. It was another of the fringe-businesses that TNC operated under another company name. I wondered what other tech the company had invented and sold and to whom. Governments? Private intelligence agencies? Foreign military? How did they decide who to partner with? It was a world that had become nearly as fascinating to me as archaeology, but I had quickly learned that prying was not going to get me anywhere. It was when I kept my questions to myself that Hiroki would let slip some engrossing and revelatory piece of the TNC story. Just when I thought I was beginning to assemble some idea around the identity of the corporation I was contracted to for a year, I would learn some other startling fact which would change my perception entirely. It was like a multi-limbed creature with each limb operating independently of the others.

At the blinking of the amber light above Hiroki's booth, the spinning vortex inside me hummed to life. With an unnecessary flick of my fingers, the bubble of wavy air fused into existence around me. My force-field naturally put me at the nexus of itself. Its walls passed through the floor of the lab equi-distant to its arch over my head. It had always moved with me, like a shadow. If I shifted side to side, the force-field always kept me at its middle. But was this essential to the force-fields existence? I instinctively felt it wasn't.

"I want to test something before we start." I spoke normally. Hiroki had had to remind me a few times that even though he was in a protective booth, he could hear me as well as if I were standing right next to him.

"Sure, let me know when you're ready," Hiroki's artificially amplified voice said through the sound-system.

Not without effort, I relaxed my hands. With nothing more than intention, giving a mental command that the force-field should stay put, I shifted side to side and saw with pleasure but no surprise that it did not follow me.

I approached the wall of the bubble and put my hand up to touch it. Nothing. No sensation. No, wait. There was a sensation, but it was mere warmth and a delicate tingle. I passed my hand through the wall and then stepped through to follow with the rest of my body. Once on the other side, I turned to observe my force-field from the outside. It looked the same as it did from the inside—just a faint circle, more mirage than anything else. If I hadn't known to look for it, it would be completely invisible, even to my eye.

I turned and caught Hiroki's eye. He looked faintly confused.

"It's there." I made a curving gesture with my hands to show him where the dome was. "I'm outside it!"

He shook his head slowly at me in wonderment.

Stepping back inside my force-field, I felt the tic inside me as it reconnected and once more moved as my shadow.

"Okay, fire when ready," I said.

There was a popping sound as a yellow ball fired from one of the guns. It bounced off my bubble and ricocheted harmlessly against the wall. I cocked my head at the information the force-field sent to the vortex spinning through my center—the frequency of the foam ball. Interesting. Now I had data. The ball rolled a couple of feet before dropping into some unseen channel beneath the floor to get cued up for another discharge.

"Fire another."

A popping sound originated behind me and I spun to watch the next ball explode in a poof of green plastic dust. It shimmered and drifted slowly to the floor, making a pile of green dirt.

"How did you do that?" Hiroki asked.

"Same way I shattered the glass in the cave in Libya," I explained. "I changed the frequency of the force-field to match that of the ball."

"Huh. I wouldn't have thought something made of soft plastic could be destroyed that way. Frequency should be too slow, material too pliable."

I shrugged, feeling a little smug. "You're the scientist. There has to be an explanation."

"Not necessarily," came Hiroki's surprising answer. "We're dealing with a supernatural ability, here. At some point, science becomes irrelevant and the 'super' part takes over. This is when all of my education and knowledge become useless. Your abilities are the way they are, scientifically explainable or not. And not only that..."

I knew what he was going to say. "I'm one of a kind."

Hiroki nodded. "Exactly. As far as we know, there is only one Euroklydon and there can only *ever* be one Euroklydon at a time."

This statement caught me in a thicket of emotions. My mind took me to my recurring dream—the one of the man who looked like me. The man who seemed to be trapped in a world that moved in slow-motion, whose warning was never explicit enough and never came fast enough. The dream was always frustrating. Always confusion. Always disconcerting.

Run.

It was all he ever said—no, mouthed—and my dismay at these dreams was getting old.

Popping sounds pulled me from my musings. Three multicolored explosions of plastic fluff appeared against the walls of my bubble. A fourth popping sound with a higher pitch sent a tennis ball bouncing off; the information about that ball passed through my core like a radio signal. When a second tennis ball followed less than half a second later, it too exploded into shreds of rubber.

I smiled, a little surprised to find that I was enjoying this. "That the best you got?" I crooked my fingers at the booth in a gesture of challenge. "Bring it on, 'Roki."

A loud bang followed my invitation and a metal ball the size of my fist bounced off the force-field to hit the lab wall with a loud crack. When a second identical metal ball fired milliseconds after the first, I was ready for it. There was another loud crack and the ball exploded into a million metal fragments.

"This could get expensive," I said with a grin.

"TNC has deep pockets," answered Hiroki, and his voice also had a smile in it. "What happens if I fire two different projectiles at the same time?"

Before I could answer, he did just that.

The popping sound of a nerf ball firing to my right, accompanied by the much louder bang of the metal ball at the same time, resulted in both projectiles bursting into fragments simultaneously.

"Whoa," said Hiroki. "Cool. Did the force-field do that automatically, or did you have to change something?"

"I heard the sound and knew what was coming. It all happens so fast that it's not really conscious."

"Remarkable."

The shining heat of confidence was steadily growing in me. "You want to try live ammunition, now?" I laughed. "Not that a metal ball wouldn't be considered 'live.' That thing could have taken my head off."

"Can we?" Hiroki sounded disbelieving and ignored my comment about being beheaded.

"Sure."

There was a sound like some faraway engine powering down. A moment later, Hiroki stepped out of the booth.

"Aren't you going to fire something deadly at me?" I asked. "Arrows? Bullets? Bombs?"

"Not here. This lab isn't equipped for it. We'll have to go outside." Hiroki unhooked the small hand-held radio from his belt. At the same time, he flicked a switch on a blue panel in the wall and the door to the lab slid open, letting in natural light.

I followed Hiroki from the lab and stepped onto the metal staircase leading up to ground level.

Hiroki spoke into the radio as we ascended the stairs. "How fast can we get cued up for a live ammo test with the Euroklydon?"

The voice that responded sounded mildly boyish. "Really?"

"Really." Hiroki looked over his shoulder and winked at me as we stepped into the hallway which led to one of the canteens.

"The team has been waiting for this ever since she signed the contract," the voice answered. "Give us twenty to set up."

"Perfect. We'll grab a coffee and meet you in clearing number twelve?"

"Clearing seven has already been pre-approved. I'll send a rover to pick you up."

"Copy that." Hiroki clipped his radio back into place as we entered the canteen.

A low murmur of voices from a group of people at one of the tables grew quieter. I felt several sets of eyes on me and made an attempt to smile at one of the women who wore a fatigue-colored skirt. The corners of her mouth twitched but she quickly looked away.

"The Euroklydon?" I asked as we grabbed coffee at the machine on the counter. "Is that how I'm referred to around here? Not Petra?"

Hiroki nodded, nonplussed, and took a sip of his espresso. "Don't take it personally. It's just easier in this line of work not to get too personal."

"Why would that be, I wonder?" I took my hot cappuccino out from under the nozzle and opened a packet of brown sugar. This was both a sarcastic and rhetorical question. I had already been warned not to foster friendships with the other employees of the TNC field-station.

"Shit happens," Hiroki said, casually.

My brows shot up. It was the first time I'd ever heard Hiroki curse. For brief moments sometimes, I would catch glimpses of the human side of Hiroki, woven through the scientist. A joke, more and more displays of emotion, a new expression on his face. He had been a scientist to me when I'd first met him, but now I saw him as fully human. A man with passions, pursuits, emotions, humor, goals, pride.

Yet, it seemed that the favor was not being returned to the same extent. The other people here didn't even refer to me by my name. The canteen seemed somehow colder and I suppressed a shiver.

Relationships were professional, conversations with anyone save Hiroki were curt and short. In one way, I didn't mind. Given that after a year of working for TNC I planned to study at Cambridge and build a world-class career in archaeology, these relationships had a short shelf-life. In another way, though, the cold professionalism grated on me. I never knew, when encountering a TNC employee, whether I was dealing with a human or a supernatural.

I had once tried to read Hiroki's mind, just for a moment, to see if I could learn something more about the employees at FS11. I hadn't been able to do it. This had left me confused and wondering if I'd lost the ability. But later that same day I had easily read the mind of a clerk at the grocery store. I hadn't wanted to out-and-out ask Hiroki about this because I didn't want him to know I'd tried to use my telepathy on him. As a result, I was left to wonder about what might be stopping my telepathic abilities and who else at TNC had supernatural abilities. So far, the only other confirmed supernatural I'd encountered through TNC was Ibukun, an Inconquo, a Metal Elemental. But she was back home in London, presumably at work for the TNC offices there.

My cell phone buzzed from my jacket pocket. I looked at the screen but didn't recognize the local number.

"Sorry, Hiroki. Excuse me a minute?"

He waved me off so I shot him a grateful smile and moved away for some privacy.

I pressed the talk button and put the phone to my ear. "Hello?"

"Petra Kara?" The voice was a woman's, and familiar.

"Mrs. Shale?" Violet Shale was one of the people who worked at the child services office in Saltford. I hadn't had a call from them since I'd been emancipated.

"You remember me?" she asked.

"Of course, I do."

Mrs. Shale had always been kind to me. She'd often gifted me with books about history, and books full of photographs documenting artifacts found in some of the more popular and spectacular archeological digs. She'd seemed to understand and maybe even share my obsession with archaeology.

"How are you? I understand you had a dig in Libya?"

"Yes, last spring," I said. "It was...an enlightening experience."

"Oh, that's nice. Good for you. I'm happy to see you pursuing your dreams." Something about her tone said that she'd not called to chit chat. "Well, I'm sorry to be the one to tell you this, Petra, but your therapist, Mr. Pierce, he passed away earlier today."

I felt like I'd been slugged in the gut with a bag full of flour. It took me several seconds to find my voice.

"Petra? Are you there?"

"Noel is...dead?" Noel had been by no means elderly, or frail. I had seen him in February and he'd seemed perfectly fit and healthy.

"I'm sorry. He had an aneurysm. An ambulance was called, but I'm afraid he died on the way to the hospital. I'm so sorry, Petra. I know you were close."

"When is the funeral?" My mouth felt like it was filled with sawdust and tears pricked at my eyes. Noel had always been kind to me. He was the only one I had trusted enough to share my secrets with before I left for Libya. I was going to miss him terribly.

"A few days' time. I don't have more information yet, but I'll be sure to call you as soon as I know."

"Okay. Thank you. I'll be waiting." I hung up the phone and closed my eyes against the news. Shockwaves of grief washed over me like breakers on the beach, stealing my breath.

"Everything okay?" I felt Hiroki's hand on my shoulder. "You look a little green around the gills."

I opened my eyes. "Do you mind if we do the ammo test another time? I really need to go home."

2

SAXONY

I took the steps up to Georjie's house two at a time with a grin pasted across my face and my heart beating with excitement. I reached the landing at the Sutherland's front door and turned to wave as my dad drove away in our van. Setting down my duffle bag, I turned to face the door.

I paused, my hands hovering just over the metal door knocker. I bit my lip. I was dying to see my friends and share our summer adventures, but was I going to tell them I was a fire mage? My hand trembled.

The truth was, I still hadn't fully decided. Basil Chaplin, my soon-to-be instructor at Arcturus, a fire mage school near Dover, had been clear that he was strictly against anyone knowing except my family. But I did consider these girls to be family. They were my sisters in every sense except blood. I had never asked Basil directly because I was afraid he'd forbid it and not let me into Arcturus as punishment if I did tell them. What was that saying? It's better to ask for forgiveness than permission? What was the harm if I trusted them? They would never betray me. I didn't doubt that they would pick up on the changes in me, anyway. My strange reflective eyes, my burnt-out voice.

Basil would never know I'd spilled my secret, and what he didn't know couldn't hurt me, could it?

I still hadn't moved. My hand hovered there, immobile.

The door swung open and Georjie stood, holding it wide, her ethereal face alight. "Saxony! I thought I heard someone on the porch, but then it went quiet."

"Hi!" The hairs on my body swept to attention at the sight of her. There was something different about her, but I couldn't put my finger on what. Something in her expression, a kind of *knowing* in her brown eyes.

She stepped out onto the front deck and we hugged each other hard, almost violently.

"Oh my gawd, I missed you so much!" she said into my hair. "I didn't realize just how much. It's so good to see you."

I squeezed her back, enjoying the solid feel of her. I swallowed back the sudden urge to cry. "I missed you too, Georjie."

We stepped back and grinned at one another. Georjie scanned my features intently, a line appearing briefly between her brows. I could guess why—my voice. Our generation (so my father likes to say) relies more on texting than phone calls. Georjie and I hadn't actually talked all summer, and I'd avoided leaving voice texts for anyone. This was the first time she'd heard me speak since Isaia gave me the fire.

"You look great!" I said, taking her in again. Her hair had grown over the summer and was freshly washed and undone, falling over her shoulders in a cascade of beachy blond waves. Her light brown eyes were clear and sparkling. She wore jean shorts and two plain layered tank tops in white and teal. A batch of freckles lay in sprinkles on her cheeks and across the bridge of her nose, a testament to the sunny weather Saltford had been enjoying. She was barefoot, which struck me as odd. I didn't think I'd ever seen Georjie without some kind of footwear unless she was in the pool. Even swimming in the ocean, she'd always worn water-shoes. It was a thing she did.

"You do too." Georjie heaved my overnight bag, throwing it over her shoulder. She stepped into the house and waved me inside. "Get in here."

Stepping into the house, I took a deep breath. It smelled fresh and green and the air felt humid. I looked around the wide foyer for familiar jackets and shoes. "No Akiko or Targa yet?"

"Nope. You're the first." Georjie closed the door.

I toed off my sneakers and peered down the stairs into the basement toward their indoor pool. A warm golden light flickered from the lower level.

"What's going on down there?"

Georjie stepped between me and the sweeping staircase. "It's a surprise. Do you mind waiting? I want to show you all at once. You're going to love it."

"If I *must*," I replied with an eye-roll. "How's Liz?"

Georjie had come home early from Ireland to be with her mom, who had been hospitalized for exhaustion and dehydration. Her mom had made a rapid and full recovery in the three weeks since Georjie had been home.

"She's good. It's weird but her illness was one of the best things that could have happened to us—for our relationship, I mean."

I thought of Isaia and how his affliction had so changed my life. More and more, I believed it was for the better although at the time it hadn't felt like it. I nodded in agreement. "I can understand that."

My gaze fell on a stack of books and papers on the table near the door. A photograph lay half-hidden inside a book, but I recognized the blond hair at its edges. I slipped the photo out from between the pages.

The image was of Georjie but her eyes were filled with a bright white light. Her hair flew up and out, making a blond corona around her head. Behind her was a sea of green foliage. She was wearing shorts and her feet were bare in the soil. It looked like dirt was crawling up her legs. Her mouth was open and her fingers were flexed as though she were casting a spell. Her hands were filthy up to the elbows with dirt, and there was even a smudge of dirt across her cheek and lip. The look on her face was both awesome and frightening. It was amazing what Photoshop could do.

"Wow," I said. "Is this from the photography course you did over the summer? Did they teach you photo-manipulation too?"

"Something like that," Georjie replied with a shy lift at one corner of her mouth. "Mom printed it without asking me. I hadn't meant for anyone to see it."

"Why not? It's beautiful!"

"Thank you," she said.

"Interesting artistic choices here," I said, mimicking our grade nine art teacher who'd been from Turkey and had a strong accent and smoked about four packs of cigarettes a day. "I'm enjoying the filth coating the woman's hands and feet. A clear statement about the dirty deeds of the youth of today."

Georjie snatched the photo out of my hand, laughing. "That was a good impression. She always did sound husky, like a jazz singer." Georjie's brows pinched together as she tucked the photograph back between the pages of the book. "Are you sick, by the way? You sound like you've got a sore throat."

"No, I'm right as rain." I opened my mouth to form some kind of lie as to why my voice was rough and husky, but someone knocked at the door.

We turned, lightning quick, to open it. Targa stood on the front deck, backpack slung over one shoulder. She grinned and my breath felt short. Something about her was *very* different, not in a subtle way like how Georjie was different. Targa's new look hadn't just been a filter over the photo she'd sent of herself and Mira at the gala in Poland.

"D'awwwwwww." Targa wrapped her arms around both of us. "You guys look so beautiful!"

"You too, Targa." Georjie stepped back and we stood side by side, staring at Targa unabashedly. "Like, *really*."

"Yeah," I said. "I mean, you've always been a fox, but *damn*, girl!"

"Uh, thanks." Targa shifted from foot to foot, letting the backpack drop from her shoulder. "Can I come in?"

"Oh, geez. Sorry." Georjie waved her inside and we stood in the foyer, the door still open behind Targa. Georjie and I couldn't take our eyes off her.

"Did you dye your hair black?" I blurted. "And your skin..."

Her skin was so pale, so opaque and flawless looking. I could have sworn she used to have a little acne scar at the tip of her right eyebrow, but it was gone now. I was also sure she'd had a few moles on her arms that were no longer there. I took her hand and examined it. The faint blue veins that normally threaded the backs of her hands were invisible.

"Uh, no..." Targa replied, withdrawing her hand gently. Her brows pulled together the way Georjie's had done only moments before. "Are you fighting a cold?"

I ignored the question. "And your eyes, they're so blue! I have never seen them so bright. Don't you think, Georjie? Come on, back me up here." I elbowed Georjayna.

"Yeah, you do look different, Targa," she agreed.

Targa made a *tsk* sound. "Gone for a couple of months and even your besties forget what you look like."

"You say that as if we don't have photographic evidence that your hair is darker, your eyes are brighter, and your skin is just...different than it used to be." Georjie finally closed the door behind Targa.

"Photos lie," Targa replied smoothly. "The blonde here can tell you all about that."

She peered down the stairs as Georjie and I shared a look over her head.

"No Akiko yet?" she asked.

"Not yet," I replied. "Georjie wants to wait to go downstairs until she gets here. Apparently there is a surprise." I waggled my eyebrows. "Aside from your enhanced good looks."

"Ha ha," Targa said with an enigmatic smile. "How's your mom, Georjie?"

"All good now. She's away at that conference so I've got the place to myself."

The sounds of light footsteps on the front porch reached our ears, and Targa threw the door open as Akiko was reaching for the knocker. Her face split in a wide smile that lit her entire countenance. I didn't think I'd ever seen her look more happy and open.

"Hello, strangers," she said, her voice soft. She stepped inside to be swallowed in a group hug. "Someone smells like jasmine," came her muffled voice.

"That's probably me," said Georjie as we broke apart. "Good nose, you have."

"Jasmine has always been one of my favorite scents." Akiko inhaled. Her discerning gaze fell on Targa and she canted her head. "You look different. Are you wearing colored contacts? And when did you dye your hair? It looks great black."

Georjie and I both gave Targa a *we-told-you-so* look.

Targa rolled her eyes. "Honestly, you guys." Her eyes seemed to search for something, anything. "You took the carpet off the stairs. They look way better as hardwood."

"Thanks! On that note, leave your cell phones at the door and..." Georjie made a 'follow me' gesture with her head and went down the stairs.

Akiko, Targa, and I shared a bemused look, took our cell phones out, and left them on the table by the door.

The humidity and sweet smell grew as we descended the stairs. By the time we reached the bottom, the air had become damp and cloying.

Previously, there had been a hallway with a number of doors leading to various rooms; the pool, two spare bedrooms, a storage and laundry room, and the garage. Now, there was a glass wall partitioning the pool from the ground floor landing. The glass was misted up with condensation and a green blur of plants could be seen through it.

"You've turned it into a greenhouse?" Akiko exclaimed.

At the same time, Targa said, "You changed your pool to saltwater!"

Georjie paused with her hand on the handle of the sliding glass door. She leveled Targa with an amazed look. "How can you tell that?"

"There's no chlorine in the air anymore," Targa answered, sniffing.

She was right. I took a deep inhale. "It smells like a jungle."

I closed my eyes, breathing in the fresh clean scents.

Georjie slid the door back. "That's a pretty apt description. Welcome to the jungle."

She stepped through and we followed her.

The pool was the same shape as before but the room was barely recognizable. Butterflies fluttered from plant to plant and greenery burst from every corner of the room. Blossoms of all kinds and colors dotted a backdrop of lush jungle. The ceiling, which had previously been low and filled with pot-lights, had been lifted and replaced with glass. Trees brushed against the glass ceiling, their branches making crisscrossed silhouettes against the dying evening light.

My eyes were immediately drawn to the tiki torches placed throughout the room. It might have been my imagination, but they seemed to flicker toward us, the tongues of flames inviting us in. Gone were the tiles and plastic sunbathing beds and tables. Moss coated the floor in places. The double sliding glass doors leading out into the yard were open to the warm autumn day.

"I don't understand." Targa's vibrant aqua eyes roamed the floor to the ceiling, following the twisted form of what looked like a fig tree. "There are trees growing in here. I can see the roots." She pointed and I saw she was right. Gnarly roots appeared and disappeared in the soil like some serpentine underwater creature.

"But this is impossible!" Akiko pulled off her socks and walked into the space in her bare feet, toes hugging the moss. "You can't have changed the space this much in the time you've been home. How did you transplant such big plants? How did you break up all that concrete and get rid of it in the time you've had?"

Georjie gave us a secretive smile. "I was so inspired by my Aunt Faith's greenhouse that I asked my mom if we could renovate. It wasn't very hard to convince her. She gave me a generous budget and away I went."

"It's amazing, Georjie!" I stripped off my socks and walked alongside the pool, enjoying the feeling of moss and soil beneath my feet. "I'm surprised Liz let you do all this. The maintenance alone-"

"It's my responsibility." Georjie gestured to a small clearing beside the pool where a patchwork blanket had been laid out. A low table held a stack of glasses, plates of veggies and dip, and jugs of water and juice. The Adirondack chairs which had been around the firepit in the back yard had been moved to a space beside the pool. "Want to go for a swim?"

"Absolutely." Targa hefted her bag.

We changed into our suits and splashed around, getting some exercise and enjoying the enchanting atmosphere.

"So, who's going to start?" I put my feet down on the pool's bottom and stood, water sluicing from my hair. "We've got a lot of catching up to do."

Georjie looked from me to Targa to Akiko, waiting.

"Why don't you go, Saxony?" Targa rested her elbows on the edge of the pool. "I'm surprised you haven't started talking already."

Butterflies spiraled through my stomach and I opened my mouth. No words formed. I didn't know how to start.

"I'll go," Akiko said quietly.

We stared at her.

"I'm pleasantly shocked," laughed Georjie. "Getting info from you is like pulling teeth, and here you are volunteering to go first?"

"This is unprecedented." Targa laughed. "You must really have something to share."

Akiko grinned. "It's difficult to know how to begin..."

I nodded, fully empathizing with her.

She took a breath. "The reason jasmine is one of my favorite scents is because my sister and I used to gather it every spring for our home and our neighbors' homes."

I blinked, thinking I had misheard her. "Your...sister?"

"Yes. I have a sister."

For the space of a few heartbeats there was no sound but the sloshing of water against the sides of the pool.

"Why didn't you tell us?" Targa asked. "If you used to pick jasmine with her every spring, then it means you didn't just meet her this past summer. You've had a sister this whole time and never told us."

Akiko nodded. "Aimi and I were raised together but were torn apart by circumstances out of our control."

"Aimi," Georjie echoed.

"I haven't been able to talk about my life because I've been bound to keep my mouth shut. Until the events of this past summer, I wasn't free to share anything with you. I am sorry for that. But everything is different now."

The words flowed from her lips, relaxed and casual, but their impact was far from casual. Georjie, Targa, and I shared looks of surprise.

I pulled myself out of the pool and wrapped a towel around myself. Georjie followed me and we settled with Akiko on the blanket. Targa stayed in the water but rested her elbows on the side of the pool. She put her chin on the back of her hand, her discerning gaze on Akiko.

"Is Aimi older or younger than you? And when can we meet her?" Georjie folded her long legs beneath her, her towel draped around her shoulders.

"She's older," Akiko said this with an enigmatic smile. "Much older, I think."

"You *think*?" Targa dropped her chin and stared at Akiko. "You *don't know*?"

Akiko shook her head. "I have been trying to think of the best way to share my story without shocking you, or making you think I'm making it all up." She shrugged. "I don't know any other way of doing it than just telling it straight."

I thought back to the moment Isaia had pushed the fire into my body. I couldn't imagine Akiko having anything to tell that was more unbelievable than my own story.

"Just tell us the truth," Georjie said, using the corner of the towel to wipe moisture from her face. "We'll believe you."

"All right." Akiko let out a long breath and then spoke slowly. "The truth is, I am not human and neither is my sister." Her words seemed to echo across the pool and the space. "I share my story with you now because I have to say goodbye and I want you to know why. I want you to know who I am and why I have to go. Why I have lied to you."

My heart began to pound and I was flooded with a confusing tangle of emotions. I found I had to open my mouth in order to get enough oxygen. *Not human? Say goodbye?*

"What are you if you're not human?" Targa sounded so calm that I glanced at her in surprise.

"I am what is known in Japan as an *Akuna Hanta*, a demon-hunter. I was born in 1908. I was conceived to human parents and, as far as I know, I was human until my sister gifted me with my tamashī—a connection to something called the Æether and the heart of my *Hanta* powers."

"You're over a century old?" breathed Targa. Remarkably, she seemed to calmly accept this confession as true.

My throat constricted and the heat of my fire flickered in my belly. If I hadn't been through my own supernatural summer, I would have thought Akiko *was* making this up. Georjie and I shared a glance and I saw my own shock reflected in her face. I had no trouble believing Akiko to have some kind of supernatural ability, but to be over one-hundred years old?

"How?" Georjie asked.

"Perhaps if I show you something, it will help." Akiko opened her right hand out to the side and a bright light appeared in the region of her heart.

Targa gasped, Georjie's hand flew to her mouth, and I blinked in awe, staring at the light.

"This is my tamashī," Akiko explained. "For over ninety years it was in the possession of Daichi, my captor."

"Daichi?" I sent Akiko a questioning look.

"I was never allowed to refer to him as anything but Grandfather," she explained, "and I only learned his true name just this past spring."

I was speechless, but Targa loosed a disgusted sound. "Ugh! I *knew* there was something off about that guy."

"He was your *captor*?" Georjie's eyes reflected the white light of the glow in Akiko's chest.

I stared at it, thinking how similar yet different it looked from my own fire. As we watched, the light began to move. It traveled along Akiko's right arm until it reached her palm. It hovered there for a second before vanishing, making the space seem much darker than before. I blinked rapidly as my eyes adjusted.

"Have you ever heard the term *kitsune*?" Akiko asked.

"Japanese mythology," Georjie answered with a nod. "A girl who can transform into a fox, or something like that."

Akiko nodded. "Aimi is a *kitsune*. She was taken in by my parents before I was born, given a home, taught our language, and cared for. As a reward, when my mother was pregnant with me, Aimi blessed the unborn child with a tamashī. She thought it would give the baby a long life and a keen intuition as well as good fortune. But the tamashī transformed me into a *Hanta*."

"Can we meet Aimi?" I asked.

"She is still in Japan."

"And Daichi?" Targa asked.

"Daichi is dead."

A beat of silence.

"Did you…kill him?" Targa's question was barely audible.

"Of course she didn't kill him!" I blurted. "Akiko doesn't have a killing bone in her body." My eyes flashed to hers as a cold thought occurred. What if Daichi had been a demon? She said she was a demon hunter. Maybe she *had* killed him. "At least for humans you don't. Right?" I added, weakly.

"I didn't kill him. He killed himself with his own sword. The one he sent me to Japan to retrieve."

"Whoa. Okay." Georjie put her palms out. "You need to start from the beginning. I am so confused right now. How and why was Daichi keeping you captive? And why was his sword left in Japan in the first place? And why did he kill himself? And why do you have to say goodbye?" She took a deep breath. "And can I put some dry clothes on before you talk? I'm getting cold."

3

SAXONY

I lay on my stomach on a towel with another draped over my back. I barely noticed the damp fabric against my skin as I stared up at Akiko with my chin propped in my hand. I had no sense of how long she'd been talking; it seemed time was no longer relevant in our little oasis of secrets.

Georjayna sat cross legged at Akiko's feet, one elbow resting on the seat of the Adirondack chair Akiko was sitting in. Georjie had put on a terrycloth hoodie and matching bottoms to keep warm, the pastel green hood was cocked over her head. Tendrils of blond hair spilled over her shoulders and out from under the hood, making her look like an elven character against the lush foliage behind her.

Targa was still in the pool, her chin resting on her forearms. Her otherworldly eyes rarely left Akiko's face. In all the years we had been friends, Akiko had never held our attention for so long or with such a firm grip.

It seemed that years of intrigue and mystery were falling away from Akiko layer by layer, like she was a flower opening slowly to the sun. Even the flickering torches appeared to be listening as she told her tale of the shape-shifting sisters, the fearsome Oni, the wakizashi she went to Japan to retrieve, the Yakuza, and her beloved Toshi. Her family had not died from a contagious illness like she'd once told us, but had gone on living after she'd been taken by Daichi. She even visited their graves when she was in Japan. She also told us about a fellow *Hanta* who had helped her retrieve the sword, a man named Yuudai.

I was dazed by the life story my friend had been forced to keep all these years, but I had no trouble believing her. I recalled Basil mentioning that fire magi were not the only supernatural beings known to him, and we weren't even the most powerful. I wondered if he knew about the *Akuna Hanta*; maybe they were even documented in his dossiers.

From time to time I would glance at Georjie and Targa, watching their faces for traces of disbelief. I found none, and this amazed me too.

When Akiko had explained how Daichi had stolen her freedom, the fire inside me raged and my face flushed with anger. It was a good thing I hadn't known how much she was suffering because with my temper, I would have done something that might have gotten me arrested.

For her part, Akiko did not seem to harbor any ill will toward Daichi or even Raiden, the Yakuza boss who nearly killed her and who would have enslaved her for his own gain. I had thought that Dante was evil incarnate, but he seemed like the Easter bunny next to the Yakuza.

The only time Akiko got emotional was when she spoke of Toshi, of their tender and hopeful love and how it was thwarted.

"I am so ashamed for thinking that my sister had plotted to get me out of the way so she could marry Toshi." Akiko's voice was solemn and heavy. "I will never forgive myself for that."

I heard Georjie sniff and looked over to see her wipe her cheek. She said with a husky voice, "I wish we could have met him. I've never seen you date or even have a crush. You always talked about the guys in school with such disdain, calling them boys." Georjie wiped her other cheek. "Now I understand why."

"You shouldn't punish yourself for thinking your sister wanted Toshi, Akiko." These the first words Targa had spoken in at least an hour. "You never know what people can be capable of."

"Ain't that the truth," I added, thinking of Dante.

"So cynical," Akiko looked from Targa to me. "I'm the centenarian here, not you. Why so embittered?"

It was Georjie who answered. "Saxony fell for a guy who turned out to be a psychopath and I found out a relative of mine was a murderer. But that doesn't explain your cynicism, Targa. Is your mother rubbing off on you?"

"Maybe." Targa's lip lifted in a smile.

"Excuse me? You have a murderer in your family, Georjie?" My jaw was on the floor. "I do not recall seeing any reference to this in your text messages this summer! You've been holding out on us, too?"

Georjie waved me off. "We'll get to me." She looked at Akiko. "So to sum up, you're a shape-shifting demon hunter with the ability to tear an evil spirit from a human body and trap it deep in the earth. You've met another *Hanta*, whose name sounds chillingly like 'you die,' your sister is a fox-shifter who can influence luck, you're actually almost one hundred and ten years old even though you look twelve."

"And she's gone through high school a few times, too," I murmured. "No wonder she's so good at trivia games."

"Don't forget that she can fly higher than a jet-plane and visit the formless void where all spirit originates," added Targa, lifting her head from her forearms.

"And you want to leave us and Saltford for good," I added sourly.

"To go rid the world of demons," Georjie said by way of defense.

"And you can see demons as well as all living beings' connection to the Æther while you're in bird form, by way of a spiraling double-helix shooting up into the sky"—Targa put her fingertips on the crown of her head—"from here."

"Like some ethereal billboard revealing that person's most innermost nature." Georjie took the hood off her hair and pulled her long locks away from her neck.

"And you want to leave us and Saltford for good," I repeated, receiving a comically withering look from Georjie. "What? Isn't anyone else bummed about this?"

Akiko was laughing. "You guys are crazy."

"Is that about the size of it, Akiko?" Targa finally got out of the pool and sat on her hip on the edge with her legs dangling in the water.

"More or less." Akiko nodded.

I sat up on my haunches and put my hands on my knees. "You know you gotta show us, right?" I reached for my glass of cranberry tonic.

"Please shift for us?" Georjie's spine straightened eagerly. She looked as though she was prepared to beg all night if that's what it was going to take. "Please?"

"If you wish."

I almost spewed my drink out at the blasé tone of Akiko's answer. Still so understated. As if we weren't all dying to see her shift. Targa burst out laughing at my snort and attempt to swallow my drink before we all ended up wearing it.

Akiko shook her head at me, smiling. She stood up and took her robe off and folded it. After tossing it behind a thick-leafed plant, she turned and saw Georjie and I share a bemused look.

"For after," Akiko said.

I got it, but Georjie still looked confused.

"'Cause she'll be naked," Targa and I said at the same time.

"Oh...right." Georjie blinked. "Of course. Your clothes don't shift with you."

There was a blurring of Akiko's form and a shimmering of the air around and through her, and suddenly she was no more. Her damp bathing suit fell to the ground in a sodden heap.

A tiny finch the color of a lemon sat on the Adirondack chair, cocking its head at us and observing us through its shining black eyes. It gave a chirp.

"Whoa," Georjie breathed.

I couldn't resist holding a finger out to the little bird. Akiko hopped onto my finger and clutched it with fragile little claws.

The air around the finch shimmered again and a raven the size of a small dog appeared on my hand. I gasped with surprise and turned my hand so she could grip my wrist and balance better.

"How can you change mass like that?" Targa asked.

"Are you kidding me?" Georjie shoved at Targa's shoulder with her foot and sent her back into the pool with a splash. "She just changed into two species of birds before our very eyes and you're asking about *mass*?"

Targa came up laughing. "I can't help it." Targa smiled through the wet hair sticking to her face. She pushed her hair back. "Logistics, you know."

"Logistics, whatever. This is magic."

The crow gave a throaty caw and Akiko took to the air, circled tightly over the pool once, and disappeared into the plants where she'd tossed her robe. I picked up her sodden bathing suit and threw it into the bush.

"Thank you," came the muffled reply.

A moment later, she stepped out of the foliage, tying the robe's belt. She was smiling, but she also looked a bit dazed.

"That was amazing!" I cried as Akiko rejoined our group and sat down. I was bursting with questions, and I wondered if she would shift on command into whatever bird species I asked for. Maybe a dodo bird? That would really throw our biology prof at Saltford High into a tizzy.

But Akiko had her eyes on Georjayna. "What have you got in here, Georjie? Silkworms or something?"

"Silk...what?" Georjie sputtered. "Why would I have silkworms in here?"

"Well you've got something because I can see their connections to the Æther."

Georjayna's smile faded and a look of understanding and wonder crossed her face. It was like drawing back a curtain on a clear blue day.

"How many?" she asked Akiko.

"I didn't count them, but quite a few. Maybe fifty. What are they?"

Targa and I shared a bemused look.

Without a hint of a joke on her face, Georjie answered, "They're faeries."

"They're what now?" Targa's eyes widened.

"Well, to be strictly accurate, they're faerie *cocoons*."

"Could this evening get any weirder?" Targa murmured.

Yes it can. I haven't told my story, yet, I thought. *Just you wait. It seemed sometime in the telling of Akiko's story, I had made peace with telling my own.*

Akiko was nodding her head like nothing was unusual. "Faeries. Cool. Show us?"

Georjayna crawled forward on her hands and knees to a potted plant with distinct trumpet-shaped flowers that I thought might be datura. "There. Can you see it?"

I squinted into the shadows, feeling like an idiot. "Uh...."

Targa bent over at the waist, peering where Georjie pointed. "I don't see anything. What are we looking for?"

Akiko was also shaking her head. "Nope. I can see their connection to the Æther while I'm in *Hanta* form, but I can't see anything now."

Georjie looked disappointed, but not surprised. "I knew Targa and Saxony probably wouldn't see them, but after your story, Akiko, I thought maybe..." She let the leaves close in again and shrugged. "Guess not."

"Faeries? Is this for real?" My faith was being stretched to its limit with this one.

Georjie nodded. "Akiko isn't the only one who had a wild supernatural summer, either. You know that photo you commented on in the foyer, Saxony?"

I nodded.

"It's not photoshopped. That's really me." Georjie took a deep, shuddering breath. "I'm a Wise, a kind of Earth Elemental... I guess. To be honest, I'm still trying to figure out what a Wise is because I can't find anything on them, not even in the memoirs my ancestor left behind. She was also a Wise."

Targa and I stared at her, our mouths agape.

Akiko was listening and nodding as she poured herself another glass of tonic.

Georgie continued, speaking more rapidly. "I don't know if you've ever heard the term before; I hadn't. But I'm not making this stuff up." She held up both palms. "It was the faeries that called me that."

Targa's vivid eyes drifted from Georjie to me and back again, swimming with bewilderment. I felt the same. When Akiko had started telling her story, I was amazed. But now, Georjie too? *What is going on here?*

"But Jasher could see them too," Georjie was saying, "so I knew I wasn't going nuts, plus the whole tree experience just before my mom called," Georjie's hands were flashing around nervously, "and the horrible thing that Mailís did…"

"Georjie, honey." I put a hand on her arm, gently pushing it down before she poked out someone's eye. "Why don't you go back to the beginning?"

"I know I sound like a crazy person," Georjie wailed. "I wasn't planning on telling anyone, except Akiko saw the faerie helix-thingies and…"

"We believe you," said Targa, who had gotten the incredulous look down to mild amazement.

"You do?"

"Of course, we do," I said. "You've got enough street-cred in our books to tell us you met King Kong at a pub in Anacullough and we'd believe you."

Georjie cracked a smile. "Really?"

"Yes." Targa took the Adirondack chair across from Akiko. "But you better go back to the beginning, because even though we believe you, nothing you just said made any sense."

"Right." Georjie took a deep breath and pulled her knees in to her chest, wrapping her arms around her legs. "The beginning."

We listened, eagerly, as Georjie told her story.

"I can't even explain what it felt like, it was so strange…" Georjie said, her brown eyes alight, her expression faraway and engrossed. "It was so wonderful and powerful. It was like my roots went hundreds of feet into the earth and told me everything about what was around me. The layers of the earth's crust and everything growing there was listening and waiting."

"For what?" Targa sounded as awed as I felt.

"To understand my will, for me to ask it for help. I towered high above the ground, even as my roots shot deep into it. Honestly, I thought I had transformed into the biggest tree in the world."

"Like an Ent." I recalled the *Lord of the Rings* films we had watched together when we were younger, and the huge walking, talking trees who joined in the battle against Saruman.

"Yes, kind of. I felt so slow-moving, but I think in real life, it all happened very fast. I lifted and tossed the soil like a salad, burying Mailís, the house, and every nasty thing left behind by the whole horrid history of that place. And then I replaced it with new life, all in an instant." She snapped her fingers. "Just because I wanted to."

"Have you done it again?" Akiko asked.

Georjie shook her head. "No, nothing like that. But I know I could if I wanted to. I can feel my connection to the earth like this amazing kinetic force that is constantly flowing from the ground. But I can tell you that when I got the call that my mom was in the hospital..." Georjie choked up and her throat worked for a moment before she continued, "it taught me that my powers are a two-edged sword."

"What do you mean?" This statement hit so close to home that I was feeling a little breathless.

"I mean, I made her sick, just by all the negative thoughts I had about her over the summer," Georjie explained. "I could have killed my own mom."

Akiko put her hand on Georjie's arm. "You don't know that for sure."

"Yes, I do. I *know* it. I could do the same to any one of you." Georjie's eyes took on a troubled cast. "I'm...*dangerous*."

"You'd never do anything to hurt us, Georjie." Targa spoke with confidence, but I knew how Georjie felt; I'd had my own struggles with temper and control.

"I'd like to think not," replied Georjie, "but these powers are new to me. I'm still learning what I am and what I'm capable of."

"Is there anyone you can talk to? Maybe Jasher knows somebody, or there's a reference in your Aunt Faith's library in Ireland that might point you to another Wise? Someone who can teach you?" Akiko shifted, pulling her legs up and crossing them beneath her.

Georjie shook her head. "Not that I know of. I've looked."

I empathized deeply with this desire. How badly I had needed to talk to someone who knew what was happening to me; how frightening it had been to change so drastically and not understand what was going on. How relieved I had been when Enzo had put me on Basil's trail, and how thankful when Basil had turned out to be more than willing to help.

"I bet there is somebody out there, Georjie," I ventured. "Don't give up. There *has* to be more beings like you."

Targa was nodding. "Absolutely."

"What makes you so sure?"

It was on the tip of my tongue to say, *because Basil told me there are many different kinds of supernaturals,* but instead I said, "Because that kind of elemental power doesn't just come out of nowhere. It must evolve over time, like every other kind of being. There have to have been Wise that existed before you."

"You healed your mom though, didn't you?" Akiko's mind was on a different track.

Georjie nodded and smiled. "I did. It was amazing. Definitely the highlight of my summer." Her cheeks tinged with pink. "That, and the kiss."

"Say what now?" I straightened. "You conveniently left that part out."

"At the very end of the summer. It was beautiful. More of a goodbye kiss, I guess."

"You're not together?"

She shook her head. "Not together, no. Jasher's got things to do. Now that he isn't being tortured by ghosts everywhere he goes, he wants to travel. Maybe I'll meet up with him somewhere, but neither of us wants a relationship right now." She blew out a long breath. "I have to sort myself out, not to mention finish high school without killing anyone."

"So, you're called a Wise?" Targa hadn't said much as Georjie told her story. She was looking thoughtful and guarded. "But you define it as an Earth Elemental?"

"I didn't call it that. Mailís did, in her diary."

"But your parents split up," Targa pointed out.

This seemed so random and strange that none of us responded at first.

"Uh..." Georjie droned. "Yes, they did. What does that have to do with–"

"Sorry." Targa blushed and made a face, like she was kicking herself. "I just had a crazy thought that your powers came from your parents. Forget I said anything." She pinched her lips together. She waved her hand at the pool and the jungle. "So, this is why you created this greenhouse?"

Georjie nodded. "We wanted to make a safe place where fae could hatch. We took out all the electrical wiring and the modem we had in here. Obviously, we can't have a chemical as powerful as chlorine in here, so we changed the pool to saltwater. The cocoons are why I asked you guys to leave your cell phones upstairs. They can destroy a cocoon in seconds. Jasher thinks there's a dearth of fae these days because of all the toxicity in the world. It wasn't easy to create the conditions they needed, but with some high-tech sprinklers that use rainwater we collect from the roof"—she pointed at the ceiling where several nozzles protruded from the ribs between the glass panels—"we figured it out."

"You're like a bee-keeper," said Akiko, "but for faeries."

Georjie laughed. "Yeah, you nailed it."

"I wish I could see them," added Targa dreamily. "How amazing to be able to see faeries."

"You're not surprised that they exist?" Georjie asked us. "I expected to have a harder time proving to you that I wasn't making all this crazy stuff up about faeries and ghosts."

At this question, there were several glances around the group.

"I was a little surprised," I admitted, "but not overly."

After the summer I'd had, faeries weren't too much of a stretch. Akiko was watching me and I was watching Targa. Akiko had no problem believing it because she'd seen their connections to the Æther, but why did Targa seem so ready to believe? Targa just shook her head, her expression impenetrable.

"And the sudden plethora of big huge jungle plants?" I asked. "I'm guessing you didn't buy these at the local greenhouse."

Not that the Sutherlands couldn't afford it, but the plants around us would have cost a small fortune. The aloe vera plant across the pool from where we were sitting would be worth hundreds of dollars by itself. I knew that because my mom had been nursing her own aloe vera collection for years and often griped about the cost of adding new ones.

Georjie smiled and raised a hand toward the datura beside us.

As we watched, the plant grew, not just visibly but rapidly. New shoots developed and thickened, fresh leaves unfurled, baby buds lengthened from its tips, and its blossoms burst open with little puffs of pollen. It was like watching a time-lapse film. The fresh growth was bright green and seemed to reach toward Georjie's fingertips, shaking and dancing under her control.

Georjie put her hand down. The plant settled and went still. It was two feet higher and its foliage much thicker. A dozen more trumpet-shaped blossoms hung from its branches. Its heady perfume filled my nose, making me feel a bit dizzy.

"Dude," was all I could think of to say. First Akiko, now Georjie... and the girls didn't know about me yet. I glanced at Targa. Did she have a secret, too?

"Yeah," Akiko agreed.

"Something really weird is going on here," I finally said out loud.

"You're not kidding," Targa agreed. "Akiko is immortal and Georjie has a serious green thumb, to understate things on a galactic level."

"Yes, but..." I held my hand out, palm up. I lit a fireball in my palm and let it flicker there. My friends gasped as my fire reflected in their shocked faces. "*Really* weird."

4

SAXONY

"I wasn't sure what my intentions were when I came here tonight," I admitted.

They had listened to my story with many more comments than when Akiko or Georjayna had told theirs, as if they'd already acclimated to our new reality.

"But how could I not tell you everything after what's happened to you," I said to Akiko, "and you." I looked at Georjie. "It made my decision pretty easy. Mind you, Basil would probably kill me if he knew that I'd told more than family members."

My burnt-out vocal chords were huskier than normal from all the talking. I took a few big gulps of water, realizing I hadn't drunk anything since I'd started telling my story, and I was beginning to feel a little too warm.

"We *are* your family, Saxony." Georjie picked up the water jug and refilled my glass.

"I know," I said, and smiled at her. "But I don't think Basil would see it that way."

"Understandable." Targa crossed her legs at the ankles and leaned back on her tailbone. "He's just trying to keep you safe. The more people know what you are, the more potential danger there is for you."

"Easy now, Targa," Georjie said, setting down the jug. "We're trying to make her feel better about sharing her most intimate secret, not worse."

"I'm just saying." Targa sounded a little defensive and her palms were up. "I would have understood if she *hadn't* told us. It's a big thing, sharing a secret like that."

"At least now I don't have to make up some story about wanting to go to a private school in England and miss out on my last year of high school with you guys," I went on. "That would have been a hard sell."

"Very." Georjie made a face. "With the potential you have of being prom queen? I never would have bought it."

"I'll try not to take offense at that," I replied with a croaky laugh. "There are far more important things to me than being prom queen." Although I had to admit that this was something I would have cared a lot about before. Oh, how things had changed.

"So, when do you leave for England?" Akiko asked.

"As soon as I get my student visa sorted out. I have to submit the application on Tuesday." I took several more gulps of water.

"Think Basil would let you have visitors who aren't your parents?" Georjie filled my glass for a third time, draining the jug. She got to her feet. "I'll get more. You were really thirsty."

"Thanks, Georjie. To answer your question, I sincerely doubt it." I put the glass back on the table. An idea struck. "Maybe if he knew I had two supernatural friends. He'd probably want me to invite you there just so he could study you."

"Appealing," Akiko murmured sarcastically.

Georjie looked thoughtful. "Still, you say Basil has been studying supernaturals for years? Would you mind asking him if he's ever studied a Wise?"

"I can ask him, but he'll wonder why I'm asking."

"I don't mind if you tell him you have a friend who is a Wise. I mean, I feel pretty alone and vulnerable with these powers. I'd really like to find someone who knows more than I do, even if it's someone who isn't a Wise themselves."

"Okay, I'll ask him next time I talk to him."

"Thank you." Georjie opened the door but looked over her shoulder. "Don't say anything until I'm back—I don't want to miss anything!"

We agreed, then waited until she returned with a full jug of water before Akiko asked the next question.

"So, what does your family think of you owing some mafia boss a favor?"

"Ha!" I gave a laugh but it came out as a squeak. I coughed to clear my throat. "James and Annette are just thrilled, I can tell you."

"No idea what he'll ask you to do?"

"Nope. Or when he'll call in the favor."

"He'll probably wait until you're finished with Arcturus," Targa ventured. "After all, it was his idea."

I nodded.

Georjie sat on the ground and dug her toes into the dirt. She shook her head. "I can't believe everything you went through and we never knew it."

"You were going through stuff, too," I pointed out.

"Yeah, but we weren't burning up from the inside," Akiko added. "Dante sounds...possessed."

"Maybe he is." Targa moved over to dangle her legs in the pool. "Maybe you should fly on over to Venice and check him out, Akiko."

"Maybe I will."

"You don't sound like you're joking," I said.

"I'm not," Akiko replied. "What else have I got to do now but what I was born for? Now that I'm not under Daichi's control, I don't want to be sitting in classrooms—much as I'll miss you guys—I want to be out hunting. I *need* to be hunting."

The fierce determination on her face gave me goosebumps. "Dante's demon should be very afraid, then," I murmured. I took another drink and then said, "What about you, Targa? You haven't told us anything at all about your summer. I've talked enough. It's your turn now. Spill."

Akiko, Georjie, and I waited expectantly, our eyes on our friend.

Targa's eyes went down to her feet, where they were crossed at the ankles and she bit her cheek. "I fell in love."

"With Antoni, we know," Georjie said. "He must be an amazing guy to have turned your head."

"He is, but he's not the only surprise."

"Finally," I rubbed my hands together and shifted closer to Targa. "We're getting to the good stuff."

"I inherited a billion-dollar multi-national company," Targa said.

A beat passed.

"That is so not what I expected you to say," I rasped.

We listened with amazement of a different kind as Targa told us about the elderly man who became attached to Targa and Mira while they worked on his salvage job with the Bluejackets team. Targa was still absorbing it herself and told the story in a halting way. She explained that Martinius had passed away shortly after she and Mira arrived home, and that Antoni himself had delivered the news along with documents for her to sign to finalize her inheritance. She had signed them, and Mira had signed for the rights to the wreck, a ship called *The Sybellen*.

While Targa told her story, I kept waiting for the other shoe to drop. There had to be more, otherwise the story didn't make sense.

"So, what are you going to do with this company, Targa?" Georjie asked.

"I don't have to do anything with it." She shrugged. "Antoni says it will run on its own just fine. I'd probably bankrupt it anyway—what do I know about shipping? Or running any company for that matter? And I don't want to sell it, that would feel like a betrayal of Martinius's memory, you know? He wouldn't have willed it to me if he'd known I would just turn around and put it on the market."

"Mira's not interested in running it until you decide what to do with it?" Akiko asked.

Targa laughed. "You need to spend more time with my mom if you think she'd be remotely interested in such a job. She can barely stand working for the Bluejackets, even with all her perks. She's on another job right now, in Nassau. You should have heard her grumble before she left."

"She must be happy about her rockstar status," added Georjie. "I've collected about a dozen articles about that woman. She's a legend."

"You have?" Targa looked surprised.

"Yeah! Your mom is a role model for me."

"You never said."

Georjie flushed. "Well, it's a little embarrassing, but I've always felt in awe of her. Not just because she's amazing at what she does. There's something else I've never really been able to put my finger on."

"Oh?" Targa cocked her head at this revelation.

"Wait a minute," I interjected. "This *can't* be it. No one else thinks there has to be more to the story?" I targeted Akiko and Georjie with this question.

"What do you mean?" Targa sounded cagey.

"It doesn't make any sense. Why would some old guy you'd never met just hand you the rights to his company? It's weird. There has to be something else. Plus, look at her." I gestured at Targa. "You can't tell me something supernatural didn't happen to her."

"She'd tell us if it did," Akiko said. "Wouldn't you, Targa?"

"I...I..." Targa stuttered.

I narrowed my eyes at my beautiful, now raven-haired friend. I pulled the fire up to my eyes and let them glow like lanterns. "I *know* you haven't told us everything. We've all spilled *our* secrets."

"She'll tell us when she's ready," said Akiko.

"No. I call bullshit." My eyes were flaming now. "We love you, Targa. Whatever you went through or are going through right now, we only want what's best for you."

Targa's lips pressed together. She dropped her eyes.

"Friendship *is* a two-way street," said Georjie, quietly.

"You don't understand," Targa said. "It's not just my secret."

Now we were getting somewhere. I said, "My secret isn't just mine either, Targa. Jack is involved now, as are Gage and Ryan, and Basil, and a host of other magi."

"I made a promise when I was barely old enough to understand what a promise was," Targa explained. "I don't want to betray—" Her eyes went glassy and a tear slipped down her cheek. She wiped it away with an almost angry movement. There was only one other person I knew of who could get Targa's emotions all stirred up like this.

"Your mother?" I guessed.

The look on her face told me I was right.

"Whatever you are, it's genetic, isn't it?" I asked.

"It's easier if I just show you."

With this pronouncement, Targa slipped into the pool.

5
SAXONY

Targa's shape was a blur in the pool. She slipped off her bathing suit bottom and tossed it from the pool. It landed in a lump on the moss. She stretched her legs out and they just kept on growing. My throat tightened as her shape changed before our eyes. Her legs thickened and fused together. A long, elegant white fin swayed gently in the water.

I forgot to breathe.

"She's a *mermaid*," Georjie said on an exhale. She looked up at Akiko and me in shock. "Is *that* why Mira is such a diving legend? Do you think the Bluejackets know?" She blinked and mimed her brain exploding. "Mind-blowing!"

I shook my head. "There's no way. Targa wouldn't have had such a hard time telling us if a whole team of divers in Saltford already knew."

Targa began to circle the pool in graceful, sinuous loops, her tail appearing to propel her effortlessly, her long black hair flowing behind her like a pennant. It was as though she'd transformed into a liquid, so smooth and silky were her movements. Her tail was pearly white at the back and a metallic silver on the front—a mercurial glimmering hue that was no color and all colors at the same time.

Her skin seemed iridescent and transitioned smoothly into scales at her waist. Her tail was full and thick—muscular looking.

Her gleaming head broke the surface, her vibrant eyes open. Water trickled over her face and neck and down her hair. Her lips parted as she looked at us. On her face was a thicket of emotions: relief, anxiety, love, wonder, and a question.

"Mira would be very unhappy with me to know that I have shared our secret." Targa's white shoulders lifted and her expression said, *but what else could I do*? "I have to trust that after everything you have all shared, I was supposed to share this with you. You now understand how important keeping your identity a secret is." She swam toward us and came half out of the water. She held out her hands.

Akiko, Georjie, and I went to the pool's edge and grasped her hands.

"Promise me," Targa began. She didn't have to finish her request, but she did anyway. "You'll tell no one what you know about me and my mother, and I will keep your secrets, too."

We promised. It was unnecessary, yet necessary at the same time. Somehow, saying the words made everything feel more real, more sacred.

Targa's face lost some of its worry. We released our hands.

"Did this just happen to you this past summer?" I asked.

Targa nodded. "I was born to a siren..."

"A siren?" Akiko cocked her head. "I thought sirens were different from mermaids?"

"There are many varying mythologies about sirens and mermaids," Targa explained. "I've read pretty much everything that has ever been written about us, and most of it is wrong. Even the stuff that seems like it was written by someone who met a mermaid doesn't get it all right. Maybe there are other creatures called sirens who are more like the bird-women of Greek mythology, but we mermaids have hypnotic and irresistible voices which we can use to make humans do whatever we wish. Most mermaids use this voice to win themselves a mate and ensure the survival of the species with the strongest human male they can find. My mother and my father—"

"Nathan," said Georjie, her eyes sad. "What a sweet man your dad was. He was your biological father?"

Targa nodded. "They were so in love. My mother didn't use her siren voice on him and the outcome was me. At first, we thought I was a dud. Turns out I had never made the transformation because we didn't know how to trigger my siren genes. For most mermaids, all it takes is exposure to salt-water when we're very young. For me..." She gave a secret smile. "It was a little more complicated than that. I had to die."

"You had to what, now?" I croaked.

"I had to drown. I had to take seawater into my lungs, and my heart had to stop and then start again before my mermaid genes were fully expressed."

"You *died* this past summer?" Georjie squeaked. "Geez. I think that wins the prize."

"I believe that is what happened." Targa nodded. "Antoni and I got caught in a storm. I drowned. When I came to, I had this." She gestured toward her tail. "And a lot more power than even Mira has."

"Powers over water?" Akiko was leaning so far out over the pool, peering at Targa, that I thought she was going to fall in. I resisted the urge to give her a little push.

"Show us?"

Targa sank into the pool and swam backwards. Behind her, an explosion of water sprayed upward, making a backdrop that framed her. With a crackling sound, the entire wave turned to ice. A hail of ice chips splattered into the pool like rain, but the main body of the wave stayed intact and bobbed in the water like an ice cube. Targa was smiling.

The girls and I laughed with delight.

Targa lifted her arms, fingers spread wide, and before our eyes, she lifted herself on a pillar of water high enough to touch the glass ceiling.

"Show off," called Georjie.

"Nah," Targa called back with a glimmer in her eye. "*This* is showing off."

The water reversed direction. The pillar Targa had been riding sank back into the pool and continued descending, a dimple formed, around which Targa circled. The water at the edges of the pool climbed, and kept climbing. The pool did not overspill its banks, but rose while keeping its square shape.

Akiko reached out and touched the water, swirling it back and forth in front of our faces.

Georjie and I did the same. The water closed over my hand but when I pulled it back, it dried instantly, as though the water was not allowed past where Targa had put it. I put both hands in the water and swept them in circles. I tried to splash Georjie, but the water wouldn't do my bidding.

Targa's shape swam past us and I reached out and touched her tail, feeling the smooth scales. The water became noticeably warmer. I gasped and looked at Georjie, who looked back at me, feeling it too.

"Is there anything you can't do with water?" I asked.

Targa circled and poked her head out of the wall of water. It was a bizarre sight as all the water squeezed out of her hair and from her face. Her head emerged, totally dry, her long hair dangled and swayed.

Targa just shrugged and smiled. Her shoulders emerged, then her chest and stomach. She was out of the water to the waist now, her spine bending as she held herself upright. Her tail moved sinuously behind her.

"That's so weird," Georjie said, pulling back to take a better look. "You look like one of those stuffed animal heads mounted on a wall."

Targa slid backwards, swallowed up once again. She released the water with a crash and the three of us squealed as we were soaked from head to foot. Plants dripped and saltwater landed in our drinks.

"Ack!" Akiko's hair was plastered to her face and when she pushed it back it stuck out in all directions.

"That was for telling her she looked weird," I gasped, water dripping off my nose.

Georjie flicked her hands and arms to get rid of some of the water and started to wring out her hair.

I cranked up my internal flame until my clothes and hair started steaming.

Georjie and Akiko watched as I evaporated all of the water on me with a smug smile.

"Brat." Akiko shook her head.

Targa emerged from the pool in her human form and pulled on her bikini bottoms. "Got a little wet, did ya?"

"Yeah, thanks for that." Georjie pulled her sodden hoodie away from her body. "Gross. Now I have to go change again." Her eyes were sparkling.

Targa noticed my fluffy, curly hair and dry clothes. I shot her a flinty, arrogant grin and crossed my arms.

With a flick of her wrist, a wave jumped out of the pool and splashed over only me. The water was freezing and shocked the breath out of me.

Georjie and Akiko bellowed laughter as I sat there in frozen wet surprise. "You know," I gasped, "it's not like I can't burn all your hair off if I wanted to."

"Go on then," she taunted me.

"Gawd, four seconds into sharing our most intimate secrets and you two already want to do battle." Akiko had her robe off and was wringing it out over the pool. "Seriously."

Again I used my inner fire to steam off all the water from my clothes, skin, and hair. Vapor misted off my body.

"You can't get off that easy," Georjie called from the sliding door where she stood with her palm on the handle. Her eyes flickered white.

"Don't you—" I started.

A green vine came out of nowhere from across the pool, snaked around my waist and jerked me backward into the water. As soon as the plant released me, I stood up, coughing and gasping.

"—dare," I finished.

I glared at Georjie, one corner of my mouth lifted. I turned up the heat until the water around me started bubbling and boiling.

Thick steam clouded the greenhouse, obscuring everything from view—the plants, my friends, even the pool. The water drained around me as it evaporated at high-speed. Only when it was thigh-deep did I turn off the heat.

It began to rain. Not just rain, but pour in heavy sheets. The girls squealed and laughed.

"You are in so much trouble," I heard Georjie yell from the doorway.

The sound of a torrential downpour was so loud I fought the urge to cover my ears. I could see my friends crouching beneath the deluge. I climbed out of the pool as the water rose, and I took shelter under a broad-leafed plant.

Akiko groaned as the rain began to let up. "You're worse than guys! Seriously? Enough with the pissing contest!"

Targa raised her arms. Her fingers beckoned to all corners of the room as she turned. Watching her was hypnotic.

Saltwater ran from every surface; off plants, off our clothes and hair, from the moss surrounding the pool. It poured back into the pool, every last drop. Everything was dry again, and it was as though nothing had happened. Targa put her hands down.

"Are we done now?" she asked.

Georjie returned from where she'd been near the door, her hair and clothing dry.

"I am if you are," she shot at me. She looked ready to raise her hands and call some of her plant friends into mischief.

I put my palms up. "I'm good. I think we've established who is the most powerful around here."

"Have we?" Targa canted her head.

"Well, *obviously*." I said. "Fire is clearly the most dangerous and powerful element. It destroys everything."

"Here we go." Akiko rolled her eyes. "I'm surrounded by children."

"Water puts out fire. I don't get how you think fire is more powerful." Targa rocked back on her tailbone and wrapped her arms around her shins.

"Fire dissolves water, didn't I just prove that?"

"But it can't destroy it," Targa shot back.

"I'll bury you both in about four tons of earth right now if you don't quit it." Georjie settled herself into an Adirondack chair and crossed her legs.

Akiko smacked her palm against her forehead. "Elementals," she groaned.

"Elementals," Georjayna echoed. "That's what we are." She put an index finger to her chest. "Earth." She pointed at me. "Fire." She swung her finger to Targa. "Water."

We all looked at Akiko and I said, "Air."

Akiko shook her head. "I'm not Air. I have no power over air. I don't even think I'm an Elemental."

I frowned. "But it fits. You said you can fly to the Æther, thirty-thousand feet above the earth's surface. If that's not an Air Elemental, what is?"

"But shouldn't I be able to make storms and high winds or something? I can't do that. Plus, Æther is not considered an element by most cultures. Æther is something different, belonging more to the realm of spirit than flesh."

"Whatever you are, you're a supernatural," Targa said. "We're all supernatural. We all know each other, we've been friends for years. So, why us? And why this summer?"

"You know why *you*," I said to Targa. "With you, it's genetic. Your mom is a mermaid. You've always had the genes in you."

Targa nodded. "But you and Georjie aren't from supernatural parents, as far as you know."

"My mother is definitely not supernatural," Georjie said with a laugh.

"My parents aren't, but my brother Jack..." I began to say this without really thinking about it, then stopped. Would Jack mind if I told the girls about his power? I thought not, since they knew about mine and they all had their own, but I wasn't sure. On the other hand, after the way I'd pressured Targa, it wasn't really fair to keep any more secrets. This was an all-in situation.

"Jack, what?" Akiko encouraged.

"Jack is some kind of supercharged empath," I explained. "He and

I butted heads hard when I first arrived home, because of all those arson incidents in Saltford."

Targa's eyes widened. "He thought that was *you*?"

"*Thank you*," I said, grateful that she didn't even question my innocence. "Yes, he did. The twit. Although," I shrugged a shoulder, "can't blame him for thinking it. Every time he came near me, all he could feel was heat."

"Sorry, but what's an empath?" asked Georjie. "I don't think I've heard that term before."

"Someone who can pick up on the mental or emotional states of others," Akiko explained. "But you mean this in a paranormal way, I presume, not just that he's sensitive?"

"Yeah, seriously paranormal. He could tell me how I felt about telling my parents my secret and how much I want to attend Arcturus. It was unnerving. Feels like I can't have any secrets from him, like ever, now."

"So, is it the fact that we know one another and are close that this happened to us? Or do you think it's happening to lots of people and we just don't know it?" Akiko wondered.

"I have a theory about that–" Georjie began.

The knocker on the front door sounded off three times.

"Who could that be, at..." I grabbed my watch from where I'd stuffed it into the toe of my shoe. "Great Scott! It's eight in the morning!"

"The sun was up over an hour ago, Saxony." Targa laughed at me.

"Great Scott?" Akiko raised an eyebrow at me as Georjie was getting to her feet. "Sleep deprivation transforms you into Christopher Lloyd?"

My jaw cracked with a yawn as I got to my feet to follow Georjie. "Who is Christopher Lloyd?"

Akiko rolled her eyes. "Millennials."

"Centenarians," I mimicked, shoving her sideways toward the pool.

"Hey!" She staggered and caught herself before falling in.

We followed Georjie out of the greenhouse and up the steps to the front foyer. Georjie stopped at the top step and laughed at the cluster of us behind her. "I can answer the door by myself, you guys."

"I wanted to check my phone anyway." I reached for my mobile.

"Me too," said Targa, reaching for hers.

"I just love your company so much I didn't want to be without y'all," Akiko drawled.

I clicked on my phone. "Crikey, I can't believe we were up all night!"

"Crikey? You must have learned that one from Basil." Georjie unlocked the door and swung it open.

6

PETRA

The sky was a fetching palette of autumn blues and peaches as the sun worked its way into the sky over the Atlantic. A smudge of clouds hugged the horizon, but it promised to be a glorious fall day.

I turned off my car and glanced at my cell phone to check the time: 7:55. I peered through the window at the palatial white house with the four columns along the porch and the green trim around the windows.

I frowned. Eight a.m. was awfully early on a Sunday to be knocking on strangers' doors, but Jody assured me that this morning would be the best time. I got out, closed my car door, and crossed the street.

My stomach was aflutter with nerves. I had my pitch relatively straight, I thought. The objective was simply to get the girls to attend a presentation at the field station. No other commitment would be required. If I could do that, my first assignment would be considered a success.

Alright then.

I took the steps two at a time and used the door knocker. A

minute later, I heard voices and soft footfalls of people moving either up or down a set of stairs.

The door opened and four girls peered out at me curiously.

"Can I help you?" the tall blond one asked.

"I'm Air," I said, as Jody had instructed me to introduce myself. I felt stupid, but she'd insisted they would respond better to this introduction than any other. Since they were Elementals, it would tell them a lot without having to make a long explanation.

The shock on all four faces was instant and profound. I had shaken them, and badly. I immediately regretted listening to Jody.

"I'm sorry," I amended. "My name is Petra. I'm an Elemental, like you. I was wondering if I could chat with you? It won't take long. I believe we might be able to help each other."

The shock seemed to deepen and the air felt laden with bewilderment. Apparently, I had just made things worse. I opened my mouth to offer some kind of comfort when the petite girl with honey-colored eyes said, "You'd better come in."

"Thanks." I gave a relieved exhale. "I'm sorry, I can tell I've upset you. It wasn't my intention."

"Wait," the vivacious looking redhead with the strange reflective eyes said, raising a hand. She held a cell phone in her hand, face up as though she'd just been looking at it. Her voice rasped nicely over my eardrums. This girl *had* to be the fire mage. She might as well have had 'fire' tattooed on her forehead.

"How did you know we were here?" Fire demanded. "Who are you? Besides...'Air'?" She said the last word with a slight curl of her upper lip.

I sensed mistrust from her that was absent in the other women. Whatever her story was, she'd been through something that had made her extremely wary.

"I knew you'd be here because my supervisor told me you'd be here. I don't know how she knew, but she did. And I can explain further out here on your porch, but I think this conversation would best be done in private." I said all this without any attitude or suggestion of threat in my voice. It wasn't easy. The redhead was now glaring at me. I stomped on the desire to read her mind. It was too early in the day for a headache. I could always fall back on telepathy if things deteriorated.

"Your supervisor?" the tiny Asian girl asked. She was the one I had been told the least about, since she wasn't of interest to TNC. She couldn't have weighed more than ninety pounds soaking wet. Though she had the stature of a child, her eyes sent a shiver through me. They looked old. Ancient, even. *What are you*? I wondered. I realized, now that I was really looking at her, that I had seen her face before.

"Just come in," said the blond one who looked like she'd spent most of the summer lying in the sunshine. "I apologize for my rude friend." She elbowed the redhead and shot her a glare, then extended a hand to me. "I'm Georjayna."

I took her hand, gladly. "Petra Kara."

"Georjie," the redhead husked in a tone full of warning, clearly not pleased but hesitating to say why in my presence.

"Really?" Georjayna answered her friend. "Are you *really* afraid of her? Look at her!" She waved a long arm in my direction. "She's just a kid, like us."

Georjayna shut the door behind me.

I couldn't help but smile at the implication Georjayna was making. Why should they be afraid of me? These girls had supernatural abilities. They were exponentially better equipped to protect themselves and one another than any normal human.

"And she's one of us," the blond continued. "Weren't we just saying it would be nice to meet someone like us? Someone with some answers?" She swung her brown eyes in my direction. "*Do* you have answers?"

"Depends what the questions are, but if I don't have answers, I can hook you up with someone who might." Hiroki seemed to know everything about supernaturals. I felt sure he'd love to help these girls the same way he'd been helping me.

"There, you see?" Georjayna put her hands on her hips.

The redhead did not see. Clearly, the idea of taking them to someone who might have answers had not done the trick. Her pouty mouth tightened and the corners turned down as she assessed me coldly. Funny how Fire could feel so icy.

"You must be the fire mage." I fixed a friendly and relaxed look on my face. "Saxony, right?" I held out my hand.

Her strange green eyes widened and she crossed her arms while uttering a curse under her breath. Then, "Who do you work for?"

The question was like a barbed spear thrust in my direction, but I was glad for the segue.

"A company called The Nakesh Corporation, TNC for short. Have you heard of it?"

The raven-haired woman with the otherworldly blue eyes (definitely the mermaid, as Jody had described her coloring to me) gave a small intake of breath. "Mr. Nakesh's corporation? The billionaire tech tycoon?"

"The same," I replied. "So you've heard of it."

"If you'll excuse me," Saxony interrupted. "I need to make a phone call before this goes any further." She pointed a finger at me. "Say nothing else until I'm back."

It wasn't a request. I decided right there and then that I liked this feisty redhead, even if she didn't like me much. Yet.

"As you wish," I replied, palms up. "I can't proceed without you anyway."

"Why's that?" She arched an elegant red brow, the eye beneath it judging, assessing.

"This is an all or none proposition. Except for you," I said to the most petite one of the group whose name I'd been told but had forgotten since she wasn't part of the assignment. Jody had said that if the girls insisted on her presence, I had permission to allow it, but they preferred she not attend. "Sorry, I hope that doesn't offend you. TNC has an offer for these three, which will be shared at a presentation." I gestured toward her friends. I held my hand out to her. "Lovely to meet you, though…"

I waited for her name.

She grasped my hand and shook, but her face was an enigmatic mask. "Akiko. No offense taken."

"Wait a second," the mermaid—Targa—spoke up. Her voice had an enchanting layered quality and I immediately wished for her to speak again. She was doll-like in her perfection, yet gave off the aura of a predator. Her energy was appealing in the same way many of the most beautiful and deadly creatures of the sea were attractive, times one-hundred. I wanted to reach out and touch her but thought that if I did, I risked drawing back a bloody stump. The little I had learned about Water Elementals was limited to what they could do with water and the fact that they could shape-shift into mermaids, but I had a feeling that her abilities could be far more seductive than making waves.

"Targa?" I held out my hand.

She opened her mouth, closed it, then shook my hand with the briefest of touches, her beautiful eyes laced with concerned. "First off, it's very disconcerting that you know our names. Second, you want to make us a proposition, but without including Akiko? Why?"

"I don't know, to be honest, but if you'll let me tell my story and agree to what I'm asking, you can ask my supervisor all the questions you want."

Georjayna and Targa shared a bewildered glance and they all looked at Akiko.

Akiko shrugged as if to say, *what do you want me to do about it*?

"Just when I thought things couldn't get any weirder," Targa said.

I turned to Saxony where she was hovering at my elbow. "You wanted to make a call?"

Saxony nodded. "Give me a few minutes. I'll be right back." She turned and left the house and the door snicked shut behind her.

7

SAXONY

I took the stairs down from Georjie's porch and went up the sidewalk, my cell clutched in my hand. I searched for Basil's number and hit dial. Surely, if this woman was hiding some sinister motive, or if the company she worked for was the kind of corporation Basil had repeatedly warned me about, he would know it. I walked a distance from the house, listening to the ring in my ear.

"Saxony?" Basil's rich accented voice filled me with warmth. I couldn't help but smile.

"Hello, Basil. How are you?"

"Busy preparing for the year but very well. Yourself?"

"I'm good too. Listen, I won't take up much of your time. I just have a question."

"I have nothing but ears and time for you, Saxony."

"Oh, thank you." I cleared my throat. There was something about Basil's tone that always kept me guessing whether he was being serious or just having fun with me. "Ever heard of a company called The Nakesh Corporation? TNC for short."

"Of course. Mr. Nakesh is famous in tech. His company is always in the news for some invention or breakthrough or another. Why?"

I heard no alarm in his voice. "They're not one of the evil corporations you've been watching?"

Basil chuckled. "Saxony, TNC is single-handedly responsible for giving clean water to something like five-hundred villages in Africa. Mr. Nakesh has a patent on a self-cleaning filtration system. Once installed, these systems require no maintenance. Other corporations would install systems that require upgrades and filter-changes in order to create a source of revenue, but TNC didn't do that."

I began to feel badly about how I had reacted to Petra. "Oh."

"Why do you ask?"

"One of their employees, an Air Elemental, has approached me to attend a presentation. She knew who I was and where to find me. It kind of freaked me out."

"An Air Elemental?"

"That's what she said."

"Hmph."

"What, *hmph*? What does *hmph* mean?"

"I've been archiving supernaturals for years; there is only one Air Elemental that I've ever heard of and it's highly unlikely that this girl is in that category."

"Why is it unlikely?"

"Because—there is only one."

My brows arched in surprise. "Like, only one in all of existence?"

"That's right. If she is what she says she is, she is one in seven billion." He paused. "I would like to meet her. Maybe she has some kind of supernatural power and doesn't know how else to label it."

"So, what can she do? Like, create storms, or something?"

Basil chuckled. "My portfolio for this kind of Elemental is rather skinny, as I've never met one, and my information gathering has always been from second- or third-hand sources; but if she is a true Air Elemental, she is capable of a lot more than that."

"Like what?"

"Well, why don't you ask her to show you? She wants you to attend a presentation. Why don't you ask for something in return? Proof."

This made sense, but if I asked her to prove herself to us and she did, then by this logic we'd be bound to say yes to her pitch. Which, all things considered, wasn't really a big ask.

"Silence?" Basil prompted.

"Sorry, I'm just thinking."

"Have I helped?"

"Yes. You've helped a lot. Thanks. I won't keep you."

"You'll let me know what happens with this woman, though? What did you say her name was?"

"Petra...Petra something. I've forgotten her last name."

There was a low grunt. "Never heard of her. Honestly, I would wager you'll catch her in a lie, or you'll be sorely disappointed with her skills. If that's the case, then you can just part ways and tell her you're not interested."

"I'm not interested, regardless. I want to come to Arcturus."

"Arcturus will always be here for you, Saxony. You can come at any time, but I have to admit I am glad to hear you say that." He let out a breath into the receiver and it sounded like wind in my ear. "There is no harm in listening to her. You might learn something you can pass on to me and it will have cost us nothing. I would be curious to hear what TNC is up to these days. They're secretive about their projects, to say the least."

The gears in my mind were clicking along at a rapid pace. I was glad I had Basil in my back pocket. His advice solidified it for me. I would ask Petra to prove herself. Based on that, we could either tell her to bug off, or we'd have made a new supernatural friend.

"Thank you, Basil. I appreciate your time."

"Of course. My pleasure. And, Saxony?"

"Yes?"

"Would you try and get her abilities on video for me? It's not likely she'll let you, but you can at least ask. Video footage is very valuable to my library."

"Sure. I'll try. Bye, Basil."

"Good bye—"

"Oh, wait!" I remembered what I'd promised Georjie.

"What?"

"Have you got anything in your archives about a supernatural called a Wise?"

There was a pause. Then, "How do you know that term?"

"I'll have to tell you another time. Long story."

Basil grunted. "I do, but not very much. Earth Elemental. Much rarer than fire magi. In comparison, we are a dime a dozen."

"Oh?" I wasn't sure if learning that would make Georjie happy or unhappy. She wanted someone to talk to about her powers, but wasn't it nice to know she was exceptional in the world of supernaturals? As much as I hated going through what Dante had put me through, the fact that my powers were unrivaled among my kind felt kind of good. No one fancied being a dime a dozen. "Interesting. What about in comparison to a fire mage who's been through a burning?"

Basil chuckled. "Feeling a little trivial now, are we?"

"No, I—" I pressed my lips together. I was, and Basil knew it. He was so intuitive.

"If my research is accurate, and I'm not saying it is, you're as rare as a Wise. But Wise are very shy and they tend not to live in populated areas, so who can say for sure."

That made sense given what Georjie's skills were and how sensitive she'd said the fae were to pollution. Why wouldn't a Wise just live in a jungle away from civilization? I couldn't picture Georjie ever wanting to do that, though; she was an urban girl through and through. Just the fact that she now liked to go around barefoot was astonishing.

"Why do you ask about the Wise?" Basil paused. His voice was infused with a sudden and palpable hope. "Have you come across one?"

I couldn't help but grin. *You have no idea,* I thought. *Seems like everyone I know is some kind of supernatural.* I opened my mouth to ask him if he'd ever heard of multiple supernaturals emerging from a single city or town, but then remembered that everyone was waiting for me, and they were probably standing in the foyer staring at Petra awkwardly. "I'll tell you another time. But maybe you can dig up what you have for me?"

I also wanted to ask him to dig up anything he had about mermaids and *Hanta*, but one thing at a time. That would really tip him off.

"I'll look into it, but I won't know if I can share it with you until I look at it. Some files are more classified than others, depending on who they're about. If I am able to share it with you, I won't send you anything electronically, you'll have to wait until you're here to see it. I don't mess around when it comes to risking the identity of anyone in my dossiers. If supernaturals think they can't trust me, they'll never talk to me."

"Okay, I understand. Thank you." I hung up the phone, feeling better, and headed back to the house.

8
PETRA

When Saxony returned, she seemed a lot more relaxed. I didn't know who she'd just been talking to or what they'd told her, but I sent them a mental thank you.

Saxony shot her friends a smile and a nod.

"Why don't we go into the kitchen. Would you like a coffee?" Georjayna offered. "We have an amazing coffee machine my mother had shipped all the way from Naples."

I grinned and shucked my denim jacket. "How can I turn that down?"

"You can't," Saxony said as we went up the stairs and into the bright and airy kitchen.

Everything was spotless, done up in modern finishing with a lot of white and gray and stainless steel. Georjayna's family was obviously not standing in line for government cheese.

I gave the redhead a curious look and she answered it with apologetic smile. "Sorry I was rude before. I'm the cautious type."

"As you should be." I draped my jacket over the back of one of the tall chairs at the kitchen island.

Targa leaned on the counter and Akiko sat on the stool at the far end. She yawned and put her chin in her hands. Come to think of it, all the girls looked a bit tired.

Akiko apologized for yawning. "We haven't had any sleep yet."

"You've been up all night?" I looked from one face to another and only then noticed the faint smudges of blue under their eyes.

"We haven't seen each other all summer," replied Targa. "There was a lot of catching up to do."

"Speaking of being one of us," Saxony continued, perching on a stool. "We'd like to make a deal with you."

"We would?" Georjayna turned around, her brown eyes full of alarm as she stared at her friend. She held two espresso cups in her hands.

"We'd like to see a demonstration of your power before we go any further." Saxony looked me boldly in the eyes, her face full of challenge and curiosity.

"Oh. Yes, we would." Georjayna looked relieved, her shoulders dropped an inch. She put the cups down on the metal tray under the glossy machine with the eagle icon sitting on its top. "Just don't wreck anything, please."

I smiled. "I'd be happy to give you a demo."

"Do you mind if I get it on video?" Saxony pulled her cell phone out of her pocket.

I shook my head. "That I can't agree to, I'm sorry."

"Oh." Her face fell but she tucked her phone away. She folded her hands on the countertop in front of her. "Do you need anything? Should we like, tie down our hair and hide all the breakables or something?"

I laughed. "That won't be necessary." I looked at Georjayna. "Do you have any more of those cups?"

"Lots. How many do you want?"

"Three should do."

Georjie opened a cupboard and pulled down three matching white espresso cups with red hearts enameled on the handles. She put them down on the counter in front of me. I could feel their expectant gazes on me. I picked up the cups with both hands and in one smooth movement, opened my palms and sent them hovering in the air. I put them into orbit so they followed one another in a circle like a little family of ducklings, and then put my hands down. "Will this do?" I asked.

The girls stared at the cups.

"I thought you were going to make a wind or something," Saxony said, "but this is cool too." She didn't look impressed, but she didn't look disappointed either.

"This is what an Air Elemental does?" Targa sounded surprised. "Moves things telekinetically?"

"Among other things," I replied.

"Like what?" Saxony reached out a finger and poked one of the cups. It jiggled and swung out of orbit before moving obediently back into line.

"Come on, Saxony," said Georjie. "She did what you asked. Let her get on with it."

"It's all right," I said. "I can create wind, but I can also lift heavy things by producing sound. I can also make a force-field."

I wasn't about to tell the girls that I could read minds—that would not foster trust.

"Now that's cool!" Saxony finally looked impressed. "Show us?"

I let the cups down and thanked Georjayna. She nodded and took them back and continued to make the coffee.

I used my hands to make a small hollow ball, a bubble of my force-field. "Can you see it? It's hard to see if you're not looking for it."

"I can," Akiko said, "just barely."

I noticed Saxony squinting at the air, looking for the near-invisible barrier. "You can touch it if you like," I invited. "It's just here," I pointed both index fingers at the space in front of my belly.

Saxony reached out and poked it with her finger. I felt Saxony's frequency vibrate through my core and picked up a psychic impression of her. A wave of heat passed through me and was gone.

"It's warm and so solid!" she made a face as she touched it again. "It feels a bit slimy. No, powdery." She rubbed her fingers together.

Georjie reached a hand across the island and touched the force-field too. "Wow. So cool."

Targa followed, and the three of them were touching the force-field. A battery of frequencies twanged through my core and I blinked at how very different they all were; different from each other, and very different from Hiroki, who was not supernatural. I sent Akiko an inviting look but she shook her head and stayed where she was.

The fancy coffee machine made a hissing sound and Georjie turned to retrieve a cup. She put the coffee at my elbow and I let the force-field dissipate.

"Enough?" I asked.

"Thanks," said Saxony. "Sorry, I hope that wasn't weird, I had to ask."

"I understand."

"I think we've gone way past weird anyway," Akiko murmured.

"I know you," I said to her. "Is it possible you went to Saltford District Collegiate? Or maybe you have a sister who looks a lot like you who went to my school?"

Akiko's pale pink lips parted and her fine brows arched. "I did go to that school."

I nodded. "I saw your school photo when I went to a meeting a Saltford High last spring. I was sure I knew you from somewhere."

"Are you born and raised in Saltford?" Targa asked.

I nodded.

Georjayna yawned.

"Why don't we get started, I have a feeling you guys could all use a nap."

They agreed, so I began.

"As you know, I work for TNC. I signed a one-year contract in return for a full-ride scholarship to the university of my choice starting next September, as well as some other perks like a new vehicle and apartment. Although, I haven't moved yet as I haven't had a lot of time to go house hunting. They've been keeping me busy lately."

"What do you do for them?" Saxony asked, propping her chin in her hand.

"So far it's been nothing but learning how to use my powers. My first assignment is actually," I spread my palms, "talking to you guys."

"*Learning* to use your powers?" Targa's coffee stopped halfway to her lips and she raised her brows. "You don't know how to use your powers?"

"I just acquired them a few months ago."

Looks of shock were shared at this. "So did we," said Georjayna.

"Really?" This was not a piece of information Jody or Hiroki had armed me with. I looked from one face to another. "Everyone?"

Saxony nodded. "Part of the reason we haven't slept is because we've been up all night talking about what happened to each of us. Prior to this summer, we were all just... normal humans. Well, Akiko wasn't," she amended, "but she was being held captive and was unable to use her powers. She just got them back this summer."

"Wow." My eyes drifted back to Akiko, concern flooding me. "Who was keeping you captive?"

"It's a very long story." She took a sip of her coffee very slowly to signal that she wasn't in the mood to tell it again.

"Fair enough." I took a breath. "Hiroki is a scientist who works at one of the TNC labs. He's got all kinds of amazing technology that is built to help supernaturals develop their skills."

"Interesting," Saxony murmured.

"TNC is very hierarchical though, and very secretive. If you don't need to know something, they don't tell you. A good example of this is that I've been given the task of inviting you to a presentation, but I don't know what the presentation is about because I'm supposed to see it for the first time along with you."

"That's it? That's your pitch?"

"Almost," I said. "If you agree to come to the presentation, you'll be picked up by a helicopter tomorrow morning-"

"Tomorrow is a holiday," interrupted Saxony.

I nodded. "TNC doesn't want to take you away from school. You'll be taken to their field station up north for the day. You'll be returned home in the evening. You will have to sign a non-disclosure agreement because you'll see things that no one else is allowed to see. If you decline, no hard feelings, you'll be thanked for your time and sent on your merry way. If you accept, you'll be given more specifics."

"And the project? You know nothing about it at all?"

I shrugged. "I'm sorry, but not really, no. I know that TNC is really excited about it. They say that it's going to change the world, make things better for all of humanity. Beyond that, I can't say."

"Geez, they really get you with curiosity," Targa murmured.

I nodded. "It's understandable that they can't really share more than that. They don't want competitors getting wind of what they're doing."

"Until after." Saxony nodded. "A friend of mine just said something similar."

I gazed at Saxony, wondering who this friend was who had told her such a thing about TNC. I made a mental note to ask her when we knew each other better.

"But we've all got plans and things to do," said Georjayna. "Saxony is headed to school overseas, Targa inherited a huge shipping company she has to figure out what to do with. I want to finish high school. We'd have to halt all that for this project." She twisted her lips to the side in an expression of doubt. "It's not likely we'll say yes, even if it is exciting."

"You don't know that," I said. "This is the opportunity of a lifetime. It's not like there is any risk in it for you at this point. A day's worth of your time is all you're asked to give, for starters." I took a sip of the coffee and almost forgot what I was saying. "This is the best coffee I think I have ever had," I said to Georjayna.

She gave me a toothy grin. "Right?"

I saluted her with the cup, took another sip, and then set it down. "Say no if you want, but when the project hits the media, I can almost guarantee you'll wish you'd been a part of it. TNC has been helping and protecting supernaturals for generations."

"And using their powers for gain," Akiko pointed out.

I nodded. "Yes, of course. It's a mutually beneficial relationship."

"Any idea how long this project is supposed to go for?" Targa asked.

"No. I'm assuming less than a year though, because I'll be a part of it, and my contract expires in less than a year."

The kitchen fell silent.

"Why don't I leave you my cell number and give you time to talk? Call whoever you need to call, talk to whoever you need to talk to, and get back to me so I can give my supervisor an answer."

Georjie took a pad of paper and a pencil from a drawer and slid it across the counter toward me.

I scrawled my number on the pad. I stood and shrugged into my jacket. "Thanks for the coffee, Georjayna."

"I'm interested in the presentation," Saxony blurted.

I turned back, surprised.

"Me too," said Targa. "I doubt I'll take the job, just being honest, but I have to admit I'm dying of curiosity." She shrugged. "It's just one day."

Georjie nodded. "I'm pretty curious, too. What do you think, Akiko?"

I shook my head. "The invitation is just for the three of you, remember?"

Georjie frowned and looked at her friends. Saxony glowered.

"Without Akiko, we won't go. Even if she's not part of the job. She's one of us." Targa said simply. "It's all of us or none of us."

Saxony and Georjie nodded in agreement.

I looked at Akiko but she was an impenetrable wall. "Do you feel the same?"

"These are my friends," said Akiko. "I have an interest in their safety and while I'm sure TNC will treat them with the utmost respect, I would feel better going along. If you don't agree to take me," she shifted in her seat and I thought the look on her face grew a trifle smug, "I'll go on my own."

"You don't know where it is." I scanned her face but it was nothing but secrets. When she didn't respond, I narrowed my eyes. "What are you, again?"

"I never said." Akiko closed her mouth and again it was clear she wasn't going to say anything more.

"Well." I took a breath. "I guess we aren't going to do any better than that. It's a yes then?"

"Yes," said Saxony. "As long as Akiko can come."

Georjayna and Targa looked at one another. "Yes," they both said.

"My supervisor will be happy. You know the chopper pad behind the fire station on Victoria street?"

"We know it," said Targa.

"Be there at six-thirty tomorrow morning." I smiled at the girls. "Even if you say no after the presentation, you're in for the most incredible day of your lives."

Saxony laughed. "I sincerely doubt that."

9

PETRA

I pulled my Toyota into the parallel parking along Victoria street, turned off the engine, and got out. I buttoned up my jean jacket against the chill of the fall morning. The sun was a mere suggestion on the horizon and my breath hung in the air in front of my face. Cars along the street were slick with dew and the streetlights were shrouded with misty halos. A shiver went through my body and I regretted not wearing a thicker jacket.

I made my way down the silent street to the walkway which led to the fire station and the helipad behind it. A restless excitement fluttered in my gut. I was looking forward to spending the day with supernaturals. It was even more amazing to me that we were all young women and all from Saltford.

But today was exciting for another reason, too. Today, we would learn more about this project which had been so tightly kept under lock and key.

I scanned the streets for the girls, but the city seemed like a ghost town this morning. Most residents would be sleeping in or having a lazy Labor Day morning.

As I turned the corner from the sidewalk to the much narrower walkway, a loud and unexpected telephone ring made my heart vault into my throat. I gasped and almost tripped as my hand clutched at my chest. If my pulse had been jumping before, it was galloping now.

The ring was coming from the run-down old telephone box across the street. How many times had I been down this way and never noticed that phone box? It looked like it had been out of service for at least a decade and the city just hadn't gotten around to removing it yet.

The ringing continued.

I took another sweep of the street. Squinting at the filthy glass of the phone box, I expected to see someone inside, but there was no one there. A creeping sensation made its way across my skin, starting at the back of my neck and working its way down my arms. Why did I have the strangest feeling that the call was for me?

I dismissed the thought and laughed at my own silly superstition. Someone had made an appointment for a call but had gotten their wires crossed. Or it was a telemarketer calling a randomly generated phone number. I expected each ring to be its last.

But it kept ringing.

I crossed the street toward the ringing phone. Stepping up on the sidewalk, I peered in through the half open door and looked at the scratched and worn phone, unsure of what to do. From the look of the rust on the hinges of the door and the weeds choking the base of it, it wasn't likely to move easily. I went closer, observing the worn handle of the phone, once a glossy black, now a stippled dark gray. The metal cord was wrapped around itself in a tight figure-eight.

I stepped close enough to reach inside and pick up the receiver. A smell of stale urine wafted to my nose and I made a face and retreated.

The phone stopped ringing.

"Petra!"

As though waking from a dream, I turned to the voice I would now know anywhere. No one else I knew had a voice like a dry husk.

"Good morning, Saxony." I smiled at the redhead as she and the other girls walked down the sidewalk in pairs. "You guys have a good rest?"

"I didn't sleep a wink, but I've had three coffees already." Saxony was wearing a hunter-green puffy vest and a plaid flannel shirt with dark denim and a tall pair of brown boots. She looked like the poster girl for Canada. Her appearance said she hadn't wanted to try too hard to impress, but still wanted look good for whatever she was facing today.

"I slept like the dead," Georjayna said as they stopped in front of me. She jammed her hands in her pockets and shivered. Her blond locks spilled out from underneath a floppy knit cap. She wore a mauve turtleneck under an oversized gray sweatshirt. "I needed a crane to get me out of bed this morning. How about you, Petra?"

"I slept well, thanks." I took the lead as we entered the narrow walkway. I glanced over my shoulder at Targa and Akiko. "All right?"

Akiko nodded but didn't say anything. She was dressed like someone who wanted to be invisible. Black jeans, black boots, black hoodie with the hood drawn up.

Targa gave a yawn that made me wonder if she could dislocate her jaw, but said that she'd slept well. She wore a mid-thigh length trench-coat tied at the waist. Her long black hair spilled over the khaki-colored fabric. Knee-high tan boots with a short square heel and laces all the way up the front gave her a few extra inches.

Given that I hadn't told the girls what to wear, I thought they'd done rather well considering they were about the meet a billionaire and be given access to a high-security field station. The girls looked like themselves, but prepared for anything. I felt a surprising and unexpected surge of pride in them.

I led them through the narrow walkway to where the pilot, Sy, was waiting for us. He was bundled up against the chill in his usual aviator jacket.

He nodded at me. "Petra." It was difficult to see where he was looking from behind the mirrored sunglasses, which I rarely saw him without, even in dim light like this morning.

"Morning, Sy."

"These are the Elementals, then?" Sy nodded at the girls but his expression didn't change.

If he was impressed by how young they were, it did not come through. He was, as most TNC employees were, the consummate professional. He shook their hands in turn, then opened the gate for us and led us up the switchback metallic steps that brought us to the helipad.

We piled into the back of the chopper and buckled up.

"Before you put your head-gear on," Sy said from the cockpit, "I'll need you to read over and sign these non-disclosure agreement papers." He glanced at me. "I'm guessing you warned them about these already?"

I nodded and took the papers from him and distributed them to the girls. They each took a copy and sat back to read it over.

After a few minutes, Georjayna said, "So, basically, we're not allowed to tell anyone anything about the location of the field station, the identities of anyone we interact with, and anything about the project we're going to be pitched today, under pain of a massive fine no one except Oprah could ever afford to pay."

"That sounds about right." Sy smiled. "Keep your lips sealed and there'll be no issues."

The girls signed and gave their copies to me. I passed them up to Sy, who folded them and tucked them into his jacket.

"Your parents must be a bunch of pretty cool cats to let you guys come along on a mysterious mission like this," Sy said.

When no one answered, he turned back to the group again with a curious look.

"My mom is working." Targa said as she pulled her helmet down over her glossy black hair. "But she'd be cool with it. In fact, she'd probably want to come. Just so you know, I'm only here out of curiosity, and to be with them." She gestured to the other three.

"Fair enough. Although I'm sure Miss Marks will be disappointed to learn you've already written the project off." Sy raised his eyebrows at Georjayna. "You?"

"My mom is at a conference." Georjayna shrugged. "She wouldn't care if I rented a Cessna and flew to New York for the weekend."

"You know how to fly?" Sy looked impressed.

"No. But we have good insurance." She gave that heart-stopping grin.

Sy laughed and his eyes drifted to Saxony. "What about you, Red?"

"I got a pass from my Prof." Saxony sat back and clicked her seatbelt into place. "That's all the permission I needed."

"Your...Prof?" Sy wrinkled his nose, perplexed.

"It's a long story."

"How about you?" Sy looked at Akiko. "Which parent did you have to bribe to be here?"

Her face impassive, she said, "I know I look like a minor, but I'm not. Every human I care about is in this helicopter. I'm exactly where I need to be."

"Alright then." Sy faced front and flicked a bunch of switches. "Good enough. Let's go." A low hum vibrated through the chopper and the blades began to turn.

"Sure I can't take a photo? Just one?" Saxony grinned at me from under her helmet. "We look so hot right now."

Targa turned her head toward Saxony. The dark glasses looked huge on her face. "You look like a bug."

I laughed and shook my head. They knew they wouldn't be allowed to record any of today's events in any way.

"How is it that TNC has clearance to use this helipad?" Georjie asked, her voice sounding slightly metallic through the headgear.

I opened my mouth to respond, but Akiko got there first.

"My guess is that TNC made a healthy donation to the fire department's upgrade back in two-thousand-three."

I nodded. "You'd be right." I had asked Sy this very question on one of my trips to the field station. It struck me that Akiko was much worldlier than she seemed. Most high school kids wouldn't jump to the conclusion that there'd been some donation made in order to use a private asset like a fire department's helipad, even though this was the way the world worked. Most high school kids wouldn't even ask such a question, so I supposed all the girls were rather worldly for their age.

Saltford fell away and the girls became absorbed with the view of their hometown as it shrank beneath us. City gave way to agricultural land, farms gave way to forest, and the forest went on forever. The chopper picked up speed and angled for the coastline, keeping it just in view on our right for most of the journey.

When the modular buildings of FS11 appeared in the distance, jutting up from the tight forest of evergreens, the girls strained at their seat belts for a better look.

"What's that?" Akiko asked, pointing beyond the compound. To me it seemed as though she was pointing at where the forest met the sky. I squinted in the direction she indicated, but it took me a full minute to see what she was talking about. I shot a side-glance at her. Her eyesight *couldn't* be *that* good.

"I don't know," I answered truthfully. Where she was pointing seemed so far away I thought it had to be outside the borders of TNC's property.

Now that we were closer, there was clearly a large patch of earth which had been clear-cut. It was close to the Atlantic and appeared to be a near perfect circle.

"What's that, Sy?" Saxony asked when I failed to produce an answer.

"You'll have to ask Hiroki or Miss Marks." Sy turned his face half-toward us between the two front seats of the cockpit. "I'm just the chauffeur."

The clear-cut patch of earth went out of view beyond a hill as Sy steered the helicopter toward the pad on the top of the highest TNC building, the one with the biggest lab beneath it. Sy cut the engines and instructed us to wait a minute before getting out. The whirring blades droned as they slowed, and then came to a sudden halt.

Leaving our headgear on the seats, we piled out of the helicopter and stepped out into the brisk morning air.

Hiroki was waiting for us at the corner of the helipad, wrapped up in a black oilskin jacket and wearing a gray knit hat jammed down around his ears. His expression was as close to excited as I'd ever seen it.

"Welcome, welcome, ladies!" He stepped forward and grabbed

Saxony's hand, jiggling her arm enthusiastically and grinning into her face. "Welcome!"

I watched, bemused, as he passed through the line, shaking the girls' hands each in turn and making sure he'd gotten their names right.

"Akiko," he said, nodding to the tiniest member of the group with a warm look which I respected him for. "Let's get out of this chilly breeze."

We followed him down the steps and into the building. He led us to a boardroom where an impressive spread of food had been laid out.

"Oh, man." Saxony unzipped her vest and shucked it. "Fresh croissants? Are those scones? It smells like a bakery in here. I'm suddenly starving."

"Have a seat and help yourself." Hiroki poured himself a coffee from the machine in the corner. "If you'd like a hit of caffeine after the early morning you've had, help yourself. This baby will make you whatever you want. I have to say, I quite fancy the vanilla-bean latte myself."

I cocked an eyebrow at Hiroki, and he shot me a 'who, me?' look of innocence accompanied by a barely perceptible shrug of the shoulder. Hiroki was schmoozing them. Hard. The girls wouldn't know it, but this was not the Hiroki I knew. I wasn't sure whether to be amused or concerned by this behavior.

"Why, thank you, Hiroki," I said, mimicking his cavalier tone. "Vanilla bean, did you say? Don't mind if I do."

"Sounds great," said Georjayna, stepping up to the machine. "Oooh, chai. I love chai. Targa, there's a mocha setting. Want one?"

The girls began to relax. They doffed their hats and coats and helped themselves to the aromatic food. A general air of anticipation and companionship permeated the room.

I sat and filled a plate with breakfast as I observed Hiroki chatting with the girls. I was so taken off-guard by his charming behavior that I didn't join in the conversation. I just listened and observed the group dynamics as Hiroki drew the girls out of their shells. He asked them how their studies were going, about their family lives, how long they'd known one another, how they'd met. He never once mentioned supernatural abilities. In fact, his questions seemed to make the girls feel like they were talking to a family acquaintance, maybe even a friend. I could see them relax more and more with every minute that went by, their guards lowering, their smiles coming easier and faster.

His approach was smart...and manipulative.

I began to grow uncomfortable as the chit-chat went on and I had to bite my tongue to keep from telling Hiroki to drop the charade. It began to irritate me that he thought it was okay with me that he behave in a way that I knew was not in his true nature. Hiroki insisted on keeping a professional distance with me, as TNC expected, but here he was asking about their lives and relationships. Why would he be so obviously one way with me in private, and so different with them?

For the first time since embarking upon my contract with TNC, I felt uneasy.

10

SAXONY

"That was the best breakfast I've had in a long time," I said, putting a hand on my belly. I looked down at the still overflowing spread before us. "Were you expecting an army or something? There is a ton of leftovers."

"I'm glad you liked it," Hiroki said just as there was a tap at the door. "Come in."

A woman with her hair tied back in a severe bun poked her head in and nodded to us in general before saying to Hiroki, "They're ready for you now. Theatre three."

"Theatre?" Georjie mouthed at me.

I shrugged.

"Excellent." Hiroki got to his feet. "Before we go in, does anyone need to visit the restroom?"

We did, so Hiroki showed us where the facilities were, then waited until we finished. Then he bade us leave our coats and hats and follow him.

He led us down a hallway past several closed doors which I assumed were offices. We passed two sets of double doors labeled Theatre 1 and Theatre 2 before stopping at the third. Hiroki pushed the doors open and stepped aside to let us enter.

Inside was an intimate theatre with enough seats for no more than thirty people. The room was dimly lit and a dark curtain was drawn across what I assumed was a stage. There was no one else in the space aside from us.

"Take a seat for a moment, ladies," Hiroki said. "I'll just go check on Miss Marks."

We made our way down the gently sloping floor to the row in front of the stage where we sat down in plush seats. The five of us gawked at the small but clearly state-of-the-art theatre. It was impeccably clean. Each seat reclined and had a panel full of buttons on the armrest. I couldn't begin to guess what that many buttons were needed for in a theatre. Ordering popcorn delivered directly? From the look on Petra's face, I guessed she'd never been in this theatre, either.

"This just gets more and more intriguing," murmured Targa.

"Tell me about it," muttered Petra.

"You really don't know anything more than we do?" Akiko shifted in her seat to face Petra.

Petra shook her head. "They've been careful not to tell me anything. It's important to Miss Marks that the four of us learn about the project all at the same time."

"Who is Miss Marks?" I asked, keeping my voice low. Something about being in a dark theatre automatically made me feel like I should be quiet.

"She's the CEO of this division of TNC."

"And have you ever met Mr. Nakesh?" Georjie asked, also keeping her voice low.

"Nope, but Hiroki says we will today. I guess that's one thing I knew that you didn't." Petra looked momentarily struck. "I have no idea if I was supposed to tell you that or not. Honestly, all the layers of secrecy in this place are enough to drive me mental."

"Ladies." A voice which did not belong to Hiroki had us shift in our seats to look back at the open double doors.

A tall slender woman in a white suit had her back to us and was just closing the double doors. She clicked them shut and turned to walk silently down the carpeted floor in white patent-leather high heels. Right away I thought that this woman and Georjie's mother might have a lot in common; she looked like she'd come from the womb in a power-suit. She walked with her chest held up and out so that her posture was perfect, her shoulders thrown back confidently. Her perfectly tailored skirt and jacket had thin gray pinstripes running down them. Her hair was a uniform light gray and pinned up in a clean french twist. Her bangs were trimmed straight across and hid her forehead. Her face was unlined, but whether that was because she never expressed herself or she'd had work done, who knew. The silver hair suggested experience and the flawless complexion suggested money and meticulous care. The eyes that took us in with an almost hungry gaze were yellow-brown, a similar color to the wood used to make expensive yachts.

"Hello, ladies," she said smoothly. "We meet at last. I have been looking forward to this moment more than I can say. I'm Jody Marks." She walked past us and perched against the stage, crossing her legs at the ankles. There was an undercurrent of excitement in the way she spoke, as though she really was thrilled to meet us but was trying not to let too much emotion leak through. "You can call me Miss Marks." Her teak-colored eyes fell on Petra and she gave her a polite nod and a smile that didn't quite make it to her eyes. "Miss Kara."

"Miss Marks," Petra murmured, and returned the closed-mouth smile.

I thought that a look passed from Jody to Petra that seemed very calculated.

"I'm sure you're all dying of curiosity," Miss Marks said with a hollow chuckle. She folded her hands together and I noticed her fingernails were done up in a french manicure. "Before we get to the good stuff, I want to thank you for coming. No matter how today turns out, no matter what you choose, I want you to know that TNC is eternally grateful for the time you've taken from your lives to be here today. You've made the decision to meet with us based on very little information."

I watched, impressed, as she lifted a hand to her heart. She seemed really sincere.

She continued, "And that decision shows a level of faith in us that we've yet to earn. Hopefully you'll allow us to reward that faith." She arched a fine silver eyebrow. "We compensate our supernaturals in the seven-figure range and sometimes even eight, depending on their abilities."

Georjie and I shared a look. Georjie's expression, much like I knew my own would be, was one of amazement and raging curiosity. Seven and sometimes eight figures? What on earth did these people have in mind? With that kind of money, I could change the lives of my family. We were solidly middle-class and had never wanted for the necessities of life, but with the kind of money she was talking about, possibilities were blown wide open. The build-up to this reveal was making me feel like I was going to crawl out of my skin with anticipation.

"I have received your paperwork, thank you also for that," Miss Marks was saying. She inclined her head with gratitude. "I must impress upon you, we take our contracts seriously and will prosecute should we have any reason to believe that details of the project we've shared with you today have been leaked to the outside world. We are a multi-billion-dollar company with numerous powerful competitors. We did not become this successful by being cavalier about..." She paused thoughtfully. "...Well, about anything. We are professionals, and we will treat you as though you are professionals also."

My throat had gone a little dry and I wished I'd brought a bottle of water from the breakfast table. She hadn't said any of this with a threatening tone, but the words sure nailed things home well enough. Secrecy. Got it.

"Petra has told you that we have a special interest in hiring and grooming supernaturals for some of our projects." As she said this, she lifted a wrist and tugged back the sleeve of her suit jacket to look at her watch. She frowned, the corners of her mouth tugging down delicately, almost imperceptibly, like she'd trained her face to go no farther since it might mar her perfect features.

Targa shifted uncomfortably in her seat and I thought I knew what she was thinking. *More* people who knew about her supernatural nature. And not just anyone—powerful people.

Miss Marks looked up, just missing Targa's discomfited movements. She looked up high on the back wall and squinted. She seemed to be addressing someone behind the black windows at the back of the theatre. "I was expecting Mr. Nakesh to have joined us by now, but he seems to be running late. Let's go ahead without him. I'm sure he'll join us as soon as he can."

In response, the curtain began to open on a silent runner. What it revealed surprised me. The stage was circular. A long, curved console accompanied by several keyboards and complicated control panels ringed the platform. Black chairs were slid in under the console. In the center of the circular space was a low indented desk with dark glass, making it look like a large cyclopean eye jutting up from the floor.

It felt like a place rockets were launched from, or a war-room or something. Chrome and shining black screens and fixtures gleamed neatly from the stage. My breath hitched with surprise and my pulse sped up. The whole thing made Basil's high-tech testing facility look hokey.

"Whoa," Georjie said on an exhale beside me. She shot me a look of incredulity.

"Do these people work for Tony Stark or something?" I said it on the barest whisper, but it still earned me an elbow in the arm.

"Come on." Miss Marks straightened and climbed the short set of steps leading up to the space station/war-room. "This will be interactive to a degree. We like to have everyone comfortable and able to move around if they wish. Different vantage points are important since this presentation is done in-the-round, to borrow some theatre lingo." She chuckled at her own wittiness.

We followed her up the steps and onto the stage where she directed us to grab our chairs and roll them to face the eye in the center. In spite of her claims about this being a round presentation and we could spread out as we wished, the five of us brought our chairs into a semi-circular line on one side of the space. Miss Marks stood opposite us.

The double doors opened and Hiroki entered. The doors snicked shut behind him, sealing out the light of the hallway. He made his way down to the stage and joined us. His brow gleamed with sweat and he took out a kerchief and mopped it. It wasn't particularly warm in the theatre, but I thought perhaps he had a bit of stage-fright. That simple gesture, of cleaning moisture off his brow, did more to send the message home: it was very important to them that they impress us; this was a one-shot deal for them. Whatever they wanted from us, they wanted it bad.

Jody leaned close to Hiroki and asked something in a quiet voice. Her eyes flicked to Targa once, but I thought I heard her say Mr. Nakesh's name again.

Hiroki looked down at his watch and gave her a shrug that said, *I don't know*.

"Right," Miss Marks said, turning her attention from Hiroki to us. Her expression was serious.

I wondered if she was sweating under that expensive-looking suit. I wished she would relax, maybe put on a hoodie and a pair of running shoes and chill out. She was making me nervous.

She said, "The projects we employ supernaturals for are the most exciting and most classified projects we execute. They cost the most money, take the biggest risks, and have the most impact. This particular project, one we're calling Project Expansion, for now–"

"The name is a working title," Hiroki added with a chuckle. "Let us know once you understand what we're doing if you want to pitch a new name. We're open to suggestions."

Miss Marks shot Hiroki a mild look that could only be described as long-suffering.

"Are you serious about that?" I asked, with more of a desire to interact and break down the ice wall that stood between Miss Marks and the rest of us.

"Yes," said Hiroki emphatically, and wrinkles sprang to life on his forehead.

"No," said Miss Marks, just as emphatically, but without the wrinkles. "Let's stay on track, please."

Hiroki leaned back so that he was out of Miss Marks's periphery and nodded at me while mouthing the words, 'Yes it is.' He widened his eyes, and he opened his mouth so wide a bird could have flown inside.

I bit back a smile and heard Targa cover a laugh by turning it into a cough. Akiko shifted in her seat with her face tucked down in shadow. Georjie rubbed a hand across her mouth to hide her smile. At least the tension had eased a little, thanks to Hiroki's theatrics.

"If our objectives are achieved," Miss Marks continued, either oblivious to Hiroki's clowning around or choosing to ignore him, "Project Expansion has the potential to improve millions of lives and alter the trajectory of destruction our planet is currently on."

Trajectory of destruction? She had to be talking about climate change and pollution. Okay, so this project was environmental in nature. A puzzle piece clicked home in my brain: we were Elementals, able to control aspects of nature. It made sense that a corporation might want to use our abilities to improve the state of the planet.

Intrigued, I perched my feet on the foot of my chair, leaned forward, and rested my elbows on my knees.

A blue glow appeared over the center circle and I immediately sat back again, startled by the bright light. The central eye was a hologram projector.

A hologram of Earth, slowly rotating in a galaxy of stars, flickered to life before us in vibrant colors. It looked so substantial I wanted to reach out and touch it to see if something had actually materialized there.

"Behold, our home," Hiroki said, gesturing to the hologram. "Our beloved planet is in trouble. By 2050, our oceans will contain more plastic than fish. Weather is becoming extreme and dangerous at an unprecedented pace, destroying billions of dollars' worth of crops every year. In 2017, the US alone suffered a record year of 306 billion dollars' worth of weather damage. Drought and rising temperatures have left millions of people in south and east Africa facing famine.

Dead zones in our oceans, areas where nothing can survive except for jellyfish because the water has become too acidic, are expanding at an alarming rate. Whole countries are starving to death, while others throw away food every day. Some might argue we are on the brink of World War III as tensions mount between the world's major powers."

Gooseflesh rose on my skin as images illustrating Hiroki's narration appeared beside the spinning globe. Each image looked real enough to step into, and a low, tense soundtrack had begun to issue from speakers around the room. The images depicted beaches buried in plastic garbage, dust blowing across a cracked and inhospitable desert, an emaciated mother holding a child so hungry and tired he could do nothing more than lie still in his mother's arms. A whale wrapped in a fishing net so tightly that the ropes were cutting into its skin. An underwater panorama that showed nothing but huge jellyfish clogging the sea for what looked like miles. A smoggy and filthy city street crowded with people covering their mouths as red dust filled the air and garbage blew across the broken pavement.

A lump formed in my throat as I witnessed the emotional and devastating images paired with the dramatic music. The soundtrack was loud enough to be heard, but not so loud it drowned out Hiroki's voice.

"The picture I paint is grim for a reason," the scientist went on. "This is our current reality, and our future, but one we have the ability to change. Which is why we've asked you here today. TNC has a wildly imaginative and bold plan to provide humanity with a new lease on life."

He took a breath and glanced at Miss Marks, who gave him an encouraging nod.

"The surface of land on our earth is approximately one hundred forty-eight million square kilometers," Hiroki continued.

The disturbing images faded away and the spinning Earth took center stage again. Sections of green light appeared on the hologram, highlighting large tracts of land on the continents. Splotches of red were also illuminated throughout, with the majority of the red areas being the Arctic and Antarctica.

"Thirty-three percent of that land is desert."

Splotches of yellow marked out the deserts in regions of Africa, South America, North America, Central Australia, and Asia. Hiroki shifted to the side so he didn't disappear from view as the hologram increased in size. "And twenty-four percent is mountainous. That makes for over sixty-three million square kilometers of uninhabitable land. Some of that land could be revitalized, brought to life, made stable and productive and used to provide a safe and self-sustaining place to live. If you'll allow me to shift gears for a moment, what I'll say next will seem strange—possibly unbelievable—but trust me as I attempt to illustrate the way you can help us achieve this."

I shared a look with Georjie on my right, and leaned forward to catch a glimpse of Targa's profile. In spite of myself, I was intrigued and impressed, not only by the altruistic objective but also the sheer scope of TNC's project. Georjie tucked her chin against her shoulder and mouthed *wow*. I nodded my agreement. Wow, indeed.

The hologram of the Earth faded away and what replaced it was an image of a familiar painting. It depicted a square ocean with a dragon crouched beneath it. Two ships sailed in the waters. One ship tilted dangerously and was in the process of falling over the side of an ocean that simply ended. Water poured off into space. A white fluffy face in the clouds blew a nasty wind to hurry the ships toward their doom.

"Ancient cultures ascribed to the idea of a flat-earth, before Aristotle provided empirical evidence for the spherical shape we're familiar with today. What we're left with from this old belief system is some beautiful imagery of how artists of the age thought the Earth might have looked. Consider this one made relatively recently, in 1893, by a fellow named Orland Ferguson."

The painting changed into another. This one was not familiar to me. It was more map than art. Rendered in black and white, it portrayed a large square slab of land with a circular indentation, like a giant had pressed the bottom of a bowl into the ground. The indentation cradled all of the oceans and the continents. Four angels hovered at each corner, keeping watch over the world.

"What's the white stripe around the outside?" I asked. A ring of white surrounded the indentation's outer edge. The white ring was smooth around the outside but jagged and crooked around the inside where it met the waters of the world.

"Ah. Glad you asked." Hiroki grinned and I gathered that he was enjoying this foray into the ridiculous. "That is the ice-wall which the artist proposed kept our oceans and seas from leaking out and falling off the edge."

"Oh."

"To be fair, I don't know if the artist was commissioned by a scientist or if he made this piece to satisfy his own desire to illustrate a world lived on-the-flat." Hiroki chuckled. "As ridiculous as it might seem given what we know now, the Flat-earth Society still exists today and contrary to popular belief, it's not full of loons and crackpots, but includes some startlingly brilliant scientific minds."

"If they're so scientific," Targa said, "how can they possibly believe in a flat world? I mean…it's preposterous. What's holding the whole thing up? A giant turtle? What makes the seasons if the world isn't round and spinning around a huge central star?"

"All good questions," Hiroki replied, nodding. "Flat-earth speculation is not the subject of our presentation today but I suggest that should you ever find yourself in a room with one of those who still believe in it, simply ask them. You may be astonished to find—in spite of your fervent investment in our global system and infinite universe—yourself being swayed. I myself—a resolute globalist like the majority of scientists—upon spending some time reading their materials, found myself both reluctantly fascinated and impressed with how they explain the science of this type"—he waved toward the map—"of system. To quote a book I recently read: 'Even the smartest people tend to seek out evidence that confirms what they already think, rather than new information that would give them a more robust view of reality.' I like to consider myself an open-minded person, so I indulged them and left my cynicism and ridicule at the door.

"This is a difficult thing to do, but the attitude of child-like wonder is what gives birth to discovery. What I came away with," he said, his eyes gleaming, "was an idea so brilliant that it captured the imagination, not to mention the pocketbook, of one of the world's richest and most powerful men." He looked at his watch and added, "A man who is never on time."

The hologram shifted again, this time to an animated and much more realistic looking flat-earth system, complete with a small rotating sun and moon, chasing each other in eternal orbit over the disc of the world.

"Modern flat-earth science gave me this," Hiroki explained. "An animation that helped me understand better how they proposed this wildly unbelievable system might work."

The hologram zoomed in to show its mechanics more clearly. I sat forward in my seat, fascinated.

"In this structure," Hiroki said, "the sun is much smaller than our actual sun and the moon even tinier yet. The two rotate over the land, disappearing from view due to perspective rather than curvature. In this way, they still provide night and day, just as we experience it in our universe. The orbits they follow swell in and out, providing us with seasons."

The animation showed the orbits moving just as Hiroki said.

He continued, "The sun, being much closer to us in this system, works more like a giant spotlight. It lights the land below and just beyond, providing the heat and energy which plants need. The moon follows along, reflecting the sun's light and providing the lesser light that rules the night." Hiroki passed behind the hologram and appeared on the other side. "In order to become useful to us, and I might say, truly revolutionary, something is missing in this scenario."

Akiko said something inaudible. She was furthest from me so I leaned forward and was about to ask her to repeat herself when Hiroki spoke again with genuine surprise on his face.

"That's right, clever girl. That is what's missing."

"What did she say?" I whispered to Georjie.

"A dome."

As Georjie answered my question, a transparent dome appeared overtop of the earth. A galaxy full of stars, which looked embedded in the walls of the dome, rotated along with the planets, sun, and moon.

"Or," said Hiroki with an eye on Petra, "a force-field, if you will. Ancient texts referred to it as a firmament."

I bent forward to catch a glimpse of Petra. She looked a bit stunned. Her lips parted and I strained to hear her whisper. She coughed to clear her throat and repeated herself, but all she'd said was, "A force-field?"

Hiroki nodded, his look both somber and triumphant. "With such a dome in place," he went on, "the land beneath would be protected from ominous forces such as extreme weather, dangerous radiation and solar flares, and even powerful impacts such as those from missiles and meteors. Such a territory would be safe in a way no land ever has been to our present knowledge, even to the destruction of our planet, in theory. I'll show you how we think it might be possible."

The hologram began to shrink and spin and morph into something that looked more like a snow-globe with the flat-earth universe going straight across the interior. The dome was now a full sphere. Beside the sphere, planet Earth appeared, rotating slowly, and the green, red and yellow patches reappeared. The sphere containing the flat-earth model shrank while the planet grew larger, part of it disappearing out of the hologram altogether as we zoomed in on Africa.

There was a sound effect, a heavy boom from the speaker system as the sphere was planted in the middle of a yellow patch on the globe, in the Sahara Desert. The sphere was half buried in the Earth's crust, leaving the flat-earth inside on the same level as the terrain of the planet. Now the visual clearly showed the force-field as a dome which we understood was actually the visible half of the sphere. Apparent through the clear field and protected under the dome, was a place of verdant green life, bodies of water, roaming animals, and small cities complete with the tiny figures of people, all apparently living in harmony. Outside the dome, the sands of the desert and the hot sun raged and baked without mercy.

A solar flare burst came from off-screen, lighting one side. A meteor hurtled out of space and struck Earth with a terrific explosion of fire, smoke, and a spray of rocks. When the mess cleared, the sphere with the flat-earth system inside it was intact.

"Obviously, this is a grim picture, and not what we anticipate will happen to Earth. We animated it just to give you the idea of how stable we think this system could be. Ladies," Hiroki said, resting his hands on the edge of the console and looking at each of us in turn, "Elementals. TNC has secured some of this uninhabitable land with the intention of transforming it into safe and habitable territory. We have been doing the math on this project for years, and while we might manage to at least partially realize our vision with technology and pure grit, it will happen much, *much* faster with your help."

One could have heard a pin drop.

"You want..." I began, and then halted, not sure I should voice it for fear I'd misunderstood and would sound completely ridiculous. "You want us to help you make...*a dome*?"

Hiroki nodded. "A prototype first, naturally, to study and test. Then a full-scale model once we've worked out any kinks. After that..." He shrugged. "Multiples."

"Is this for real?" Georjie's voice was pregnant with doubt.

"I assure you it is." Miss Marks shifted against the outer console, the first movement she'd made since Hiroki's presentation had begun in earnest. "It is a project you can be proud of. Not only would you be compensated beyond your wildest dreams, you would be helping to make life on this planet better through giving people hope and offering them a place of safety."

Akiko spoke up. "You don't think it makes more sense to try and reverse the environmental issues we're facing, instead of creating something to hide under?"

Hiroki said, "We like to approach problems from two sides. TNC has departments whose sole focus and purpose is to alleviate some of the problems I mentioned earlier, most specifically to do with the environment. Cleaning up our oceans, working on the acid and alkaline balance, and studying why weather is becoming more volatile with every passing year are some of the aims of those departments. Believe me, we are working on reversing the current trajectory. But that is not the aim of this particular department. We are tackling world issues from a different angle. Suppose we are not successful in reversing the colossal wheels of destruction already in motion? Suppose we are struck by a meteor? Suppose the poles do reverse? Suppose a solar flare large enough to bake half the planet does occur? Suppose all life in our oceans dies, coral reefs gone, fish gone, seventy percent of our oxygen supply, gone."

I raised an eyebrow, waiting to see where he was going with this.

"Ladies, those are the incidences we are executing this project for. The project's aim is to preserve life, should the planet face destruction. Imagine, even in the event of a meteor strike which sends us spinning out of orbit and away from our sun! With your help, life can go on. Life could even begin on other planets! This possibility is not overreaching."

His answer impressed me. I eyeballed the little rotating sun in the animation.

"I have a question," I put up a finger.

"Please," Hiroki gestured to continue.

"Why do you need a miniature sun and moon if the dome is transparent and will get sunshine anyway?"

"We don't, presently," answered Hiroki, "but we want to test our ability to provide them as an optional extra for the event of, say, a nuclear winter or meteor strike. The impact wouldn't even have to push the Earth out of orbit for the miniature sun to be helpful, because the dust alone would block out our sun—as happened during the dinosaur extinction—leaving those inside the dome with a need for a new light source."

"Oh." Seemed Hiroki had an answer for everything.

"Good question, though. Keep them coming." Hiroki winked at me.

Miss Marks crossed behind the hologram and stood on the other side, looking from face to face. She clasped her hands behind her back. "What you would be involved in with Project Expansion, we believe, is not unique in the world of space exploration and aeronautic research."

This statement was contradictory to what Hiroki had implied. I glanced at him but he didn't defend his earlier position.

"But no one has as yet thought to apply it to our own planet," Miss Marks said. "It is only a matter of time before our competitors come to a similar conclusion and begin work on it, if they haven't already." She stopped walking and turned to face us.

I stared back at her, conscious of my friends next to me who were also intrigued.

Miss Marks continued, "But our competitors don't have you. If you agree to work with us, you'll be protected and nurtured by a team of scientists who are already working with supernaturals. Your families will also be protected and provided for." Her expression grew sober. "Walk away, and we cannot protect you. You are very valuable and if we know you exist, believe me, others know you exist too. You are lucky that we happened to get to you first."

"You can't imagine that they'll give you an answer today?" Akiko said, incredulous. "This is a huge commitment, and if I'm being honest, it seems rife with potential problems."

"Would you like to speak for yourselves?" Miss Marks asked Targa, Georjie, Petra, and me, while ignoring Akiko.

"She's right," Targa said, nodding. "Your project looks incredible and in spite of having a million questions about it, I like the idea in theory. But you're asking a lot. We have lives we would have to walk away from. You can't expect us to make a decision right now, or even in the next couple of days."

Hiroki gave a hearty laugh. "And we don't. Please don't feel pressured. I would very much like the opportunity to answer those questions, and if there are some I haven't got answers to yet, then all the better. I have incredible AI here at the labs which is capable of doing millions of calculations, analyzing millions of outcomes in a moment. If there is something you ask that I haven't yet answered, then I would love the opportunity to do just that." He clapped his hands together once. "I think we've had enough for the moment. Why don't we take a break? Use the facilities, have a snack or a coffee or whatever your hearts' desire. I'd like to begin the second part in an hour. If you're amenable, of course."

"What's the second part of the day?" Petra asked as we got up from our seats.

Hiroki flicked a switch on the dashboard and the hologram vanished. "Making the prototype!"

11

SAXONY

We entered the boardroom where we'd eaten breakfast. My friends looked dazed, amazed, and doubtful. What my friends were doubtful about, I couldn't say, but I was doubtful both about the viability of the project and the sanity of its creators.

I barely noticed that a new spread of fragrant food and tasty looking drinks had been laid out on the table. We took our former seats. Hiroki and Miss Marks had followed us into the boardroom, but they didn't sit down. I was hoping they'd leave us alone for a bit.

As though she could read my mind, Miss Marks said, "You'll be in need of some time to absorb this initial presentation, as well as some privacy to talk. Hiroki and I will leave you and be back in a little less than an hour." They turned to go, but she paused at the door and said, "We may be back sooner if Mr. Nakesh shows up, as I know he'll want to meet you without delay."

They left and shut the doors.

"Do you think they've got recording devices in here?" Akiko was scanning the corners and eyeballing the screen at the front of the room dubiously.

"I can almost guarantee it," Petra replied.

"Isn't that illegal? To record someone without their permission?" Georjie reached for a jug of water and began to fill glasses for everyone.

"It is, but you only need consent from one of the people in the conversation and they've already got mine." Petra took a glass from Georjie with a nod of thanks. "Just so you know. I looked it up when I first signed on with TNC. When I signed my contract, I agreed to let them record all of my activities at FS11."

"FS11?" I asked, taking my glass from Georjie.

"Field Station Eleven."

"Oh, right."

"So, what do you guys think?" Petra reached for an apple from the bowl overflowing with fruit. Seemed she wasn't having the same difficulties with her appetite as I was. Food was the last thing I was interested in.

"The whole thing sounds a bit nuts," I said, my palms out. "Do they really think it can work?"

"Why not?" Petra looked at me with surprise. "I mean, it's ambitious for sure, but a little over a hundred years ago, people thought horseless carriages were an impossibility, same with flying and sending people into space. Those things are all the norm now."

"It's got its challenges," added Georjie, also not touching the food. "But it's intriguing. I mean, I love the idea of making uninhabitable land viable. That is an awesome objective, don't you think?"

I nodded. "Yeah, for comic book characters." I turned to Akiko. "What do you think of these loony-tunes?"

Akiko's mouth was a flat line. "I instinctively don't trust corporations, no matter how prettily they paint their intentions. The idea is amazing, but it's fraught with potential problems."

"What potential problems would those be?" said a jovial voice. "Pour them on me!"

We turned to see a man's face poking in the door.

"Can I come in?" He grinned and came in without waiting for an invitation.

This had to be Mr. Nakesh.

He was not obviously an extremely rich and successful man, dressed the way he was. Yet, if I had spotted him walking down the street I would have said there was something in his movements and expression that oozed confidence and importance. He wore faded blue jeans and white sneakers combined with a white t-shirt and a violently purple twill blazer overtop. His hair was so blond it was almost white. His features were fine and sharp and his hair cropped short. From beneath a wide brow blazed intelligent eyes of bright blue. They were not ethereal or vibrant the way Targa's and her mother's were, but they were arresting in their own way.

"I'm so sorry I missed the presentation." He began to shake hands with each of us. "I'm Mr. Nakesh and I am *beyond* happy to meet you guys."

He leaned back a little, bent at the knees, to emphasize just how happy he was.

He continued, "I've read all your files—"

I saw Akiko and Targa share a cocked eyebrow at the idea that we had files. This didn't surprise me so much after meeting Basil.

"-And what an honor, just an absolute honor it is to have supernaturals of your caliber even *considering* working with us." He gave a laugh that might be better described as a giggle. "Of course, we are the best, so why wouldn't you, but still..."

There was a frenetic and slightly desperate energy about Mr. Nakesh. He spun out a chair and sat in it backwards, facing us eagerly. He tapped out a rhythm on the wooden back of the seat.

I got the sense that he was either high on some drug or he was the type of person I labeled a chihuahua–-high-strung, hyperactive, and incapable of sitting still. I knew the type well. There was one in every class. I observed him observing us, feeling faintly amused.

"It's an honor to meet you, too," Georjie said, very politely.

"So, what did you guys think of the presentation?" He didn't wait for us to answer and began to speak rapidly. "I've seen it so many times I know it by heart. I helped build it, in my own way, you know with feedback and stuff." He waved a hand. "But I'm sorry I didn't get to see your faces when you first caught wind of our idea. What do you think? What do you think?"

He enunciated all of his consonants, which gave him a robotic air.

We glanced at one another, not sure what to say. I wondered what Miss Marks might think of her boss's tactic of mining for a reaction before we were ready to give one.

Finally, Akiko responded. "It's...ambitious, to say the least."

Mr. Nakesh nodded vigorously. "Of course, we don't do anything if it isn't ambitious, otherwise what's the point? Who wants to do things that are boring? We have the means to rock the world with this project. So, you have questions? Well, come on, let's get into it."

The door opened and Miss Marks burst into the room with Hiroki on her heels.

"You're here!" A spot of color had appeared on each cheekbone. "Thank goodness. But I was hoping to give you a proper introduction." She smiled at us apologetically and took a deep breath. "Let's do this properly."

There was a lot of body language going on while she spoke. Miss Marks seemed both frazzled and embarrassed, but exerting enormous will to hide both. Hiroki's movements were both wooden and animated. He had taken off his glasses, put them back on again, removed a clipboard that had been tucked up under his arm, transferred it to under his other arm, shuffled backward to the wall, decided not to stand there and shuffled forward again. The whole effect was comical and made me feel like I'd been thrust into a slapstick play.

"...He's, uh, founded a dozen tech firms worldwide..." Miss Marks was going on about Mr. Nakesh's accomplishments when Hiroki finally settled on taking the empty seat between Georjie and Mr. Nakesh.

"It's all right, Jody. They don't need my entire resume." Mr. Nakesh laughed and waved her off, mid-sentence. "Let's get to the good stuff. Project Expansion."

I tried not to look at my friends—I was afraid their expressions would set me to giggling.

He spun the chair and put his back to Miss Marks, facing us once again. He slapped Hiroki's back. "Nice to see you, my man." He pointed a finger-gun in Hiroki's direction. "Picked this dude up from MIT and right out from under NASA's nose. No one more brilliant in astrophysics has ever been born."

Hiroki shifted uncomfortably under this. His entire face flushed cherry red. "Well, I..."

I noticed Petra stared at the two of them, bemused. I wondered what she was thinking.

"Whatever your questions are, don't leave any out. Hiroki here is writing a project pitch, thousands of pages long. He and his team are preparing a document answering in detail all of the questions you can think of as well as many you'll never think of. No one embarks upon a project of this magnitude and expense with a doubt factor of more than one percent. We have sales to make and they don't happen without a thorough F-A-Q sheet... in this case, maybe an F-A-Q tome." Mr. Nakesh chuckled at his own joke.

"Sales?" Targa came to life at this statement. "What are you selling?"

"Property inside the domes, of course," Mr. Nakesh replied, with another hand-tapping rhythm on the back of his chair.

"You're already selling property?" Confusion clouded her face. "But the domes don't even exist yet."

"It's all conditional," Mr. Nakesh said with another floppy wave of his hand. "If the project fails then the sales don't go through, naturally. We're investing billions in this project, we have to make our money back or we'll go under. This is the way things work in business. One of our competitors has already sold property on another planet..."

"How do you sell something that doesn't belong to you?" Akiko narrowed her eyes at the billionaire.

"It belongs to whoever can reach it first, then viably explore and develop it. This is how it has always been. But let's not get off track—"

"Who are you selling the properties inside the domes to?" Targa asked.

"Just like any developer with a large tract of land, we've plotted maps and zoned them for residential, commercial, agricultural, and recreational. But before you get the idea that this project is strictly for profit, we also intend to offer a heavily-subsidized portion for middle-income families—to be won by impartial lottery—and we've also set aside a percentage for charity."

Georjie leaned forward in her chair and asked, "Just how large are these domes supposed to be?"

"Huge," Mr. Nakesh said. "Big as countries, some of them."

Georjie blinked a couple of times and stared at him, as though calculating the amount of work that would be required.

"How will people get in and out of the domes? What about oxygen and weather and crops?" I asked. "I'm more concerned about this than how you'll divvy up the property. How can it possibly be sustainable?"

"All great questions," Mr. Nakesh said smoothly. "Hiroki is working with Petra on how to create a doorway in the force-fields. While it's something we haven't figured out yet, I am fully confident we will. We just need more time with her kind of technology."

"What about jobs and businesses?" Georjie asked.

"This is simple," Mr. Nakesh spread his hands and shrugged. "Economy is fueled by supply and demand, and it would be no different inside the domes. We've already documented and laid out solutions for these very questions. The things that we are not yet able to solve require the prototype to be built first, as we need to work from a living model. Everything moves in stages. We risk getting lost in the weeds if we focus on these later details. Do you all understand the general thrust of the project?" Mr. Nakesh tucked his chin down and gazed at each of us in turn.

"Yes, I get it," Georjie said. "There is a lot I don't understand, and so many things that seem like they might not work, but I get what you're trying to do."

"Yes, I understand," I added. "In principle."

Akiko just nodded and said, "I get your objectives."

Petra and Targa also said they understood.

"Good." Mr. Nakesh looked at his watch and then stood. "Continue to ask Hiroki questions. He may not have a satisfactory answer yet, he may not have an answer at all, but one thing you can know for certain is that we understand that you will not sign any contracts until you're satisfied."

Hiroki nodded and added, "We get that."

"I would do no different," Mr. Nakesh went on, "and it is the least I would expect from intelligent young people such as yourselves. This is a huge project, the terms of which we can work out together when the time is right. But trust me please when I say that making this prototype is not just for our benefit, but also for yours. I'm confident that when you put your skills to this use, you will need no further inspiration from us."

Miss Marks stepped in again. "You'll be chomping at the bit to make it a reality."

Mr. Nakesh glanced at Miss Marks as though he'd forgotten for a moment that she was in the room, then went on. "Building a small prototype is on the schedule for today, but only if you agree. So," he gave us a glittering grin, "can we proceed with this next step?"

Targa spoke up first. "I'm game to try."

I looked at her with surprise. Of all of us, I had thought Targa would be the first to walk away. After all, she had Antoni waiting for her in Poland, and she'd inherited a huge company she had to figure out what to do with. This project could keep her busy for years if she agreed to it.

"Really? I'm surprised, Targa." Georjie evidently shared my feelings.

"Why?" Targa shrugged. "I'm curious to see if it might actually work. Like Mr. Nakesh said, we're not committing to anything other than this next step." Her bright blue eyes caught mine and held them, issuing a good-natured challenge. "You can't tell me you're not itching to unleash your powers on this?"

"I..." I swallowed. She wasn't wrong, but...Arcturus...

"I'm in," Georjie said when I didn't finish my answer. "I was in as soon as I understood what this could mean for humanity."

Mr. Nakesh and Hiroki exchanged an enthusiastic look. Even Miss Marks was now beaming with joy.

Georjie held up her hands. "Don't get too excited. I'm not saying I'm signing the contract or anything. I'm just saying, if my friends are game to build this prototype with me, then I'm up for it." She turned to me. "So? What do you say, Saxony?"

Georjie and Targa's enthusiasm gave me the little push I needed. I kept reminding myself that I hadn't signed anything yet, and there was no pressure. Yet. This was a chance to put our powers together to create something bigger than ourselves. I blinked at this realization and gazed at my friends. Between us, we held the powers of creation—this was why TNC wanted to work with us. I finally allowed the possibility that this crazy plan might actually work to seep in.

I smiled. "If you guys are in, then I'm in."

"Yeah!" Hiroki gave a fist-pump that looked so hilarious on the scientist that the room burst out laughing. The energy and feeling of camaraderie was building among our little group.

"And what do you think, Akiko?" Mr. Nakesh surprised me by asking for her opinion directly. "I know you're important to these ladies," he said, giving her a tiny bow of the head, "and whoever is important to them is important to me."

Akiko looked as surprised as the rest of us were. "I guess I'm taking the fifth," she finally said. "After all, TNC isn't looking for anything from me. But since you've all decided to build this prototype, you can bet I want a front row seat."

"That's it then," Georjie said, turning to Mr. Nakesh and standing up. "Bring it on."

12

SAXONY

"The diameter of the earth is 12,742 kilometers," Hiroki said as we walked from the all-purpose vehicles which had carried us through the woods toward the land they'd earmarked for the prototype. He was carrying a bag of tools over his shoulder and I eyeballed it, wondering what kind of equipment a scientist would need for a project like this. "We've plotted out 2.7 kilometers of land, the borders of which just reach the shores of the Atlantic." He gave Targa a smile. "That was done with you in mind."

The sound of waves and seabirds could be heard in the distance. Mr. Nakesh and Miss Marks trailed behind us. We walked with Hiroki while he gave us further instruction. Ahead of us, the land which had been clear-cut was occupied by a single crane. Dangling from the crane was a platform with a railing. The platform looked large enough to hold half a dozen people. I squinted at the crane's cockpit and saw there was a man sitting inside studying something in his hand like a book or a map. He looked up as we approached.

"In terms of the visual acuity of the human eye," Hiroki said, "the curvature of the earth drops at 7.85 centimeters per kilometer. We aren't able to mimic the visual effect of the sun disappearing below the horizon at the size of our prototype, so you'll just have to trust me that once scaled up, we will be able to mimic the optics of a real sunrise, sunset, and the moon's orbit. You won't even know the difference."

"Are you following all this?" I muttered to Akiko, falling back a little. "I don't get it."

She nodded. "A healthy human eye can see as far as fifty kilometers. At just under three clicks across, the prototype is too small to enable the sun to appear like the real sun because it can't disappear below the horizon. But in a dome that is thousands of kilometers across, a small sun should, in theory, disappear in the distance due to perspective. Provided the land inside the dome is actually flat and doesn't follow the curve of the earth." She shrugged. "If it does, then the sun and moon would simply disappear below the horizon as normal."

My face must have looked blank because Akiko stopped talking. She had an amused tilt at the corner of her mouth. She jerked her chin toward Hiroki. "Just pay attention."

Hiroki and Petra were walking together with Georjie and Targa on either side, listening. Hiroki talked with his hands. Akiko and I caught up.

Hiroki said, "The fellow in the crane is Mr. Biden. He's agreed to help us out today."

Hiroki waved to Mr. Biden and the arm of the crane lowered the platform to the ground where Hiroki had us step onto it. Mr. Nakesh and Miss Marks stepped up with us. Miss Marks had traded her power suit for khaki pants and a fatigue jacket, with a cute pair of white sneakers. Cat-eye sunglasses hid her eyes, while a pair of mirrored aviators perched on Mr. Nakesh's nose.

"The masks, Hiroki?" Miss Marks murmured.

Hiroki blinked. "I almost forgot." He bent to his bag and retrieved a bunch of tinted goggles and face masks. He handed them out to us. "Better put these on."

We all put the glasses on and settled the masks over our mouths and noses. Miss Marks tucked her sunglasses into a fancy pearly case and dropped them into the shoulder bag she carried. Mr. Nakesh hooked his on his collar.

"The first step is you two." Hiroki beckoned to Georjie and Targa. "Step up beside me at the railing here. I want to show you something that will help. It's a blueprint of sorts."

The crane lifted us into the air while we shifted around to let Georjie and Targa have the best view of the land below.

"See the border flags?" Hiroki pointed to the small orange flags nearly lost in the ground cover. They staked out a broad arch which swung behind us and curved off gently to either side. Given that we were making a round dome, I presumed they marked out a full circle.

The platform came to a halt and swayed gently. "Now, if you watch, you'll see something else that we've delineated." He picked up a remote control the size of a key-fob and flicked a switch. "Watch."

Thin, neon green lines appeared. They appeared to have no obvious order. They were being projected onto the ground by lasers fixed to the crane's arm.

"My team did a lot of calculations for this part of the prototype," Hiroki said, leaning his elbows on the railing of our platform. He pointed a finger down at the lines before us, tracing them. "You won't be able to tell because it's too big, but the laser maps out the continents as they looked on early maps when people thought the world was flat. We took our inspiration from the United Nations flag and logo. It closely resembles a flat-earth map as well. Because we're creating a place for humans to live that is, if we consider within the dome the only safe zone for life, not actually a globe but under a dome, we thought we would take an existing model rather than trying to create our own." He pointed to the edges of the dome. "The Arctic would technically be a shelf that runs around the perimeter of the dome, but we've left that part out, too. We really just need the main continents for our experiment today."

"The actual domes wouldn't be laid out this way, would they?" Akiko asked.

"No," Hiroki shook his head. "We thought that following a flat-earth map would be interesting and challenging for you guys. Give you a chance to really show off your powers. We needed a template to work with, and the flat-earth map already existed, so it was easy for us to borrow."

He turned to address Georjie and Targa. "Working together, can the two of you put the water where it is supposed to be, and the continents where they are supposed to be, as mapped out by the lasers? I can help guide you, as it'll be difficult at first."

Targa and Georjie looked at each other.

"At the same time?" Georjie asked Hiroki.

"As you wish," he answered. "However suits you."

"I need to have my feet in the dirt," Georjie said.

"Oh!" Hiroki looked surprised. He signaled the crane operator again, his cheeks pink. "Of course," he said, as though he'd known it all along. "I just wanted you to have an overhead view of the project first."

I shared a look with Akiko. It was clear Hiroki hadn't known Georjie needed to have her feet in the soil. No big deal. He wasn't omniscient. So why did he feel the need to cover it up and pretend he'd known all along?

The platform began to move again, lowering us to the ground. Once close enough, Georjie kicked off her sneakers and jumped down, landing barefoot in the soil.

"Can you still see the lasers?" Hiroki asked.

"I'll be able to in a moment," Georjie replied, cryptically. She pushed her goggles up into her hair and pulled the mask away from her mouth. "These are just annoying," she muttered.

Hiroki turned to Targa and hefted his bag. He seemed flustered. "We can go back to the vehicles and drive you down to the ocean, Targa."

But Targa shook her head. "I don't need to be in the water to control it."

"Ah, of course." Hiroki's cheeks flushed pink and I noticed Jody and Mr. Nakesh sharing what I thought was an unhappy glance. Hiroki put his bag down again and signaled to Mr. Biden, and we were hoisted into the sky.

Once again, Hiroki had shown ignorance about Elementals. These two bits of evidence left me wondering just how many supernaturals Hiroki had actually worked with. I glanced at Petra and there was a wrinkle of concern between her brows which I could see even under the goggles. I wondered if she had noticed Hiroki's blunders.

Georjayna's feet were planted in the soil, ankle-deep.

A dull and deep groaning sound rose to our ears. My heart began to pound in response, as it sounded like the very ground underneath us had a serious bellyache. Higher pitched twangs as well as loud snapping sounds punctuated the yawning growl of displeasure. It took me several seconds to realize what we were hearing—roots deep underground, stretching and breaking. The pure force Georjie had to be exerting was eye-watering.

We leaned over the railing, watching the terrain for signs of movement. Vertigo swept over me as the topography began to heave and shift. Cracks appeared in the dirt, yawning open and then collapsing. Lumpy mounds rose rapidly as though punched violently from underneath. The crackling and groaning sounds popped and echoed and reverberated through the air. It sounded like some colossal wooden hinge badly in need of lubrication was being pried open by Herculean fingers.

Then all movement and sound ceased.

We looked down at Georjie and she looked up at us, her hands hovering in the air and a look of amazement on her face.

"This earth is full of seeds!" she called up to us.

"Isn't the earth always full of seeds?" Akiko called back.

"Not like this. There are literally hundreds of thousands of species, many of them not native to Canada. If I made them grow, we would have the world's most diverse and colossal greenhouse right here—not to mention a problem with the law."

"That's the idea," Mr. Nakesh called down at her. He bobbed his head. "Not the problem with the law part, just the greenhouse bit."

There was a beat while Georjie absorbed this. "*You* put them here?"

"My team did, yes," Hiroki answered. He cleared his throat, still seeming a bit uncomfortable.

"Ohhhh...." Georjie let out a long understanding sigh and her expression and body language conveyed that her entire being was melting with pleasure. "You want me to develop them?"

"Yes, once you've shifted the continents into place, if you'd like, you can populate them with plants."

Facing front, Georjie said, "It's like the best theme park game ever." She spoke as though to herself, but the words drifted up and we laughed. She looked up again. "But some of these species are invasive."

"That's what the dome is for," Petra replied. "They'll never escape the barrier."

Georjie let out a long breath. "If you say so. If you're wrong I'll have to kill them all later, and that would suck." She returned to her work.

The cacophony started up again and the world below us shifted and swayed, dropped and rose. The topography began to make some sense of itself when the swells and dips of the land began to follow the laser lines. Replica continents rose as the floors of replica oceans and seas sank away. Jagged rocks appeared as Georjie unearthed stones and assembled them haphazardly. The optics of random rocks emerging and rolling around in the dirt to congeal and climb one another was bizarre and mesmerizing. The air was filled with dust and I was grateful for the goggles and the face masks.

The earth between the continents began to darken, and soon water seeped from underground.

I looked over at Targa and saw that she had also taken the goggles and mask off and was concentrating in the direction of the Atlantic, drawing it through the ground. Dirty water swelled and churned as it bubbled up through the earth, filling the caverns Georjie had built.

Goosebumps marbled the skin of my arms as we watched the heaving, churning real-life map of the world being constructed by Georjie and Targa. It was messy, filthy, and disorganized, and a little sickening to the senses, but through it all I was thoroughly amazed.

At first it looked like a mud pit, but as we watched the water began to clear. The land continued to shift into place, roiling and seething, and the water crept higher and higher. The air was so rich with the smell of soil and water, even through my mask, that it reminded me of the greenhouse in Georjie's basement.

The first of the plants began to appear, sprouting out of the earth like tiny hairs in a million shades of green. Wiggling and vibrating in response to Georjie's power, everything grew rapidly. Grasses, flowers, shrubs, vegetables, and herbs burst into bloom and filled our eyes with verdant shades of green speckled with yellows, pinks, and blues, while the taller plants continued onward and upward.

The oceans and seas were now full of shifting, slopping water, which began to calm as Targa let them be. Georjie was now a slash of blond hair in the sea of green below us. The tops of the trees were lush, and a canopy had formed along the fresh banks of dark water. Vines looped through tree branches while mosses crept over bark.

Georjie's arms came to rest at her sides and she looked up. "How's that?"

"Beautiful," Hiroki called down to her. "Marvelous job, both of you."

For several moments, we gazed out at the incredible scene before us. It looked like a huge swamp dotted with large forested islands.

"It's so quiet," Akiko murmured, who had now abandoned her mask and goggles too. I glanced at Petra, who had her goggles up in her hair and her mask hanging around her throat. I smiled at our quiet rebellion and slipped mine off as well. The dust was clearing and it felt nice to breath the air.

"Yeah, like it needs birds and animals and bugs," I added.

"Of course," Mr. Nakesh said. "We will introduce those to the domes as well. We want the experience of living in a dome to be as natural as possible. Like a paradise, or an Eden." He rubbed his hands together and turned to gaze at Petra with an expression akin to adoration. "Let's get to the next part. It's the most exciting. Our Euroklydon will now make our impenetrable dome."

13

SAXONY

"Its borders will follow the flags we've set out." Hiroki said as he took out his kerchief and mopped his forehead.

Georjie had rejoined us on the platform and we were once again hovering over the ground. She leaned over and whispered to Petra, "Euroklydon, that's what they call you?"

Petra nodded.

Hiroki continued, "Petra has a remarkable ability to allow material through the field while keeping out everything else. If I live to be a thousand I don't think any science could ever explain it."

Petra stepped away from us and a look of concentration came over her face. She held her hands apart, palms facing one another, and then let them rest slowly at her side. Her eyes had an unfocused look.

"You won't be able to see it," Hiroki said. "It's invisible to all except Petra."

"I can see it," said Akiko.

"You can?" Hiroki sounded shocked.

Akiko nodded. "It looks like heat, sort of. If you didn't know it was there, you'd never see it. Your eyes wouldn't know how to focus on it."

Hiroki took out a notepad from his chest pocket and jotted something down before tucking it away again. I stole a glance at his notes but his scrawl was hard to make out. The only word I caught was 'cryptochromes.' What was that? I made a mental note to look it up later.

"But you have to get it around us." I was looking at Petra. "How do you do that?"

"You each have a unique signature," Petra said. "I can feel it, and then I make the atoms of the force-field pass through yours."

At the look of alarm on our faces she added quickly, "Without hurting you. Kind of like this." She held the fingers of both hands spread open and passed the fingers through the spaces of the opposite hand, between each digit. "Touch it again," she directed me.

As I did, the solid surface of the force-field seemed to vanish as my fingers passed through it. "That's so bizarre," I said. "It's like a shadow passing over your skin."

"Now, I'll make it bigger."

The shadow passed over my skin, went up my body and disappeared. I looked up. There was nothing to see but clear blue sky.

A beat later and Petra said, "Okay, Hiroki. It's up."

"Great." Hiroki bent to his bag and pulled out a plastic flare-gun. "Just to demonstrate the efficacy of the barrier." He cocked the gun and fired it into the sky.

A red flare of light shot from the gun with a pop and hurtled into the sky. It hit the invisible barrier and exploded into a million sparking fragments.

"Can I try?" I asked.

"Absolutely," said Hiroki, putting the gun down and smiling at me. "Have at 'er."

I cocked my arm and released a fireball as hard as I could. Rather than flying up, like the flare had, it flew across the land at a blazing speed. Much brighter and faster than the flare, it hit the force-field with a dry crackle and exploded. A blue wave of ripples shot outward across the wall of the barrier. Against the forest beyond, it looked like a computer-generated effect.

"Wow!" Georjie laughed with amazement. "There it is! Did you do that?" she asked Petra.

Petra shook her head, looking mildly dazed herself. She was gazing at me with something akin to awe. "Nope. The force-field did it all by itself. I guess there was some juice behind that fireball."

I grinned, feeling a little cocky. "Some."

"Crank it up a notch, just for fun," Hiroki suggested.

"Don't fry us, Saxony," Targa said.

"I won't." I drew back my arm again, stoking the fire and drawing more heat up my arm as I released a larger, hotter fireball. I threw it in the other direction. Everyone squinted as it streaked into the air.

"I can feel the heat of that thing on my face," cried Petra, with her hand up to protect her eyes. Her hand bumped her goggles and she slid them down over her eyes again.

My fireball hit the inside wall of the dome with a light dry thud which didn't do justice to the heat I had packed into it. But the corona of blue ripples and the burst of fiery light that followed had all of us making sounds of appreciation. This time the blue ripples lasted a long time and the force-field seemed to waver before settling back into its quiet and invisible existence.

"What about fresh air?" Akiko asked Petra.

"Petra can make a barrier which air can permeate, if she wishes to. That's one of the most remarkable things about it," Hiroki explained. "It's impenetrable but permeable. Truly magical."

He turned to me. "Are you ready for your part?"

I gulped and my stomach did a little flip. "I've never made a sun before. It's going to be very hot."

"You can do it," Hiroki said. "If you have any trouble, we can get you there with coaching. Besides, you'll have Petra to help you. So we don't have any accidents, move away from us and into that clearing." He pointed. "Petra will lift the sun telekinetically while you increase its size slowly. Does that make sense?"

Petra and I nodded. Hiroki signaled the crane driver to lower us to the ground where Petra and I stepped off into a wonderland of lush green life. Petra put her goggles back up on her head.

"I did some rough calculations," Hiroki said from the platform, "but I had to guess a bit because I don't know how hot your fire is or how dense your fireball might be. I figure, if you make it roughly twelve feet in diameter, it will suffice for today's work."

"Twelve feet." I could do that. "I don't know if it will burn in perpetuity, though," I said. "I've never just left a fireball to burn before."

"That's all right," said Hiroki. "Let's just get the thing up there for starters. We can work on its lifespan later."

Hiroki stepped back onto the platform and had the crane lift it again. Targa gave me an encouraging wink as she peered over the side, then she slid her goggles into place and spoke to Georjie and Akiko, who both seemed to agree that now was finally a good time to wear the goggles, too. Mr. Nakesh and Miss Marks stood on Hiroki's other side, out of my view.

Petra and I made our way to the clearing Hiroki had appointed and stopped.

I looked into Petra's strange, silver-gray eyes, and she gazed back.

"Nervous?" she asked.

"A little," I admitted.

"I've had more coaching than I'd like to admit," she said with a quirky smile. "Georjie and Targa have put me to shame with how well they manage their powers. I'm sure you will too. I'll stand behind you. I don't really fancy being roasted today."

She took a step behind me.

"Heat doesn't bother me so I'm trusting you to lift it as fast as you need to so you won't burn," I said over my shoulder to her. "I'll make it small, then toss it up. Can you make sure it doesn't come down as I blow it up?"

"Piece of cake," Petra called as she took a few more steps back.

She put her goggles back into place. I didn't bother with mine. Light from fire had never hurt my eyes, even when I was surrounded by it or when my whole body had been aflame. If anything, it had taken my eyesight to a whole new level.

I waited until Petra was well behind me, then took a deep breath and closed my eyes, visualizing the fireball I wanted to make. I spread my hands apart and sent two small jet-streams of flame toward one another where they collided and swirled in a messy blur of fire. Rolling my hands in small circles, the misshapen ball began to form a rough sphere. It boiled and flickered and seethed in the air, spinning slowly and licking flames outward like it didn't know which direction was up.

I tossed the ball into the sky and watched as it paused and hovered. Petra was controlling it now. She pushed it up into the air, farther and farther from us.

Focusing, I compressed it, asking it to take up less space yet remain bright and hot. It did my bidding, becoming brighter and denser. Petra continued to lift the ball high into the air above our heads. As she did so, I asked the fire to condense further, and I gave it more fuel. It shrank, but brightened. It was too small still, so I sent jet-streams of fire from both hands to meet it in the air. It increased in size and the heat and light now coming off it was immense.

I continued to pack it tightly as Petra lifted. I added more fire, brightened it, and turned up the heat. I couldn't help but smile as I looked at the creation—it really did look like a small sun.

"Higher, Petra," Hiroki called from the platform.

Mr. Nakesh added, "Wonderful! Both of you!"

Our shadows darkened, their lines becoming sharper as the artificial sun rose overhead. Georjie and Targa made sounds of amazement. I looked back and up, catching Akiko shaking her head with wonder.

"You're all wonders of the world." Akiko's words drifted on the air.

"Big enough," Hiroki said.

I relaxed my hands and let the fire be, feeling a bit like I had just sent a kid off to kindergarten for their first day. Who knew I could create a sun-like object, even if it was minuscule? How big could I make it—as big as the sun? With Petra's help, could we create new stars? I swayed a little on my feet at the impact of what Hiroki was having us do. Alone, a supernatural was a force of nature. Together, we were like demi-gods or something.

"Okay, Petra, that's good. Leave it there."

The sun stopped moving and hovered in our artificial sky, sending heat and light down over us and the plants. The crane lowered the platform again so Petra and I could step on board.

At this point, everyone except for Miss Marks removed their goggles and masks and gazed at the effects of having a much closer light source.

"I have an issue for you to note," Georjie said to Hiroki.

He turned to her and took out his notepad. "What's that?"

"That sun doesn't throw the right spectrum of light for plants to grow."

Hiroki's pen scratched on the pad. "Thanks for bringing that up. I've made a note for later." He tucked the pad and pen away then said, "Okay, Georjayna, you're up again."

"I am?" She sounded excited, and had a *lemme at it* look on her face.

Hiroki pulled a box out of his bag. He opened it and held it out so we could see inside.

I peered in, curiously, but my face must have fallen with disappointment because Hiroki laughed.

Georjie reached into the box and picked up a boring gray rock from the pile. "It's just a bunch of common minerals."

She easily broke the piece apart with her hands. It crumbled back into the box and a bit of dust puffed up.

"That is what it seems like, yes," Hiroki said. "But these minerals were specially gathered by a friend of Petra's."

"They were?" Petra looked as surprised at this as the rest of us were. Then her face slipped into understanding. "Oh, Ibby."

"Yes. Ibukun is one of our supernaturals."

"What kind?" Georjie asked this and then seemed to hold her breath. "If she knows minerals..."

I knew what she was thinking and hoping—that Ibby was also a Wise.

"She's an Inconquo," Hiroki explained. "A Metal Elemental. She's in your category, Georjayna, but doesn't have your breadth of power. What she's gathered for you here are the various lunar minerals we need to create a synthetic moon. They aren't in the proper proportions to solidify and reflect the sun's light the way the actual moon can, but that's where you come in. Think of them like the ingredients for a cake all mixed together. They just need to be separated and rearranged properly. Think you can do that?"

"I can feel the different minerals. They're just like what we have here on earth." She glanced at Hiroki. "I'm assuming Ibukun didn't go to the moon to get these?"

"No. She just had a list from me and procured them," Hiroki explained. "Mostly from the desert, I think."

Georjie's fingers shifted through the dust and rock in the box. "Pyroxene, olivine, iron, anorthosite, and some others. If you tell me the proportions, I'll see what I can do with them."

"Sure, hang on a minute." Hiroki handed the box to Georjie.

She took the box off the platform, set it on the ground, and knelt beside it, rolling up her sleeves. She looked up and her brow wrinkled in the light of my sun.

"Any chance you could move the sun away, Petra?" she asked. "It's a bit intense."

"Oh, sure." Petra raised her face to the fireball and it shifted over the land, sending our shadows reeling in response. The sun skidded across the sky. It slid to a stop and remained aloft and still.

"Thanks."

"Okay, here we go." Hiroki pulled out a notebook and went over the proportions of the moon's makeup for Georjie, who listened intently.

"Don't worry about making the core," Hiroki said. "It's not necessary. It would just be nice if you're able to make it appear moon-like."

Georjie was already packing a ball into shape, her hands hovering above the box, her bare feet and toes half buried in the ground. The gray dust arranged itself into a ball and then seethed and churned in the same way the soil had under Georjie's command. Dust and pebbles and fractured bits of rock fell back into the box. The 'moon' became a gray ball of dirt, not entirely smooth, but nowhere near as pockmarked looking as our real moon.

"That's about as big as I can make it with what you have here," Georjie said, standing. She left it sitting on the ground in a bed of grass. It was about the size of a beach ball.

Petra held a hand out to the ball and it began to levitate. It rose above our heads, shrinking and shrinking as it climbed.

"Better stop there, Petra." Hiroki had his hands on his hips and was looking up at the sun and moon. He frowned. "It's not the right proportions, but that's okay for today. In the actual domes, we'll have all the correct calculations done to make everything much more realistic."

"It'll be like paint-by-numbers." Mr. Nakesh gave that strange giggle again.

Hiroki nodded at Petra. "Send the sun and moon to their positions across from one another, please."

Our shadows leaned and spun as the sun moved across the sky toward the other side of the dome. Petra pushed the moon into place, opposite the sun. We fell into shadow as the moon came to sit over us and the sun was too far away to saturate us with light.

"We won't get the proper effect of moon-glow in a dome this small," Hiroki explained. "The dome has to be big enough for the 'sun' to disappear out of view before the minerals of the moon will do their job." He shrugged. "There are some things we won't know until we go to make our first dome for real."

"And," Petra whispered without taking her eyes from the sun, "orbit."

The sun and moon began to move in tandem in the same direction. We all watched this, captivated. It was starting to really feel like a livable dome in here.

The light increased as the sun swept by overhead, licking our skin with heat. The temperature dropped rapidly as the sun passed beyond us, shrinking in the distance.

"Congratulations," Hiroki said to us. "You've just created the world's first true bio-dome."

I glanced at Targa and Georjie. They looked mildly dazed. My heart was pounding with the exhilaration of what we had just done. It had worked. TNC's mad plan was working.

Now, I had a real problem.

I wanted to go to Arcturus, but how could I go when there was a possibility of making such a positive impact for people on Earth? Maybe, the impossible had just happened in my own life. Maybe, just maybe, I wanted to work for TNC instead of going to work with Basil. I could see that Georjie and Petra were both captured by the TNC project, but Targa was not an easy read.

After all, she had fallen in love with someone who was waiting for her in Poland. Would she say yes to this project and put off her budding romance for the greater good?

14

PETRA

Rain began to spatter lightly on the pavement as I said goodbye to the girls. I walked to where my Toyota was parked and looked back over my shoulder at the girls. I'd offered them a ride, but they'd said they preferred to walk together so they could keep talking.

As I watched them walk away, Targa lifted her hands and an arch of water appeared over their heads like an invisible umbrella. I snorted a laugh at this as the girls clustered together in the dry zone. Then Akiko said something and Targa put her hands down and the rain drenched them again. I laughed again, guessing that Akiko had reminded Targa that if someone saw them, they'd catch trouble.

What we'd been through today had bound us with an invisible cord. I didn't know them, but I had grown to both respect and care for them as the day progressed. They were good people, all of them. That was not hard to see, and I found it exciting that I might get to work with them on something as important as Project Expansion.

I got into my car and put the key in the ignition, thinking that though they had not yet finished high school, the girls seemed more mature than they should be. We hadn't had time to chit-chat, but if we were going to be working together, I intended to ask each of them for their origin stories. I expected there would be hardship in every one. Could a supernatural come about without some kind of adversity to bring the powers to the surface? I didn't think so.

As my car roared to life and I turned the heater on, my eyes drifted to the phone box across the street. This morning seemed so long ago that I half wondered if I'd dreamt that it had rung.

The car windows began to fog up so I cracked my window open. I paused, listening, before turning up the fan. No ringing. I smiled at my own silliness. It had just been a fluke the first time, and my imagination was getting away with me.

I pulled away from the curb and headed for my apartment.

The rain began to come down in earnest as I dashed from my car to my building. The sky was so thick with clouds that it blocked out any possible moon and starlight. The sound of pelting raindrops hammering against my windows greeted me as I opened the door to my apartment and locked it behind me, shivering.

I stripped off my sopping jacket and hung it on the coat rack by the door. My teeth chattering, I got out of my damp clothes and turned on the shower, leaving the water to heat up. I scampered to where the thermostat was beside the key hooks and turned it up. Then I returned to the bathroom, where steam was already fogging the mirror. I got under the spray with a long, exhausted sigh.

As I shampooed my hair I thought I heard the faintest sound of a phone ringing. I paused, suds dripping down the sides of my face, and listened.

Nothing.

I finished my shower and wrapped my wet hair up in a towel. After pulling on a pair of flannel pajamas, I crawled into bed with my hair still wrapped up.

A burning smell made me open my eyes and sniff. It took me a second to realize that the smell of burnt dust was coming from the heaters, which I hadn't used since June. I got up and opened a window a crack to let in some fresh air.

There *was* ringing!

I froze, listening. It had the same hard, old-fashioned ring as the phone box across from the fire station. It was coming from outside.

"No," I whispered with a disbelieving huff. "It *can't* be. I'm hearing things."

But I wasn't.

The ring continued to drift in through the window. The sound was faint, almost drowned out by the rain. I listened, as conflicted as two mountain rams fighting over territory. What to do? I didn't realize I was holding my breath until the ringing stopped.

After a few minutes of listening at the window and no answering sound but the driving of rain against the glass and the rooftops and pavement outside, I lay down.

The ringing started again.

"That's it!" I threw back the covers, turned on the lamp beside my bed, and rooted through my closet for some warm clothes.

As I left the apartment, key in my pocket and gloves and raincoat on, I jammed a hat down over my head. I was either going to answer the damn phone, or destroy the damn cord so I could go to sleep. Not sure which I would do until I got there, I pounded down the stairs and went out into the rain with my cheap umbrella open.

I listened, and then moved in the direction of the ring. It was coming from a payphone near the kiddie park just down the road from my apartment building.

My heart began to jump as I drew close to the ringing payphone. Unlike the first phone box, this one looked more appealing. It was clean, modern, and made of stainless steel.

I slid the door open and stepped inside, leaving my umbrella on the ground. I stared at the phone, thinking that surely every ring would be its last.

When it didn't cease, I snatched up the receiver. My heart was going like jungle drums.

"Hello?"

"Oh, Petra! Thank God!"

The masculine voice on the other end was familiar, but I was so shocked at what the voice had said that I couldn't immediately put my finger on who owned it.

"I thought I was going to have to break into your apartment and kidnap you or something," the voice continued, infused with relief—and if I wasn't mistaken, joy? "Thank you so much for answering. Listen, I know you're probably freaked out right now—"

It clicked into place, the owner of the voice. I took a sharp inhale and clutched the receiver with my other hand, heart going harder than ever.

"Jesse?"

There was a pause. Then, "You figured it out, huh. Yeah, sorry, I guess I should have said my name."

I was speechless.

"It's been a while, I know." Now he sounded guilty and uncomfortable. "I'm sorry for that."

"What...where are you? What are you doing haunting payphones? How did you know it was even me? What's happening? If you wanted to get a hold of me, you could have just called my cell."

"I couldn't, though."

Anger was now simmering underneath the elation I felt at hearing his beautiful voice again. Anger, and something else completely different—excitement. He'd finally made contact, he did care after all. It had taken him forever, but he'd finally reached out.

"I called you enough times," I said, my voice full of reproach. "I know you have my number. Do you know how long I tried to reach you for? How many times I called you? Nothing, Jesse! I got nothing from you."

"I know, and I'm sorry."

"I thought...you..." *Hated me or something.* "Were hurt or something, or, I don't know." Tears were misting in my eyes now, hot and angry tears. I squeezed my eyes shut. I hadn't been aware how much he meant to me, how much it hurt that he'd ignored me, until now. I clenched my teeth against the sob that wanted so badly to surge from my throat.

"Petra, please, we don't have much time."

I opened my eyes, brushing at them with my glove. That didn't help, my glove was wet. I bit the end of my glove and ripped it off my hand, then wiped at my eyes. "What do you mean?"

"I'm going to give you an address. I need you to come to me."

"What? Jesse, what's going on?" My head snapped up as what he'd said sank in. "Are you here? In Saltford?"

"Yes, I'm here. I can't explain more right now. I need to see you and you need to see me. Petra, you and those other girls are in danger. Other people are in danger too. Lots of other people." He let out a frustrated breath. "Will you please just—"

"Yes, yes! Of course. Tell me where and I'll come, right now."

He let out a shaky breath. "Great. Do you have a pen?"

"Just tell me. I'll remember."

He rattled off an address, twice. I said it back to him and committed it to memory. "I think I know where you are. You're near the harbor, not far from the Seadog."

"Is that the restaurant that looks like a ship?"

"That's the one."

"Yeah, I'm close. Please hurry. And Petra?"

"Yes?"

"Make sure you're not followed."

Make sure you're not followed?

Great. Yeah, no problem, I thought as I hung up the phone. This was surreal.

I grabbed my wet umbrella from the ground and jogged for my car. The streets were deserted. The rain was near-torrential, and though there were a few lights on in the buildings along my street, most of the windows were dark.

I got back into my car and turned it on, shivering, thinking about seeing Jesse again. It had been months since the dig in Libya. A whole summer had passed. I couldn't believe he was *here*, here in Saltford, my town. I had thought he was half a world away, literally, in Australia. What was he doing here? How long had he been here? How long had he been trying to find me? Why hadn't he just called my cell?

Because TNC gave you that cell, Petra.

The thought came so fast and hard that I gasped. Was that thought even my own? My blood felt like it was turning to ice in my veins.

Of course, that was why. It was the only reason that made any sense. My fingers trembled against the steering wheel as I made my way through wet and deserted streets. Rain pounded my windshield and filled the car with a sharp driving sound that was so loud it made me wince. I kept glancing into my rear-view mirror, looking for headlights or the shadow of a vehicle with the headlights off. There was nothing.

I parked a block away from the harbor in a quiet residential neighborhood. The address Jesse had given me led me to a new duplex, a building that had gone up less than a year before. I knew this area because it wasn't far from a park where Beverly used to take me when I was a kid.

I jogged up the walkway to door B. My mind raced. Would it be awkward to see him again after so much time apart? Was he here as a professional courtesy? Or was he here because he really cared about me and it was more personal than that?

A dim light could be seen through curtains on the second floor. I rapped on the door. Moments later, it opened, and Jesse was there, pulling me inside.

I barely had time to inhale as Jesse closed and locked the door behind me and yanked me into a hug. He didn't seem to care or notice that I was soaking wet.

"I'm sorry, Petra," he said into my hair. "I'm so, so sorry. For so much."

"Jesse, you're scaring me." My voice trembled. I wanted to push him away and pull him close at the same time.

He made the decision for me, holding me so tight I couldn't help but hug him back. My heart was skittering around like a fawn on ice, and my whole body felt shot through with adrenalin. I closed my eyes and breathed in his scent, tuned in to his frequency.

Desperate to understand, I slid the gate between my mind and his open, probing his thoughts. Immediately, the back of my head began to ache but worse, there was nothing. Nothing but cold and black, like a thick chunk of metal was barring the way. I closed my mind and breathed as the headache eased away.

Why could I not read his thoughts? It was just like trying to read Hiroki's had been. My pulse jumped again. My mind screamed, what is going on?

Jesse pulled back and put warm hands on either side of my face. "I'm sorry."

His hazel eyes searched mine. I could feel the heat of his body leaching through my damp clothing.

"Would you stop saying that–"

He silenced my words with a kiss.

Suddenly, we were back in that tent in Libya, making out like we'd been starved for one another. His hands worked at my coat, opening it, pushing it off my shoulders and down my arms as he kissed me hungrily. My coat dropped to the floor, taking my wet gloves with it. My hands threaded through his hair as he pressed me back against the wall.

So, not so much awkwardness then. My whole body ignited as he kissed me.

His fingers raked into my hair and squeezed. My scalp pulled pleasantly and my breath hitched. My body came alive in a way it hadn't since he'd kissed me the first time, as The Ghibli had wailed and screamed around us, throwing sand up against our tent. There had been as much passion and fury going on inside the tent during that desert storm as there was now in the foyer of this strange house.

My mind was whirling, my body was a raging torrent, and there beneath it all was Jesse and his rhythms, surging against me. His heartbeat, and a different kind of pulse, his energy signature, woke me up inside and sent my own vibrations humming. Last time we had done this, I was terrified at what matching our rhythms might do to him, but this time, there was no fear. All these months later I had a better understanding of how I worked; I was in control. I had no desire to hurt Jesse, so I wouldn't. I kissed him and my thoughts and fears flew apart like shattered glass.

He began to chuckle against my mouth.

"What?" I asked between kisses, "is so funny?"

"I just-" He pulled back, taking a breath. "I thought maybe it would be awkward between us." He bent his face to my neck and kissed me there. "I'm so glad I was wrong."

"Me too." My eyes drifted shut with pleasure. I thought I would melt into a puddle, right then and there. "But Jesse," I said hoarsely, "you need to start talking."

His head came up. "Yeah." He kissed me again, but it was a finisher, not a starter. He took my hand. "I do. Come upstairs."

"Wait." I bent and untied my wet boots and toed them off. "Whose house is this?"

I followed him up the stairs.

"I rented it."

I blinked in surprise. "Rented? How long have you been here?"

"Four days. I've been trying to reach you since I got here. I couldn't go to your apartment because it's often under surveillance, and I'm-" He stopped and gave a chuckle. "Well, I've gone rogue. If TNC finds me, they'll...well, it won't be good."

"Rogue?"

As we crested the stairs to the second floor, my jaw dropped as I looked around.

Four computers were haphazardly set up across a makeshift desk. File folders and documents spread across the floor in semi-organized disarray. A folder lay open on the desk. In it was a photograph, only partially in view, but I would recognize the face on it anywhere.

My heart skidded to a halt before resuming an erratic rhythm.

I went to the desk and picked up the printed photo, devouring the face of the man in the image with my eyes. Jesse's handwriting had scrawled the name Tareq Ghoga across the bottom of the photo. The image was in black and white but I knew without a shadow of a doubt that those eyes were silver and that skin was a dark creamy tan, just like mine.

It was the man from my dreams. But this image was real, taken by a camera. It brought him to sudden, primal life. He was not just a product of my imagination anymore.

"Where did you get this?" My voice was shaking worse now.

"I'll tell you everything, Petra. Just promise me, promise me you're not going to lose it on me." Jesse's voice had a thin thread of fear twisting through it.

I barely registered his request. "Who is this?"

My eyes met Jesse's and I was vaguely aware of the sensation of falling, even though I hadn't moved. The floor seemed to be tilting, the walls closing in. Jesse sounded so far away. Though I knew the answer already, his words still rocked my heart like it was a toy boat on an angry ocean.

"He's your father."

15

PETRA

"Tareq." The word clipped off my tongue, sharp and strong. No one in my whole life, not my therapists, not the foster care workers over the years, not any law enforcement people who had come into contact with me through my case had been able to provide the name of my father, let alone a photo of him. He had been a black hole, until now.

I tore my eyes from the image of my father and looked up at the young man who'd given me my first real link to my past.

"Where did you get this?" My lips felt numb and the muscles running up and down along my spine were quivering.

"There is so much to tell you, Petra." Jesse raked a hand through his hair, looking at the mess of papers and technology around us. His eyes found mine and they were full of sorrow. "And you're not going to like any of it."

"Start talking." My voice sounded calm and I was grateful for that. Inside, I was a storm. I knelt on the carpet in front of the documents but I didn't touch any of them, almost afraid of what I'd discover if I opened another one. "I'm listening."

"Your father, Tareq Gogha, was a Euroklydon who worked for

TNC. As far as I can make out, they picked him up in Libya, his native country, and contracted him on the spot. I haven't yet found the original contract but I'm confident it was for an insane amount of money and it was either a lifetime deal or spanned decades. I don't know whether he signed it under duress or not." Jesse's shoulders lifted. "Either way, he worked for them and came to regret it."

Jesse picked up another folder and opened it, taking another photograph and handing it to me. "This is your mom."

I took the photo and stared at the woman central to the image. She was unaware she was being photographed. She had one long-fingered hand reaching toward the handle of a car door as she looked over her shoulder and smiled at someone who was not in the photograph. She wore a long skirt and a wrap sweater around her curvy frame. Her long dark hair was in a bun at the nape of her neck, but wisps of it had escaped and were blowing fetchingly around her face. She was beautiful; with high cheekbones, smooth skin, straight white teeth, and a high brow. Big gold disc earrings swung beside her jaw and the one hand that was visible was encrusted with rings. She looked well cared for.

"Her name was Tala Kara, Tala Gogha after she married your father." Jesse plucked a swath of papers from another folder. On the pages were mostly text and some had been blacked out with a marker. "I've been digging through TNC documents for months and have pieced together a rough story. I think your father violated his contract when he married your mom. I can't say for sure, because I haven't found the contract. TNC's files are multi-layered, well encrypted, and organized in a confusing way."

"Then why do you think the marriage violated the contract?"

"Because after he got married, TNC's behavior changed toward him. They put more surveillance on him, on his personal life, even. Whatever was going on inside your parents' marriage, TNC felt it was relevant to them and spent a lot of money to make sure they knew a lot about your mom's health."

"My mom's...health?"

"More specifically, whether or not she'd become pregnant."

"Oh." Ice felt like it was coating my stomach. Why had I ever trusted this corporation? And now, I was under contract to them too. Thankfully, I'd only signed for a year, but looking at my parents' images, a year was still a year too long. "And they cared about whether she became pregnant because..."

"Read this and see for yourself." Jesse handed me a single sheet.

I took it and scanned it, understanding in a few seconds that it was a report written by either a researcher or a doctor to a corporate authority. It had been stamped CLASSIFIED & PRIVATE. It looked like a copy of a copy of a copy. There was a phrase circled in red that drew my eye.

Our discovery confirms that there can only ever be a single Euroklydon alive at any given time. The power is genetic and may or may not pass to a child from either parent. Our attempts to create two living Euroklydon have failed repeatedly [see article 137-B]. Upon conception, should the fetus have acquired the gene, the parent immediately loses 98% supernatural capacity. The remaining 2% is limited to low-grade telepathy and may or may not include some low-grade telekinesis as well. Their usefulness to the corporation being greatly diminished, we recommend contractual obligations include a commitment to refrain from conceiving a child until such time as the corporation allows, perhaps when the asset has passed prime. We recommend continued research into sperm and oocyte cryopreservation; until which time it is successful, this is our recommendation to the board.

The words burned into my skull as I read them silently three times over. I noticed a number code in the top right-hand corner which included the number 1956. "Is this the year this document was created?" I asked, Jesse, my voice hoarse. "1956?"

"Yes. Thirty years before the first successful pregnancy done with a frozen egg."

I had so many questions about this paragraph alone that I didn't know what to ask first.

"But I wasn't conceived this way..." I stumbled over the words. I had always been told I'd been born to an eclamptic mother in the

Saltford hospital. But at this point, with everything Jesse was showing me, I didn't know what to believe anymore.

"No." Jesse shook his head. "That's why I think TNC became upset with your father, because he didn't wait for their permission. This document is the only thing I've found that suggests the agreement to wait before conceiving a child might have been part of his contract. If it was, and he signed it willingly, he also broke it willingly. Your mom and he decided to have a baby in spite of TNC." He canted his head. "Or she became pregnant by accident. It's impossible to know for certain."

I let out a breath. "Why would he sign such a contract in the first place?"

Jesse shrugged. "We don't know how old he was when he signed, or what his state was. He might have been poor, desperate, very young. He might have thought he didn't want kids anyway and then later on, changed his mind. TNC would pay a Euroklydon at the very highest scale. It's tough for anyone to turn that kind of wealth down, let alone someone who might have grown up impoverished."

"*Did* he grow up impoverished?"

"I don't know that either, I'm afraid. It's just little old me doing all this digging. I haven't had time to delve into his past before TNC. I've come to you with everything I've found, because you're running out of time."

"Time? Does this have to do with Project Expansion?"

Jesse nodded. "It does, but there's more before we get to that."

"Low-grade telepathy and telekinesis," I read out loud from the pages I still held.

Jesse nodded. "That's what you had before the cave in Libya, right?"

"I never told anyone that, only my therapist."

"Yes, Noel Pierce." Jesse's mouth formed a flat line. "They got to him, too. The moment he became your therapist, they paid him a little visit. He resisted, but they got him eventually. They intimidated him into being their eyes on you while you grew up."

"He resisted," I echoed. My eyes shuttered closed as the day I revealed myself to him in his office, the day I'd seen a memory of someone beating him with the butt of a gun.

Jesse nodded. "Yeah."

"They had him ratting on me all the years he was my therapist." Cold sorrow filled my empty spaces like ice-water. "He died only a few days ago."

My throat closed up and I looked at Jesse, a question in my eyes that couldn't quite make it to my lips. I took a breath.

"Tell me he actually died of an aneurysm," I said. "Please. Please, tell me that's really how he died."

Jesse shook his head and his shoulders slumped. "We're dealing with a hydra here." He shifted to sit beside me and wrapped an arm around my shoulders. "But you're not alone. We're going to do something about this. You and me."

"What did they do to him?"

"Petra, don't do this to yourself."

"What did they do, Jesse?" I spoke around clenched teeth.

"They knew his family history. Genetically, Noel might have eventually died of an aneurysm anyway. His grandfather did, one of his uncles did, as did his great grandmother. They just gave nature a little push." Jesse swallowed so hard I could hear it. "Then they bribed the coroner. Path of least resistance. Noel wasn't of any use to them anymore. I'm so sorry, Petra. I know how much you cared for him."

Jesse put a hand on mine. Hot tears blocked out my vision. They poured over my cheeks as I squeezed my eyes shut. I rubbed my sleeve across my nose, which had begun to run.

Jesse fished in a pocket and handed me a crumpled tissue. "Sorry, I'll get you a fresh one."

He got up and disappeared through a door. I heard the click of a light-switch which also turned on a fan, the rustling of plastic, and he returned with a travel-pack of tissues.

I took it and fished one out to clean myself up with. *Oh, Noel,* I thought. *Murdered because of association with me.*

Who else had TNC interfered with because of me, or my father?

"So, my mother became pregnant," I said, crumpling the tissue and tossing it in the small wastebasket under the desk. "Then what?"

Jesse leaned back and pulled his legs into a cross-legged position. "They put your parents under house-arrest. Every move they made was monitored. Your mother's pregnancy was monitored, probably closer than any pregnancy had been monitored before. Even royalty doesn't have check-ups like your mother did. Poor Tala was very stressed, as you can imagine, and TNC found itself with the very tricky objective of helping your mother to have a safe and successful pregnancy, while keeping her and your father under lock and key."

"All that monitoring, and they couldn't prevent her eclampsia?"

Jesse let out a sigh. "They probably did know and chose not to do anything about it. Knowing TNC, they might not have minded if your mother died after you were born anyway." He made a disgusted face. "It might have even crossed their mind to allow *you* to die, too, just to see if the powers returned to your father."

"That would have been a huge risk," I said.

Jesse nodded. "And they did decide to keep you alive, so I guess they thought so, too. You were conceived in Jordan, where your father had been doing a job. TNC moved your parents to Saltford because they had a well-equipped facility nearby, and because it was easy to bring them both into the country. What they were planning to do with your folks after you were born is anyone's guess, but"—Jesse scratched his jaw and the rasp of his stubble made me notice that he hadn't shaved in quite a while—"TNC is very good at appearing to be altruistic while having devious goals. If I were your father, I would have done what he did, too."

"Let me guess," I interjected, bitterly. "They tried to escape?"

Jesse nodded. "Your father caused a diversion so that the guards watching them were drawn away from the house. Then your mother snuck out while security was diminished. They'd planned to rendezvous at a point, I'm sure." He inhaled. "I'm sure they didn't think TNC would take it as far as they did."

"They killed my father?" They'd killed Noel, what would stop them from killing Tareq once he was useless? Jesse's answer was still like a bowling ball to the gut.

"Yes. When they found out what your father had done, they shot him. Your mother—"

"Was picked up by strangers and taken to the hospital." This was where the story that I knew picked up, and seemed to fit.

"Yes, where TNC found her," Jesse said. "Since they knew where you were, and you were just an infant, not to mention an orphan, they decided the best thing to do would be to let child services put you into a foster home where they could stay out of your life but keep an eye on you."

"Okay, but then what? I grew up, but I wasn't a Euroklydon until after what happened in Libya. They were waiting for me to go to Libya? That might never have happened."

"But it did happen." Jesse looked at me, his eyes reticent and regretful.

"Are you saying I was bound to come into my powers at some point regardless? Even if I hadn't gone to Libya and fallen into that cave?"

"No, I'm saying they knew that going to Libya was what it would take for you to inherit your abilities. They *orchestrated* Libya."

I let out a disbelieving laugh. "They couldn't be that good. They might have money and technology, but they don't know the future. They might have known that I love archaeology and would want to go on a North African excavation, but they couldn't possibly know that a dig would come up in Libya. It's more than unlikely, it's preposterous."

Jesse's eyes were full of pity, and I felt a surge of anger at his expression.

"What? Why are you looking at me like that?" Then it clicked. My eyes widened in horror. My voice croaked as I said, "No."

"I'm so sorry." Jesse's eyes were on the floor, his head bent like he couldn't bear to look at me.

"Tell me it's not true, Jesse."

Tears pricked my eyes and I covered my face with my hands.

But the evidence was there. The whole thing had been faked, the entire dig. I could hardly process it. That day in the classroom when I'd read Ibby's mind and she was wondering why they were doing what they were doing to a nice girl like me. It hadn't made any sense given what I'd thought was going on, but it made sense now.

They were actors.

"All of you?" I spoke from between my fingers, tears in my voice. "TNC hired all of you? Staged the whole dig?"

"Yes," Jesse answered miserably. "The site was real, your finds were genuine. But all the rest..." He swallowed and didn't go on.

My face burned with shame and my eyes wouldn't stop streaming. But the anger, oh the anger, the deep and utter betrayal—it was all-encompassing. I pulled my hands away from my face and let the tears flow.

I looked at Jesse. "Are you even an archaeologist? Is your name even Jesse?"

"I'm not an archeologist, I'm a hacker. I worked for TNC until..." He reached for my face, but I pulled away from his touch. "Until you, Petra. My name is Jesse, and I can't even tell you how sorry I am, how much I want to make things right."

"You can't," I whispered, staring at him through vision blurred by moisture. I brushed at my eyes angrily. "How do you make this right? Why did you even agree to it?" My voice grew harder.

"TNC was my employer. I never questioned my projects until yours came along." Jesse went to his knees and reached for me, his warm fingers encircling mine. "I met you, and...I fell in love with you, Petra."

His admission of love may well have fallen on deaf ears. My mind was whirling. "What about the kidnapping? The fight? That was all TNC, too?"

Jesse shook his head. "That's where TNC lost control and got scared. It's why they ended up calling the whole thing off the day of the fight. The locals knew what you were and interfered. I heard that Miss Marks destroyed her hotel room in anger when she learned you were taken. If it weren't for Molly, you'd probably have been executed."

I felt myself tense up with the memory of being held captive.

Jesse continued, "They sent a team out from Ghat but they arrived too late to rescue you, arriving instead just after you stopped the militants." He shook his head. "Miss Marks played it so cool, but trust me, she was freaking out. Why do you think they shoved you into a vehicle and got you out of there so fast?"

"Why didn't you tell me?" I choked out.

"I couldn't, Petra." Jesse's voice cracked. "I was sworn to secrecy. You *know* how TNC is. They wouldn't allow me to talk to you afterward, and they ordered me to cut off all communication. I hated it, I hated them for that. That's why I started digging and why I've been digging ever since."

I put a hand up and he stopped talking. Silently, and with angry tears still burning tracks down my cheeks, I got up.

"Where are you going?" Jesse got up and followed me. "Petra, please don't leave."

I headed down the stairs, pulled on my boots and jacket, and put my hand on the doorknob.

Jesse sounded stricken. "I know you're angry. I would be, too."

"Jesse," I whirled to face him, my hand twisting the door knob. "Just stop talking."

"Petra..."

I opened the door and left the storm inside the house for the one outside.

The wind-driven rain pummeled me as I took the steps down to the sidewalk. I ignored Jesse yelling my name from the house, until he came out behind me while pulling on his jacket.

"Come back inside, Petra. There's more to explain. I know you're upset, you should be, but I've risked my life to find you–"

I turned back to him, my mouth an angry snarl. "Jesse."

The look on my face was enough. Jesse's own face changed from desperate to fearful. He staggered backward, one arm half coming up to shield his body. It was as though he'd never believed I could lash out at him but suddenly realized he was wrong in one earth-shaking moment.

Shame flooded me. He genuinely thought I was going to hurt him. I closed my eyes and took a breath. When I opened them, Jesse was watching me, eyes darting over my features.

"Just, give me a minute," I said.

"Of course." He nodded and held out my umbrella. "Take this."

I ignored the umbrella and marched down the walk into the black rainy night.

As I walked, unheedful of where I was headed and feeling like it didn't matter anyway, memories came at me like bats swooping out of the dark. They battered my brain and shook my emotions. I remembered the way Jesse, Ethan, and Ibby had all reacted when I'd told them the vision of my father who was telling me to run. The way I had caught Ibby and Jesse repeatedly watching me, their expressions full of guilt. Noel's reaction as I pushed the glass across the table at him—he'd not known why TNC was keeping an eye on me until that moment, I was sure of that now. Jesse and me, kissing passionately in my tent. Being grabbed in the middle of the night by a people who were so terrified of me they may well have murdered me.

I barely registered the cold water trickling down my face. Rage and humiliation made my head feel hot and my fists clench. I had been played for a fool by the corporation I was now bound to. They'd murdered my father, and as far as I was concerned, they'd killed my mother, too. They'd destroyed my family and then hid it from me. They'd exploited people in my life to keep me under their thumb. They'd been manipulating me since birth, all so they could position themselves as trustworthy and earn my loyalty.

I wondered if they'd ever controlled my foster mom, Beverly, or even had a hand in her death. TNC had manipulated me on a scale that was almost impossible to comprehend. How much had they spent to secure me? What was I worth to them now?

A growl of frustration escaped my throat when I thought about the Elemental girls. What had I done getting them involved with TNC? It was crystal clear to me now that my father had been telling me to run from this corporation, and I'd been too blind to see it; their ruse had been too thorough.

I stopped walking and looked up, realizing that I had come down to the harbor where the water churned and washed over the docks. Thoughts and emotions were so stormy and tangled I could hardly tell which was which, but one thing I did know, as clear as a cloudless day: I had to get out of TNC and keep the Elemental girls from falling into their hands, too.

I turned to look back toward Jesse's neighborhood. What else did he know? Could I trust him? Was he still working for TNC and this was some elaborate new plot?

There was only one way to know for sure.

I glowered and put the harbor to my back. When I knocked on Jesse's door, he opened it immediately. The look on his face was pure relief.

"Oh, thank God. Get in here." He reached out and pulled me inside. "I'll get you some dry clothes."

"Jesse."

He walked down the hall and opened a door under the stairs. His head and shoulders disappeared inside. "I just did some laundry. I made a bad choice with the soap and they smell like they just came out of a dishwasher, but at least they're clean."

There was the click of a dryer door closing.

"Jesse."

He backed out of the laundry room with his hands full of wrinkled clothes, which he held out to me. "They'll be too big, but–"

"Jesse."

"What?"

"Why can't I read your mind?"

His face froze for a moment in an expression of surprise. "You tried?"

I gave him a withering look. "I don't like using telepathy. It hurts my head and it feels like an invasion of privacy. Turns out I should have been using it all along. I'm such a fool. Only a fool would have powers this strong and not use them to make sure she could trust people. I wouldn't have been caught up in TNC's schemes like the world's biggest sucker. Except that when I try to read yours, I get nothing. Dead air."

I put a hand on the dry clothes he was still holding out at me and pushed them back toward him.

"I'll only stay under one condition," I said. "That you let me read your mind."

16

PETRA

"It wouldn't have mattered if you had tried to read everyone's minds, anyway," Jesse said, setting the clothes on the step behind him. "Don't you think TNC accounted for that?"

"Why wouldn't it have mattered?"

He reached into his pocket. "Because you can't get past this." He pulled a pendant out and held it on his open palm. "This is part of what else there is to tell you. Perhaps I should have started with this. My mistake. I'm just happy you came back."

On his palm lay a plain cylinder of a dull gray metal, darker than silver and about the size of a pen's cap. He held it up for me and it swayed before my eyes.

"I've seen this metal before." I reached for it and held it against my palm. It was extremely heavy for its size. Unlike everything else I ever touched, I could not detect its signature against my skin. It was dead to me.

"It's wolfram," Jesse said, watching me. "Also known as tungsten."

"Ibby had some of this." Another memory came back to me, another bat swooping at me from my past.

Jesse looked shocked. "She *showed* it to you?"

"I don't think she meant to. It fell out of her pocket along with a few other stones. She told me she collects rocks and metals." I'd had no reason to question it, even after I'd discovered she was supernatural. She was a Metal Elemental, an Inconquo, so why wouldn't she have an affinity for rocks? She'd gone to great length on wolfram, talking about its rare density and value. I hadn't suspected a thing. The girl was a good actress, I had to give her that.

"Clever woman to keep it in with a bunch of other random bits," Jesse said. "TNC gave us all a piece, which we were to wear at all times during the dig. As long as we had it on our person, it would block any efforts at telepathy. They must have known about the effects of wolfram on a Euroklydon since your father's day, if not before."

"Ibby must have forgotten to wear it the day of the briefing, when I first met you."

"You read her mind that day?" Jesse asked.

I nodded. "What she was thinking that day didn't make sense at the time, but now it does."

"Dare I ask?"

I looked up at him. "She thought I was a nice girl, and she wondered why you guys were all doing this to me."

"Oh." Jesse's eyes softened as he gazed at me. He took the metal cylinder and threw it down the hall, past the laundry room door. It hit the floor in the kitchen beyond it. "Go ahead. Read away. I want you to know you can trust me."

I stared at where the innocuous little stone lay in the shadows beyond Jesse. "All the trouble they went to, just for me."

"You are the Euroklydon," Jesse said quietly. "You're one of a kind, worth more trouble to them than any other supernatural on their staff."

My eyes narrowed. "Are you also supernatural?"

Jesse laughed. "Only if you consider mad hacking skills to be magical." He reached his hands out to me. "Here. Everything I have seen and know is yours."

I took his hands and lifted the gates between our minds.

A flood of images and emotions and desperate thoughts pelted me.

Jesse was terrified, but it wasn't of me, it was of TNC. A dull ache began to spread across the back of my skull. I closed my eyes and clenched my teeth against it as I sifted through his thoughts and memories like a playing deck of 3-D cards. Snapshots and moments in time fluttered through his conscious thoughts like he wanted me to see everything all at once.

He'd been working as a hacker for a branch of TNC in Australia called Compulox. He was handsomely paid for projects that came his way as infrequently as once a month. He'd receive an envelope in the mail detailing assignments with clear objectives. There was never any explanation as to why he was doing what he was doing, just a straightforward command. Hack into some company's mainframe and insert a virus, deliver a list of private email addresses to this safety deposit box, insert a photograph into a gallery of photographs on this website. They were simple requests which were not simple to execute, unless you were a hacker.

One day he'd received a fatter envelope than usual, detailing how they wanted him to pose as an archaeologist on an excavation in Libya. He'd never been asked to act before, and they gave him a choice to say yes or no depending on whether he thought he could be convincing.

My eyes flew open. "They paid you four million US dollars to go to Libya?"

He didn't have to answer—I could see the truth plainly. Who would say no to such an assignment?

I closed my eyes again, wincing at the pulsing pain in my head. I homed in on the details of the assignment in his thoughts. He was to pose as an archaeologist with a group of other actors hired by TNC. They were told a young woman named Petra Kara, a valuable asset to TNC, was the beneficiary of all this dramatic effort and under no circumstances was she to be let in on the scheme. They were required to study up on archaeology well enough to pass at a glance. They were required to wear the enclosed metal on their person at all times, even while sleeping. If the target (me) were to display unusual powers, this was to be received as any normal human being might react to it—with shock and awe.

I saw myself through Jesse's eyes, how he tried to distance his heart at first and how, as the dig went on, guilt began to eat away at him. How he finally fell in love with me. I saw his anguish as they told him he couldn't respond to any efforts I made to keep in touch, and I saw him throw a laptop off a desk in anger. I saw him purchasing more computers, moving away and leaving everything in his apartment just the way it was, taking pains not to leave a trail, getting on a small plane headed to Berlin where he hid behind the alias Tayler Jasper.

He spent days and nights hacking into TNC's systems, looking for me, for clues to who I was and what they wanted with me. He'd hacked into Jody Marks's private schedule and found notes about when she would ask me to recruit the Elemental girls, when the prototype would be built. It was when Jesse found this that he got on a plane to Halifax, rented a car, drove to Saltford, and hid out in this duplex.

He couldn't call my cell and he was afraid my apartment was being watched, so he'd hacked into Saltford's telecom system and began to call telephone booths positioned near where he thought I might be. He'd been making phones ring near the fire department, since he knew that was the helipad TNC used to transfer me to FS_{II}, and near my apartment, hoping against hope that I would pick it up if I heard them ringing often enough. When I hadn't picked up, he began to form a plan to break into my apartment and wait there for me.

It was enough.

I slammed the gates down and squeezed my eyes shut against the pain.

"Petra?" There was alarm in Jesse's voice and I felt his hands squeeze my biceps.

"I'll be okay in a minute," I said through a tight jaw. Already, the ache had lessened. I looked up at him. I understood, now. Not only could I trust him, but he'd risked everything to help me see the truth. If TNC found him, they'd terminate him.

Rogue, indeed.

Words hovered on my lips, but instead I pulled his face down to mine and kissed him. Not only had I seen his deep desire to bring TNC down, I'd read his sour regret at having ever gotten involved with them in the first place, and his sorrow for taking part in my deception. But shining red and bright amidst all of his thoughts and memories was his love for me.

"Am I forgiven?" he asked quietly when I pulled back, as he gazed down at me through hooded eyes.

"How can I not forgive you after seeing all of that?"

He smiled. "I should have just let you read my mind first thing. We would have avoided you storming out in the rain and almost giving me a heart attack."

"Sorry about that."

"I'll take another kiss for my troubles, please," he said with a cheeky smile.

I obliged him.

When we finally pulled away, he took my hand. "There's more I have to tell you, and it's time sensitive."

"Has to do with the project they want the Elemental girls for?"

He nodded. "Can you handle it?"

"Bring it on, Donkey Kong." I pulled my wet pants away from my thighs. "About those dry clothes?"

———

ONCE I HAD DRIED off and changed, I joined Jesse again in the large loft where his research was spread across the carpet in folders.

"There is too much to take you through in the time we have," Jesse said, eyes scanning the folders thoughtfully. "So, I'm going to cherry pick to give an idea of TNC's past behavior."

"The best predictor of future behavior is past behavior," I murmured, kneeling on the floor again.

Jesse nodded and selected one of the folders, which he slid across the carpet to me. "Exactly. This is the earliest incident I've found. It contains articles about a pesticide plant they developed with another company shortly after World War II. An accident in the loading dock released sixty tons of toxic gas in India. In one night, over four hundred thousand people in nearby towns were affected with illness, burning throats and eyes. Tens of thousands died."

I picked up the file folder and thumbed through its contents which included pictures that made my blood run cold, as well as maps with hand drawn circles and X's laying out the location of the towns, the plant, and the perimeter of the pollution. Numbers were written above surrounding towns with dashes linking the numbers to things like 'birth defects,' 'deaths,' and 'blindness.'

"Even decades after the accident, birth defects and health issues still plague the area. A human rights group has done studies on their ground water, and they have video of tons of hazardous waste being buried illegally. That human rights group tried to bring all this to international court and were squashed overnight—their founders were killed in a road accident and their website was hacked. They were obliterated." Jesse frowned. "Probably by someone like me."

"You found all this in the TNC records?"

Jesse nodded, his face grim. "I actually found it by accident. But once I started hunting, more buried evidence turned up. It's hard to find, but it's there. It's easy to make something disappear from the mainstream online world, but it's not actually gone forever and can be found by people who know where to look."

"It's horrible," I shuddered, closing the file and handing it back.

"It's just the tip of the iceberg." Jesse picked up another file folder. "This one is full of buried evidence that a radiation therapy device developed by a TNC lab and used to track dosage had a bug which resulted in hundreds of patients receiving overdoses that killed them." He grabbed another file, opened it, and slid it over the carpet toward me. "This one is about a software-induced plane crash in '97. The pilot was blamed for the crash, even though many experts knew it was a systems error. Guess who built the software?"

"TNC?" I'd begun to feel faintly ill.

Jesse nodded. "A child-company of TNC's called Soren-Tech, based in Sweden. Forty-four people died and seventy were injured. Again, evidence was buried and links to TNC disappeared."

"So...what? They are accident prone? Don't do their research? Really bad at planning?"

"I don't know, but aside from its illegal and immoral behavior, it's weird. I mean, no other huge corporations have such a diverse portfolio of industries and companies. Most big companies still specialize, but TNC is all over the place, like they're ADD and can't decide where to spend their money or something. It goes beyond disasters. If they were focused on just making money, they would become experts in a few linked industries, dominating and even making moves to monopolize. That's not what they're doing." Jesse raked both his hands through his hair, making it spike out in all directions. "It's like their business is *causing* and *hiding* disasters!"

"Why would they do that?" A chill had crept into my bones. Fury was winding its way through my incredulity and disgust. This was no longer about me, my offense, my family, the deceptions they had rained down on me. This was much, much bigger.

He let out a long, frustrated exhale. "At this point, your guess is as good as mine. I've been digging up story after story, project after wildly diverse and disastrous project, buried evidence. They're the corporate equivalent of a serial killer but for the life of me I cannot find any motivation for them to do so because every disaster costs them money. Which led me to dig into their investments, and the picture gets even weirder."

"What do you mean?"

"They own stocks in all kinds of diverse companies, and all of them are winners. TNC makes as much, and in some years, more money on the stock market than they do from their technology. It's like they can't make a wrong move."

"*All* of them are winners?"

"Every single one. Do you know what the odds of that are?"

"I don't know much about the stock market, but that sounds

impossible." I shivered and zippered Jesse's hoodie up tighter to my throat. This company was scary.

"It is. Unless you have a Magic 8-Ball or a clairvoyant who knows the future, it is." Jesse's brow wrinkled.

"Clairvoyant." We both said at the same time.

"That's not outside the realm of possibility," I said, straightening. "TNC collects supernaturals like other people collect fridge magnets. Right?"

"Maybe..." Jesse pinched his bottom lip between a thumb and forefinger, meditating.

"Maybe?"

"Well, they do hire supernaturals, but I think they lead their employees to think that there are more of them on staff than there actually are."

"Why would they do that?"

"To keep you in line," Jesse proposed. "To keep you guessing if you step out or rebel, thinking they might have someone more powerful than you on staff who could kick your teeth in."

"Hiroki told me I was the most powerful supernatural he's ever worked with," I said, softly. Given that I could put up an indestructible field of energy and destroy anything I wanted to just by touching it, I didn't think he'd been lying. Which led me to another question—just how much did Hiroki know about all of this?

"Then he made a mistake by talking to you," Jesse said. "Listen, this facility they take you to, north of the city..."

"Field Station Eleven?"

Jesse nodded. "What's it like?"

"Seems pretty high-tech."

"Have you ever actually seen anyone else displaying supernatural abilities there?"

"Just the Elemental girls, earlier today."

"Hmmm." Jesse grunted thoughtfully and went quiet, thinking.

Were Jesse's insinuations right? Was I the only supernatural at FS11? Hiroki had revealed ignorance when Georjayna had told him she needed to have her feet in the soil to be able to move earth. And he'd then assumed Targa needed to be in water, and that had been a mistake, too. Maybe he hadn't worked with as many supernaturals as he wanted me to think.

I couldn't believe anything TNC told me. They'd proven themselves to be a corporation of lies. But the question remained...why?

The corporate equivalent of a serial killer, Jesse had said.

I shuddered, feeling numb and sick. I picked up more of the file folders and flipped through them. This one documented the development of a vaccine that had killed and maimed tens of thousands in Bolivia, the next one detailed toxic piping developed and sold to unknowing contractors who then used it to build whole suburbs. Over a period of years, residents became ill and many of them died before it was ever linked to the metals which had leached into the water.

As I looked over the documents, a thread began to appear.

"All of these lead to human death and suffering," I said, shoving another folder away from me. "None of them are *purely* environmental or limited to disasters where no one got hurt. Someone always gets hurt." A vitriolic wrath was seething under the surface of my calm.

Jesse looked thoughtful. "Yes. You're right. They *all* hurt people. None of these incidents happen in remote regions or have zero human casualties. Still, the question is *why*."

It didn't matter how great Project Expansion looked, I was certain it had invisible fangs. It was no longer enough to get myself out of TNC and keep the Elemental girls out too, someone had to stop TNC for good.

I looked at my watch. It was nearly midnight. I got to my feet. "Have you got anything else I should see?"

He splayed his hands at the mess on the floor. "Just more of the same, but no real answers. What are you doing?"

I grabbed my car keys and headed for the door when a thought struck.

"Petra?" Jesse sounded nervous. He got to his feet. "Where are you going?"

"Can you make copies of all of TNC's data?"

"I already have," he said, then shrugged one shoulder. "Well, not all of it because the company is massive and has servers all over the world."

"Start with Field Station Eleven," I said. "Make copies of everything you find there. I want to know what's behind Project Expansion. Are you able to make all this information public?"

"I can, but it'll take time."

"Good." I headed down the stairs.

"Petra, wait." Jesse scrambled to his feet. "I'm coming with you."

"No." I turned back to him as I snagged his coat from its hook. It would be too big but at least it was dry. "Can I borrow this?"

"Oh...kay." He looked confused.

"I have to do this alone," I explained, pulling his coat on. "If you want to help, do what you're good at. Make a virus that will handicap their technology or better yet, bring their whole system down. Bring them down from the inside."

"What are you going to do?"

I barely paused to answer as I headed out the door. "I'm going to bring them down from the outside."

17

SAXONY

My phone buzzed against my side on my bed where I lay with my laptop, scrolling through UK government pages and making notes on everything I needed to gather for my student visa application. I still hadn't made a decision about TNC's Project, but I thought it smart to apply for my visa so that there would be no delay if we decided against the job.

Feeling sleepy and only half paying attention to what I was reading, my brain was still in the wilderness, replaying the events of the time at the field station over and over. I picked up my phone and answered it absently.

"Hello?"

"Saxony?"

"Petra?" I sat up quickly, alarmed. "Are you all right? You sound upset." She'd only said my name but her voice was saturated with something...something not good. Anger? Panic? I didn't know her well enough to guess.

"I'm fine. Listen." Her voice was so flinty, so determined.

My skin prickled. "I'm listening."

"Tell the other girls I'm really sorry, but the whole thing is off."

"Off? What do you mean?"

"Project Expansion. It's not happening anymore. I can't talk now but I learned some things about TNC." Petra sucked in a breath. "Let's just say they don't play well with others. We should not only not trust them, we should trust that they have nasty intentions."

"What do you mean? Like what?"

"I can't go into it right now, and honestly, you'd be better off just going back to your original plans, whatever they were, before we met. Just move on with your life. Forget about TNC."

How was I supposed to forget about the incredible experience of creating a viable place to live out of nonviable land? What was it Petra had learned? Whatever it was, it sounded bad. "You're scaring me, Petra. What can I do? Do you want to meet and we can talk this through? I want to help."

"That's very sweet of you, but I have to deal with them on my own, my way. Pass on my apologies to the other girls. I'm really sorry I dragged you guys into this mess."

Mess? "What mess?"

I heard a car door slam. "I gotta go, Saxony. I wish you the best, I really do. Maybe one day we can meet up and I'll be able to explain it better."

Why did she sound like she was certain that day would never come? Curiosity and concern surged like waves inside of me. "Petra, wait! Where are you? I'll come to you!"

The phone went dead.

"Ugh." I let out a frustrated sigh. Chewing my lip with frustration, I hit dial and hoped to get her back on the line. Her ringtone just droned on without answer.

I pounded out a text: *What's going on, Petra? I want to help. Please.*

I waited, but there was no response.

I checked the time. It was almost midnight. But I couldn't wait to tell my friends what had just happened so I sent the group an SOS.

I just got the weirdest call from Petra. Either the Project is off, or Petra just made our decisions for us.

Georjie wrote back immediately. *What do you mean?*

Me: *She didn't say, but she sounded upset. She's not picking up or* answering my texts. Something has gone horribly wrong. I have to submit my application tomorrow, but meet you guys at school at mid-morning break?

Georjie: *No prob, see you then.*

Targa: *I'll be there.*

Akiko chimed in with: *I'm doing a little work at the library in the morning but I'll meet you at lunch hour.*

Me: *Sounds good. See you guys tomorrow.*

18

PETRA

I turned my car down an unmarked road thickly lined with pines. I looked at my phone and watched the blinking light that represented me and how I was drawing closer and closer to the GPS coordinates for FS11 I'd taken from Jesse's notes. It was just shy of four a.m.

I'd had several calls from Saxony when I'd first left Saltford, but when I didn't answer, she'd given up. I would call her when I was done with FS11, as I knew she'd told the others right away and they'd be dying of curiosity. It was better not to tell them any more until I'd executed my plan.

I tossed my phone into the glove compartment and went on without it. It would be no good to me anyway, from the first moment I threw out an EMP.

The forest was familiar, the same kind that we had driven through to get to the plot of clear cut land where the Elemental girls and I had built the prototype.

As a clearing along the side of the road came into view, I pulled my car off the double track and parked it. After killing the engine, I got out, closed the door, and took a deep breath of the fresh night air. I continued down the road on foot.

I felt something in the pocket of the coat I'd borrowed from Jesse and pulled out a pair of sunglasses. I tucked them into a chest pocket inside the coat so I didn't lose them, then pulled up the zipper against the bite in the air.

It had not rained here the way it had in Saltford. It was cold and humid, but the ground was dry.

It was the darkest part of night, the time of night when sleep was deepest, when even dreams had ceased and the weary drew renewal from profound slumber.

Though the world was asleep, I was wide awake and I expected TNC's security would be wide awake as well.

I expected I'd meet someone soon.

A tall and solid wall came into view, running through the trees to my left and right, cutting off the rest of the world from FS11. I'd reached the compound proper, but I had never approached it from the ground before. Every time I'd come here I had been flown in by helicopter.

My sneakers were silent on the needle-carpeted road but as I rounded a gentle curve, a bright coin of light came on and threw a beam which swung from side to side. It fell on me, paused, then passed back and forth over me as though determining I was alone. It settled on me again.

"Miss Kara?!"

The voice was not familiar to me, and it sounded both surprised and relieved.

"What are you doing out here? You'd better stop there and let me check with Miss Marks. I don't have any intel that you're due to enter this side of the station, or even due here at all this morning."

I continued to walk until the light was so bright it made me squint. I waved a hand and the beam of light moved off to the side and out of my eyes. I'd given the light a gentle mental shove, but there was a thud and the sound of thick plastic breaking.

"Hey!" the voice protested. "Was that...was that *you*?" There was indiscernible muttering, probably cursing supernaturals...unless he was one, of course.

Like Jesse had implied, Ibby and I could be the only supernaturals in the whole corporation, or this compound could be riddled with them. Whatever was on the other side of these gates, I wouldn't be letting it stand in my way.

The booth and gate sharpened in my vision, also the single guard they'd stationed at this entrance. Even in the short time I had worked for TNC, I had learned that they were anything but slack on security. I could only see one guard, but others would not be far away.

There was the sound of footsteps on metallic stairs as the guard descended from the booth to the ground.

The hum in my cortex began as I threw my force-field out around me in a bubble wide enough that if something incendiary hit, I wouldn't be totally blinded by the blast.

The guard came to stand in front of me on the other side of the gate, which was a grid of thick, welded wire. He had a weapon in a holster at his hip, but he'd not drawn it. I was an employee, after all, and that knowledge gave me some benefit of the doubt. His face was a pale apparition in the darkness of the night.

"What's going on? Why are you here?"

"What's your name?" I asked calmly.

"Pete." He seemed to take some comfort from this familiar interaction. Some of the anxiety went out of his eyes.

"Pete, I've terminated my contract with TNC and you should do the same. Please open the gate. I'll only ask once."

His eyes widened and he lifted the radio in his hand to his mouth. "Requesting backup at—"

I flicked my fingers and the radio flew sideways. It landed out of sight behind the wall.

Pete stared at me, wide-eyed, before saying, "Oh, boy."

Allowing the gate to pass through my force-field, I stepped up and put my hand on the metal. I had allowed the gate to pass through the force-field without really thinking about it, and as I did, a realization struck which both amazed and delighted me. I could fracture my own force-field into sections without compromising the strength of the pieces I wanted to keep working. I could move the fractured pieces about as I wished, and the sections were just as strong as the bubble when it was whole.

"...not without losing my job..." Pete was saying.

I had been so startled by the revelation about my force-field that I'd missed part of what he'd said. It didn't matter, he wasn't going to open the gate, and I hadn't expected him to.

"Stand back, please."

Pete put up a hand, palm out, while the other went half-heartedly to the weapon at his hip. I felt sorry for him. He didn't want any trouble. "Please, don't," he said. "Whatever you're doing, don't—"

With a flick of my fingers, I sent a piece of the field up to protect Pete from shrapnel, and with the other hand I sent a wave of energy through the gate.

With a loud crack, the gate shattered into millions of metal fragments which should have seriously injured if not killed both of us. I heard the spray skitter across the fields in front of Pete and me. The multitude of blue ripples, like freckles, illustrated exactly where the fields began and ended.

Pete had crouched and brought his hands up when the gate exploded, but was now peeking out from between his arms, focused on the diminishing ripples in the air in front of his face. His expression was one of amazement. The blue ripples revealed an invisible oval barrier between his flesh and the deadly slivers of metal. It was just the same as the oval barrier in front of me.

I walked by him, letting the field in front of Pete vanish. I sealed myself in, closing the field behind me.

"Send instructions to evacuate," I said over my shoulder as I continued down the double track, "and then go home."

Without waiting for his response, I began to jog through the trees.

There was silence behind me, and then footsteps pounding on the stairs. I could hear the urgent drone of Pete's voice through the glass of the booth. He wasn't going to listen to me. Of course, he wasn't. There was nothing I could do about that.

What I hadn't expected was for him to fire at my back.

When the barks of his weapon came, they made me jump with

surprise. I turned as the first bullet ricocheted and the second and third shattered in two bright pulses of light. Blue ripples crisscrossed over me, cross-hatching and revealing my field momentarily.

I heard Pete calling for backup, sounding more frantic than ever. I turned my back and kept jogging as he fired more bullets. Underneath my calm and rational words, rage seethed like an angry bear. I kept it caged. What I was doing needed to be calculated, not emotional. I had to keep my wits about me.

My heart was pounding a quick but steady rhythm, and the vortex running through my center was humming like a generator as I closed the distance between myself and my target: the TNC labs and offices, where the schemes that destroyed my parents and goodness knew how many other lives, had been staged.

I moved off the path and into the trees, making a beeline for the first modular building. I recognized it and reoriented myself on my mental map, putting the Atlantic ahead and off to the left. The building I was approaching was the one just behind the lab where Sy had always landed the helicopter. The rear of the building was a windowless block of concrete. On either side there was a glow of light.

The distant sounds of engines and indistinct shouting came to me from the front of the building.

I squeezed my eyes shut and sent out an electromagnetic pulse. There was a deep sonic boom and the artificial lights on either side of the building went out. The sound of engines ceased immediately, and so did the sounds of human voices.

Then they swept up stronger than ever, shouting and hurling commands.

I rounded the corner of the building and into the parking lot and gravel roundabout in front. Everything was shades of blue and gray under the dim light of a setting moon. A couple of yellow flashlight beams could be seen through the trees in between the building nearest me and Hiroki's lab. I headed for the front doors. These were offices, where servers were kept.

"Stop right there," a woman's voice called sharply.

I turned, my hand outstretched, ready to blow out the door.

A woman with close-cropped dark hair stood alone on the pavement in a half-crouch. Her eyes were lit like embers, and she held up both hands, which flickered with red flames. Saxony had looked much like this when she'd created the artificial sun for the prototype.

"Hello, mage." I faced her, unafraid.

"I'm not alone," she said as three more people, eyes lit in the same way, hands aflame, emerged from the trees and joined her, ready for a fight.

I turned my back on them, reaching for the door again.

A blast of fire hit my force-field and lit the world around me so brightly I squinted. When the blast ceased, I turned to face the woman, who was now only a few feet from me. With a flick of my fingers I lifted her into the air and threw her back into one of her friends, who caught her and staggered back before the two of them fell to the ground in a heap.

Facing front again, I put a hand on the door and cracked the metal. Kicking the door in, I stepped inside.

The building was empty, locked down for the night. Behind me the mages were talking fiercely, arguing. I wondered how much they knew about who I was and what I could do.

"You made a mistake with me, TNC," I muttered to myself. I looked right, then left, and headed down the carpeted hall. "Big mistake."

It didn't take long to find what I was looking for. It was underground, as I knew it would be: a small room housing several Faraday cages. These cages were meant to protect the servers inside from electromagnetic radiation. Lines of blinking blue light confirmed that my EMP had not damaged the servers.

The cages on both sides of the room peeled back and folded like an accordion under my mental control, leaving the servers exposed.

Shattering them to bits took mere seconds.

I turned my back on a room that was filled with nothing but broken plastic, twisted metal, and fried electronics. The acrid stench of electricity and smoke hung in the air.

I emerged from underground and went through the offices room by room, destroying laptops, computers, phones, anything electronic I could find.

No one entered the building to stop me, and I wondered what TNC forces were up to. Still trying to recover from my EMP? Reaching out to other supernaturals in their employ who might be able to face off with the Euroklydon?

Hiroki had made the mistake of inflating my confidence, telling me there was no one like me in the world of supernaturals. He'd said I was not just rare, I was one-of-a-kind. Was it just lip-service? *Was there someone out there who could get through my force-field?* I pushed these thoughts aside and moved faster, destroying everything and anything I could find until I had gone through every room.

On the front steps of the building, when I emerged, I had something of an answer.

A group of about two dozen people in full combat gear stood in the clearing in front of the building. They'd formed a semicircle and every one of them had some kind of weapon leveled at me. The two people on the outer edges of the half-circle each hefted short, huge-barreled things on their shoulders, which, based only on movies I'd seen, might be actual bazookas.

"So," I said as I took the steps down to the ground. "We finally get the ammo test you guys have been looking forward to."

Two notions materialized in my mind. The first was that I could mentally bat their weapons out of their hands and smack them over the heads with them. The second thought stayed my hand. I wanted to see what was going to happen when they leveled all the firepower they had at me. The assault would either be too much for me and I'd die, or it would prove to both them and to me that my barrier was as indestructible as Hiroki had me believing it was.

"I intend to destroy every single piece of technology I can find in this field station. And after that, I intend to visit every single other lab, office, field station, battle-ship, tank, freaking zeppelin that TNC owns, and destroy them too." I took a step forward. "After that, I'll visit the personal residences of everyone with enough clearance to know what TNC has been up to since it first killed all those people in India after the second World War."

I couldn't make out the expressions of any of the people, hidden as they were behind full-face protection. But there was an uncomfortable shifting from a few of them. My guess was that none of them had a clue what I was talking about, but now they'd be curious.

"Come on, then." I made a beckoning motion with my fingers. "If you want to stop me, now is your chance."

I took the sunglasses out of my pocket and put them on my face. I couldn't stop my grin.

With a cry of, "Fire!" from someone, the world around my bubble exploded.

A multitude of frequencies lit through my core. Even with the sunglasses on, I had to squint against the bright lights of the assault. Starbursts and sparks went off everywhere, the blue ripples of my force-field adding to the visual chaos. It was like an over-the-top firework display happening mere feet from my face.

The light was simply too much for my poor retinas, the sunglasses were not enough protection. I crouched and hid my face in my arms, waiting.

When the assault finally ceased, I lifted my head and opened my eyes, blinking as the firing squad came into view. The acrid smell of hot metal and smoke lingered in the air. The world went still as they realized I was still here, whole and untouched.

"Are you finished?" I stood up.

A few long seconds passed before two of them parted. Hiroki was shoved through the line to the forefront. A soldier held him by the collar, pressing the barrel of a handgun to Hiroki's temple. Hiroki was pale and sweaty, looking fit to have a heart attack.

I flicked my fingers.

The gun flew out of the soldier's hand, did an arc in the air, and landed behind enemy lines. There was a murmur as they witnessed this.

I flicked my fingers again, and did what I could have done earlier.

The weapons were wrenched out of their hands to hover in the air. With a batting gesture, I send the guns into orbit, rotating like a macabre carousel high over their heads.

My eyes on Hiroki, I walked forward, anger simmering. I ignored those now gaping up at the weapons swinging in their grim merry-go-round.

"How much did you know? Did you know about Libya?"

"Petra, I'm so sorry," Hiroki stuttered.

I spoke through a tight jaw, trying to keep my teeth from clenching. "Did you work with my father?"

Hiroki wilted under my gaze. "I tried to tell them—"

I cut him off. "Did you know they killed my father? Did you know they've been watching me since birth? Did you know the whole dig in Libya was a fake? That it was all an elaborate scheme to get me on your roster?" I turned and said this to everyone present. "Do you know that people die every time TNC executes a project? Do you know who you're working for? *What* you're working for?"

No one answered me. I looked at the faces, covered in dark glass.

"Why? Can any of you tell me why?" I paused, giving time for someone to step up with a response. No one did. "Why does TNC seem to exist to hurt people?"

I couldn't see their faces to tell how they were feeling, what they might be thinking.

I narrowed in on one of them and lifted the gates between our minds, probing for answers. Nothing. There was wolfram here. I wouldn't doubt that it was lining their combat gear. I closed the gate and took a weary breath.

Someone was speaking. I turned to Hiroki, rubbing the back of my head as the pain passed.

He was stuttering. "I-I asked them not to hire you." Sweat poured down the sides of his face in streams. "I told them not to–"

"Is that supposed to make me feel better?" My lip curled in a snarl. "It doesn't even matter if you're telling the truth. I can't believe a word you say."

"He did," said a muffled but familiar voice. "He warned us not to hire you."

Miss Marks pulled off her helmet and put it under her arm. Her perfect face was ashen in the dim light. The carousel of weapons circling overhead sent shadows over her features.

She continued, "But do you know what his recommendation was?"

"Jody, don't," Hiroki said.

"He said we should terminate you instead."

Somehow this admission, which was meant to shock me, did not surprise me at all.

I stepped through the line and headed for Hiroki's lab. "You should have."

19

PETRA

I tore the guts out of it.

Destruction became almost mindless as I fried electronics and blasted computer hardware and complex tools that did goodness knew what. I shattered millions of dollars' worth of lab equipment, cracked open the hologram machines in all of the theatres, busted up the consoles and left them smoking and sparking. I even broke their coffee and vending machines. I ruptured pipes and let the water run. I sparked fires to life and let them burn.

The sun was breaching the horizon by the time I finished with TNC's offices and labs.

I stood on the road leading to the prototype, listening. If there was anyone around, they were quiet. I wondered where Mr. Nakesh was, and what the team was doing now. They couldn't stop me with any show of might, they knew that now. But were they re-strategizing? Coming up with some way that didn't involve firepower to bring a halt to the destruction I would rain down upon them?

I put the rubble of FS11 at my back and made the journey to the dome the Elemental girls and I had built the day before.

It was truly beautiful to look at, like a protected park. The curves of the dome pressed the leaves of vegetation growing next to its inner walls into a gentle curve that made it look like the plants were reaching for the sky. The small sun and moon were slowly orbiting, throwing shadows as they moved peacefully around the dome like a lazy top.

I turned the force-field around it off and the vegetation sprang outward.

A pleasant smell and the feeling of fresh and humid air rich with the scent of damp earth swept over me.

The moon Georjie had assembled drifted slowly by. I untethered it and it dropped out of the sky and crashed into the jungle below. A cloud of gray-white dust drifted up from its wreck.

With a powerful mental shove, I sent the small sun, which had lost much of its brightness, flying toward the Atlantic. It became a shooting star as it arched across the sky, trailing smoke and flaming debris. Shadows moved under its path and then vanished as it splashed with a loud hiss into the waves beyond, extinguished forever.

Unsure of what to do about the vegetation, I made a mental note to ask Georjayna about it. She had mentioned that many of the species were not native to the area, but this issue was out of my jurisdiction. If she thought it was going to be a problem, she could deal with it.

The sound of footsteps and panicked breathing made me turn.

"I wondered when you'd show," I said, crossing my arms and facing Mr. Nakesh as he came running through the trees, huffing and puffing.

His blue eyes were wide and blazing, his brow and hair pasted with sweat. His clothing was torn and muddy. He was wheezing hard but when he saw me, he still had breath enough to let out an agonized wail. He bent over at the waist and put his hands on his knees, his back heaving.

"What...have...you..." he wheezed, panting and looking the color of curdled milk, "done?"

His eyes traced the edges where the tell-tale curve of plants should have been. Then he looked up for the orbiting fake-sun and fake-moon, which were no longer there. His face seemed to cave in on itself. He shook his head and dropped his face again, moaning.

"What have *you* done, Mr. Nakesh?" I asked in a flat voice. "You were hoping that I would never find out what you did to my parents? Worse than even the personal offense, I know about the sinister side that TNC projects always have. I'd ask you to tell me why people die whenever you and your company come near them, but I don't think you're capable of saying anything that isn't a lie."

"You don't understand," he said, standing and scrubbing at his pale face with his hands. His sweaty hair gleamed in the morning sun and stuck up in all directions. "There has always been more good done than bad. It's the way it has to work."

"What are you talking about, 'more good,'" I snapped, then held up a hand. "You know what. I don't care to listen. Actions speak louder than words, and your company is about to see a whole lot of action from me."

I walked past him, fighting the urge to send him flying into the nearest tree.

He reached out for me but his hand bumped hard against my force-field and there was a crunch of knuckles.

"You don't get it," he said. "I'm due to pay up. Now is the time. It has been too long since it fed."

My skin prickled and I paused, wondering what kind of new insanity this was. I turned slowly. "It?"

His face was terrible to behold—terror, fear, desperation.

"Please," he whispered. "This is your only moment to fix this, to stop what's going to happen. Put it back. Please, put it back." His voice became conspiratorial. "Let's let it think the plan is going forward, if only to buy us a little time."

"Us?" I almost laughed. "There is no us, *Devin*." I enunciated his name.

He trembled and opened his mouth to argue. I shook my head.

"I don't know what you're talking about, but I do know this." My voice was calm in the face of his apparent mania. "I will never, *ever*, do anything you ask of me."

"Then I am a dead man, and others will die. People you love. You may be indestructible, but they are not."

My lip curled. "That already happened, in case you forgot. It's in the name of those people that I'll destroy everything you own, everything you have ever touched."

"Jesse is alive," he said, shaking his head. "Put the prototype back, or he dies."

For a moment I had no words, and scanned Devin's face for a lie.

"What did you say?" I asked, my voice low.

"We have him. We picked him up as you were blowing apart all of our hard work, all of my assets."

I narrowed my eyes. "Where did you pick him up from?"

"In Saltford. We knew when we lost track of him in Berlin that he was going to find you." He put out a hand. "Please, put the prototype back before it wakes up."

I didn't believe anything that came from his lips. The 'it' thing was just another lie, something he'd made up to get me to cave. The 'it' thing was not my problem. Jesse was. Could I afford to assume he was also lying about Jesse?

I lifted the gates between our minds and got the result I expected. Nothing. There was wolfram on his person somewhere. My eyes ran over him, looking for sign of the metal.

"I need proof that you have him," I said.

He let out a sharp exhale. "Petra, we don't have time for this. We *have* him. I'm not lying."

"How do you even know that your people found him? I fried all of your electronics. You'd have no way of hearing from anyone outside of shouting distance." My eyes traced his collar, looking for a necklace, his fingers, looking for rings. Nothing.

Then I spotted his watch. Its band was made from alternating gold and wolfram.

"We have ways, Petra." His tone was patronizing and it made my skin crawl.

"That's a nice watch, Devin."

He paled. "Wh–what?"

"Take it off."

He began to shake his head.

"You want me to believe you have Jesse? Take off the watch." I crossed my arms. "You have three seconds."

He laughed that creepy high-pitched giggle, rubbing at the back of his head frantically, like there was a serious itch there.

The wolfram was dead to me, but the gold's frequency sang out loud and clear. I gave the watch a mental yank and his arm shot out toward me.

He gave a cry of surprise and tried to pull his hand back. I held it there as he squirmed against it. Keeping my eyes on his, I flicked open the watch's gold clasp and it came shooting off his wrist. It arched over my head and landed somewhere in the trees behind me.

Lifting the gate to his mind was like opening Pandora's box. Strange scared gibberish and images flashed across the screen of my mind. A demonic face tipped with horns flew out of the refuse filling his head and I choked off a scream. I yelled out Jesse's name to help focus Devin's thinking and Jesse's face and form flashed in front of me, along with the truth.

They did not have him. They knew he was in Saltford and they were looking for him, but they did not have him.

I slammed the gates down and fought back a moan against the pain.

Devin stood before me, his eyes still wild. His hands came together and I believed he was about to resort to begging. I shuddered and swallowed the urge to throw up. I desperately wanted to take a shower, and never, ever would I fish around in his mind again.

"Goodbye." I turned and walked away.

"Wait! You don't understand!" His voice was a croak behind me.

I was several meters away when there came a sharp and heavy *boom* which vibrated through the ground. It was too deep a sound to be from a gun. The sound was somehow familiar. My eyes dropped, looking for this new threat. Then I realized why the sound was familiar. It had been the sound of terrain straining under Georjayna's power as she moved earth.

A deep crack had opened in the ground between Devin's shoes.

20

PETRA

We both staggered back, me with surprise, and Devin screaming out for help.

His already white face turned a shade of dirty gray and his eyes widened and rolled with fear. He looked up at me, his expression a grimace of mortal terror.

"It's too late," he rasped. "It's awake."

He staggered backward as the crack in the earth widened and spread with a sound like a series of breaking bones. He fell and scrambled onto his stomach in a desperate army crawl to get away.

A black tentacle made of smoke whipped out of the crevice in the earth and wrapped itself around his ankle, dragging him clawing and screaming toward the crack.

He disappeared into the earth with no other sound, along with the tentacle. The crack in the earth slammed shut with a thud. A puff of dirt drifted up and a sapling swayed back and forth before deciding to cant heavily toward the sea. Then, all went ghostly quiet.

It was as though Devin had never been there, the tentacle had never been real, and the only evidence that the earth had been disrupted was the crooked young tree.

I stood frozen in soundless shock. I wanted to scream, but my throat felt too tight. Only the sound of my labored breathing and the whisper of the wind in the pines could be heard. Every hair on my body stood at attention and for the first time, the cold hands of terror slipped around my heart.

"What just happened?" I croaked at the woods.

I lost track of time as I stood there trying to process. I had just met 'it,' or part of it. *It* had also decided that today was Devin's day to die.

My heart thudded dryly, as though all the blood had gone out of it, while I replayed his awful demise in my head. It might have been fitting, but that didn't make me feel any better about watching him die. A wave of nausea swept over me and I closed my eyes against it, swallowing hard.

The wind picked up and the sound of a distant siren made me jump. Some alarm finally decided to react to something.

"A little late," I muttered, but the sound opened my eyes and jolted me back into action.

I began to run through the trees in the direction of the front gates of FS11, back to where I had parked my car. I paced myself, but it wasn't easy. I kept glancing over my shoulder, wondering if that thing might appear again. My heart was galloping, and not just from the exertion. My hands were ice-cold while my face felt flushed with heat.

Skirting the field station buildings, I ran on, looking back every once in a while and watching the earth, half expecting more cracks to open up and a tentacle to come out and grab me. Fear was an exquisite motivator and it spurned me on, even when my breath grew ragged.

What was that thing? What did it belong to? What, exactly, had woken up as a result of the project falling apart? I didn't know the answers to these questions, other than TNC was dealing with a supernatural force that was very unhappy.

I kept my force-field intact and passed by the now useless laboratory where Hiroki had first started testing me.

After nearly twenty minutes of running and no sign of 'it,' I slowed enough so my heart could find something of its regular pace. I allowed a small but bitter smile to lift the corners of my lips as I passed the shattered gate and abandoned security booth.

It was over for this field station.

With Jesse's help, I would find the other stations and I'd destroy those, too. I didn't care if it meant I couldn't ever live a normal life again. I wasn't normal, so a normal life was not something I could expect anyway. I had a new purpose now—destroy TNC and any corporations like it. The arrogance, the pure evil of these kinds of conglomerates couldn't be fought by normal civilians. But I was not a normal civilian. I had the power and the kind of defenses necessary.

My thoughts were broken by the sound of a great groan vibrating deep beneath my feet. I froze in a half-crouch, ready to spring or run if a crack broke open.

The groan ceased. I waited, but all remained quiet. I resumed jogging. Whatever owned the tentacle that had pulled Devin into the earth, it had sounded like it had rolled over.

A minute later, the groan was back, louder this time. The earth shook and I felt the shudder go up my legs.

A long rattling hiss followed the groan and the early morning light dimmed. I looked up and watched as part of the sky went from pink to gray. My skin grew cool and my hands and face felt wet. I rubbed my fingers together, looking at them and expecting to see them dripping. But the damp I felt was invisible, and whatever was between my fingers felt more slimy than wet.

"Ugh!" I flicked my fingers, trying to get rid of the feeling. I felt my face, and it too felt coated with slime. I wiped at my skin but the feeling didn't go away. My fingers showed no visible mucous, nothing could be scraped off and examined, yet the feeling remained.

The groan became a growl.

I whirled, raking the trees for whatever made the sound.

The forest had now lost its color, just as part of the sky had. I blinked and rubbed my eyes, thinking something was wrong with my vision. When I opened my eyes again, the view was the same. The forest and sky were shifting from the dim color of early morning to shades of gray. In fact, the edges of everything were blurry, like a heavy fog was gathering between the trees.

The growl came again, from everywhere and nowhere. My heart began to gallop again in my chest.

"Where are you?" I yelled into the trees. "Show yourself!"

My answer was a deep roll of thunder...or was it a slow throaty laugh? If I hadn't seen the tentacle for myself, I would have thought this was a storm gathering.

The forest grew dark and the trees faded from view, swallowed up in the unnatural fog. Cold slime felt heavy on my skin and again I tried to remove it, scraping at my cheeks with my fingers. I let out a yell of frustration. How could I fight an enemy I couldn't see?

The fog grew thick and my clothing became heavy with moisture. Looking down at my jeans and Jesse's jacket revealed nothing unusual—the fabric was not dark, and squeezing it drew no liquid from the fibers. Yet I felt thick with it, sopping.

The thunder-like laugh, or was it laugh-like thunder, dwindled. The fog began to migrate through the trees, drawing toward a central point off to my right. As the fog moved, I felt the moisture crawl across my skin, as though it was being sucked by vacuum toward this same central point. The sensation made shivers of revulsion run up my spine. My hair did not move and yet I felt the wet viscous liquid crawl over my scalp and through my clothing, across the skin of my back. I fought down the urge to retch.

But the ooze was leaving my body, drawing away from me toward the dark mass of murkiness which was coagulating, growing darker and denser by the second.

I let out a relieved breath as the last of the muck left my body, but I watched with dawning horror as the shape of something transparent and massive formed in the clearing. It grew tall, but its shape coalesced only roughly into the shape of some hunched but powerful looking creature. Its edges did not grow sharp but remained fuzzy, as if it wasn't fully materializing.

"Who are you?" I yelled at the shape.

Whatever the thing was, it was surely the thing that pulled Devin into the ground, though I couldn't make out any tentacles. I wouldn't be giving it a chance to do the same to me. At the same time, I hoped it tried something, because the moment it touched me, I would have its signature and I could destroy it.

"Come on," I murmured, taking a few steps closer.

Color returned to the sky and the forest as the gray drew into the...whatever it was that I faced. The gray palette surrounded and followed it as it moved.

I squinted as it settled roughly into a familiar shape, a creature I had not thought of since I was a child reading about ancient mythology—a minotaur. Long, wicked-looking horns grew from its rounded skull, close together, as though the beast was not facing me but looking off at something to the south. It seemed to lift its head and sniff the wind. The forest was visible through it, laden with fog and lacking color.

The cold feeling washed over me once more as the thing swung its head and the horns squared in my direction.

"What are you?" I took another step toward it.

With a lightning-like strike, a tentacle whipped from its form and struck my shield. Blue waves reverberated and rippled across my force-field. A second strike followed, then a third and a fourth. Blue ripples crisscrossed around me, deflecting the blows.

"Good luck," I snarled at it. My words and tone were bold and confident, but inside, an ice-cold confusion took hold of my mind. This thing had no signature; it was as dead to me as tungsten. And if it was dead to me, how could I destroy it?

The thing responded with that resonant laugh that came from nowhere and everywhere. It filled my ears with thunder and my heart with dread.

Slowly, cautiously—praying that the pain of it wouldn't knock me flat—I opened the gate between my mind and the mind of the thing.

I gasped at the vast ugliness which opened up before me.

Petra, the thing thought at me. Coming from it, my name sounded like a curse. It knew my name, knew I was probing its consciousness.

I didn't answer, but neither did I close the gate, because here, in its deeply evil consciousness, I would find an answer. I had to.

What are you?

There was a long groaning growl of as I searched.

Aaaaaaaaarrrrrrrrrrkoooooooooonnnnnnnnnnn.......

The growl tapered off and the beast threw its horns back and then fell forward on its front arms, or legs, I couldn't tell. It was an effort to intimidate, to shake me off. It didn't work. Moisture crept from my eyes at the effort it took to keep the gate between us open.

Archon.

My skull felt cold and aching and yet I dug. As the beast shook its head, I felt its efforts to expel me. My headache swelled and sharpened. I gasped at the pain, but did not retreat.

A demon of the old world. The last time it had surfaced was seventy-three years ago. It was thousands of years old and it had emerged at points in history that overlapped every war, every genocide, every major act of violence and conflict. As I understood, there were more Archons; this wasn't the only one. And present during every reign of terror was this demon or something like it.

This thing had been making deals with mankind for centuries, exchanging wealth, power, long life, and other so-called gifts with weak-minded and greedy people. It had the power to manipulate, dole out curses dressed as gifts, and orchestrate events through these people. It could put those it controlled into positions of power where it could then create the outcomes it wanted.

And the outcome it wanted was fear and chaos, misery and death. These things were what it fed on. It grew strong on human tragedy the way a suckling pig grew into a powerful boar.

This Archon in front of me now was the reason TNC's projects resulted in pain and suffering. Devin had bound himself to this Archon and he owed it sustenance. Now it was angry because it had been planning a giant feast involving the domes, and the plan had been thwarted.

By Jesse, and by me.

I had read enough. I slammed the gate down. Tears rolled down my cheeks from the shock of what I had read in its consciousness. I heaved a sob and covered my face with my hands. It was so much worse than anything I could have imagined.

Underneath my horror raged my resolute fury to destroy TNC, and now this Archon.

Looking up at the Archon, I gritted my teeth and sent a wave of energy at it. I changed my frequency and sent another, and another, and another. They emitted from my body like ripples. For all my deadly powers, the ripples passed through the Archon harmlessly.

It was futile. The Archon was not fully in this world. I could not touch it.

The thunder-laugh came again, but this time it changed pitch as the dark shape turned and began to walk away from me.

Desperately, I sent out more pulses of energy. There was the sound of breaking glass in the distance, but the beast still walked. Losing shape and becoming fog again, it was nothing but an amorphous shadow moving through the trees. It was evil disguised as strange weather.

I opened the mental gate between us again, searching to understand its intent. Its thoughts were not like those of men, or perhaps like only the worst kind of men, the most twisted among us.

The domes had been its idea all along, well-hidden in layers of seemingly good intention. The projects TNC had executed which resulted in disease and death had been orchestrated so this thing could feed.

I searched for how the domes were to be used, but the Archon was dissolving and moving away, its consciousness growing weak. I grappled for what it wanted now.

The Archon was hungry.

It came to my understanding through the driving pain in the back of my skull that the Archon had suffered defeat before, many times. It had won some, it had lost some, but there had always been a consolation prize.

It had been defeated by its opposites: truth, love, courage, self-sacrifice. I understood this as a concept, but it still did not help me understand the method by which this thing could not only be defeated but destroyed, and I would not be happy with less.

In losing cases, there had always been a consolation prize, a meal to tide it over until the next deal could be made. The chaos and fear and death it needed could be found where the population was dense, and the nearest dense population was Saltford.

My hometown was the Archon's consolation prize.

"Oh, what have I done?" I whispered as I slammed the gates down between us again, feeling filthy, my head pounding. I wanted to take a bath and scrub my skin raw. It made reading Devin seem like a pleasant stroll in the country by comparison.

The dark shape faded as it moved through the trees, heading south.

I bolted in the other direction, making a bee-line for my car. How fast did that thing move? How much time did I have? I raced through the woods, ignoring the branches and leaves as they whipped across my body, tearing at my clothes.

I saw my car through the trees and urged my legs faster. A hundred meters, seventy, fifty... My heart pounded and I sucked in air.

A cracking boom and the sound of twisting metal reached my ears. My car flew into the air.

I skidded to a halt and watched, horrified, as my Toyota was catapulted above the canopy. It rotated slowly through the air in an arc, flipping once, twice, three full rotations before landing upside down on the tops of the pines. There was a terrific crack along with the sound of breaking glass and the scream of metal scraping against wood as the car broke through the branches cradling it and slid nose-first toward the ground.

Bolting into action, I reached out with my mind to catch the car and slow its descent. The car came to a halt, hovering two feet from the ground. I turned the car slowly, righting it and putting its wheels level.

Another hit came from nowhere—this one weaker and seeming almost half-hearted—but enough to send the car sideways into a large tree. It dented the driver's side door and smashed the rest of the glass out.

I let go of the car with a groan and it dropped to the ground with a final sad crunch.

That thing, that horrid ancient evil, was headed for my hometown, and I had just lost my ride.

21

SAXONY

"Tell us again what Petra said," Georjie asked, raking her hair up and tying it into a messy bun on the top of her head.

Students and teachers milled about Saltford High, chatting and laughing, stress-free on the first day of the school year. Georjie, Targa, and I were seated on one of the picnic tables in the park beside the school. Crunched up paper bags and food wrappers from our lunch rested in a lump on the table.

"I'm sorry to ask you to repeat yourself but I'm having a hard time making sense of it." Georjie grabbed the garbage, got up, and took the few steps to the nearest trash bin to toss it in. She returned to the table and sat down.

I'd already told them once what Petra had said, and they had both tried calling her with the same result—no answer.

"You're not the only one," Targa muttered. "Although, I have to say, I'm kind of relieved that I don't have to decide between going back to Poland and potentially"—she made air quotes with her fingers—"saving millions. Does that make me a bad person?"

"Terrible." Georjie eyed Targa with a sardonic tilt to her brow.

"Very bad. Shame on you for being in love and wanting to be with the guy you're in love with."

Georjie blew a raspberry, and Targa wrinkled her nose at her.

"All joking aside," Georjie said, "there's no reason you couldn't have had both. Antoni would just have to wait a bit."

They turned their attention back to me.

"So, Saxony?" Targa prompted.

"She just said the whole thing was off," I explained. "She didn't say why, she said we'd be better off going back to our lives and forgetting about everything that happened. She said that TNC wasn't transparent with their intentions and that they'd done bad things."

"I'm dying of curiosity," Targa said. "And I hope Petra is okay. She'll answer her phone one of these days..." She trailed off at the look that passed between Georjie and me. "What, you don't think she will?"

"We don't know her." I shrugged. "Just how upset is she? What had she learned? A girl with powers like that crossed with a vengeful streak isn't someone I'd want to cross. What if she did something crazy?"

"Or stupid," Georjie added.

"Or both," I finished.

The picnic table swayed back and forth. I held the edge tightly with my fists, and the three of us froze in alarm.

The bolts holding the table together squeaked and groaned as the wood shifted. My heart leapt and turned over, making me feel a bit sick to my stomach. The fire inside me flared and twisted, almost as though it too had been startled out of its sleep. It died down, but the temperature of my whole body ramped up several degrees. My eyes flared with heat before cooling again.

Somewhere in the school parking lot, several car alarms went off.

I jumped to my feet and Georjie and Targa did the same. We staggered as the ground moved beneath us again. One of the girls at a nearby table gave a shrill squawk. There were a few other screams and the glass in the school windows audibly rattled in their frames.

The earth rested.

Car alarms continued to wail and several people jogged across the parking lot to attend to their vehicles. Gradually, the sirens were silenced.

"Did we just live through our first earthquake?" Targa asked with a nervous laugh.

People were calming down, sharing incredulous looks and talking rapidly. Some were laughing with relief as it had appeared the earthquake had passed.

"It's a first for me," I said, sitting down again.

"But not a first for this region," Georjie said. "There was that one on Canada Day in Yarmouth in 2015. Remember?"

"Oh, yeah." Targa nodded as she and Georjie sat at the picnic table again.

Georjie perched on the top and Targa sat on the bench across from me with her knees up under her forearms.

"How could I forget," I said. "My mom went crazy earthquake proofing the house. She had my poor dad crawling around under the house with a hammer drill, adding steel plates to our foundation. Our televisions and paintings are still bolted down." I laughed. "Our place could probably take a six-point earthquake without breaking a sweat."

Some kids from our grade wandered by, their faces lit with excitement over what had just happened. One of them waved to us. "You guys good?"

"Okay, here," Georjie called to a tall guy with dark curly hair and ruddy cheeks. "Was that your car alarm I heard going off, Burnam?"

"The one that sounds like a kid screaming through a tin can?" He gave a honking laugh and playfully shoved the blond guy in front of him. "That was Nick's. My alarm sounds way more badass than that."

"Whatever," Nick snorted and slapped Burnam's hand away. "My alarm is your mother screaming through a tin can."

The boys with them tittered and snorted.

"Ha ha." Burnam stuck his foot forward and hooked Nick's ankle, sending him sprawling.

"Why does it always have to be about the mother?" I said under my breath, both annoyed and amused.

"Because we're surrounded by children," Georjie answered, just as quietly. "It's like preschool, as Akiko often likes to point out."

"Speaking of which," Targa said, glancing at her phone. "She just checked in. She's leaving the library. She's fine."

The boys made their way back into the school in good spirits. It seemed Saltford had passed through the little quake without any damage.

My phone vibrated in my jacket pocket and I pulled it out to see my mom was calling. I pressed the talk button. "Hi, Mom. You okay?"

"Saxony! Where are you, honey?" Her voice was tense, as expected.

"I'm at school." I kept my tone calm and even, though my heart was still running at a moderate skip.

"Inside?"

"Outside, in the little park. We're fine, Mum. I'm with the girls. Well, not Akiko, but she texted. She's okay. Did you talk to the bros?"

"I'm calling RJ next, and your dad will be talking to Jack right now. We have it worked out that in an emergency, I'll call you and RJ, and your dad will call Jack. So we don't end up calling the same kid at the same time."

"Brilliant, Mom. You know a group text would mean talking to the whole Cagney family all at once?"

She went quiet. Then, "That's a great idea. Can you start one of those?"

"Sure, Mom. Everything seems okay."

"Seems so," she replied, "but the experts say that several small quakes can sometimes indicate a big one is coming."

It was on the tip of my tongue to ask how she knew this, but of course she knew this. Annette Cagney had literally gotten on the phone with an earthquake expert after the small one happened a couple years prior.

"Geologists say they come in waves," she continued, "so I just think we need to be on our guard. There are two fault lines relatively nearby—"

"I know, Bay of Fundy and south of Shelburne." I made a rolling motion with my hand, wanting to get off the phone.

"Do the girls know to drop, cover, and hold on?"

"I'm sure they do, Mum."

Actually, earthquakes were so rare in Atlantic Canada that this wasn't something that was taught consistently in schools. For all I knew, my friends had never been told what to do in an earthquake.

My gaze drifted to Georjie. I had seen her cause a kind of earthquake with my own two eyes. Somehow, I didn't worry that she'd come out any worse for wear. But my mom didn't know any of that. A shard of guilt slipped through me as I thought about what we'd been through with TNC. My mother had no idea, and as much as it sucked keeping secrets from my family, this was one I could never let slip.

"Well, you tell them, just in case. And practice. If a big one comes, you have to react quickly." I heard her snap her fingers through the phone. "Drop to the ground, cover your head and neck with your arms, and get to a place where you're as safe from falling debris as possible."

"I'll tell them. I should let you call RJ now, yeah?"

"Okay, honey." She made a kissing sound. "I love you. Oh, and make sure to stay away from gas mains, water lines, and power lines. They can rupture and cause fires in the blink of an eye."

I almost said, *better if I'm nearby if a fire starts than someone else*, but it wasn't the right thing to say to my mom. She knew what I was but it didn't mean she had to like it and for her, the tactic that worked best was to ignore my fire as much as possible…even if I was going to Arcturus as soon as my visa came through.

"Sure, Mum," I said instead. "Talk to you later."

I hung up just as a text came through from Jack.

Jack: *All good here. You?*

I sent him a thumbs up.

I had just tucked my phone back into my bag when a heavy rumble filled the air and shook the ground. It reverberated through my soles and up my shins. My head snapped up, catching the look of shock on Georjie's and Targa's faces. It definitely had not been my imagination. Looking around the park and the lot, people were either still with their heads cocked and listening, or interrupting their friends to get them to shut up and listen.

"Now, that was the weirdest thunder I've ever heard," Georjie said, getting off the picnic table. "I don't know whether to look up to the sky or down at the ground."

"Uh"—Targa pointed toward the north, where the city met the sky—"I think up."

22

AKIKO

Visiting the community library was a bit like going back in time. They had only offered a digital catalogue of their books in the last couple of years. I was thankful that at least they had 'the interweb,' as the librarian liked to call it.

I looked up as someone got up from a squeaky chair. Then I went back to my research, scanning articles about The Nakesh Corporation and its doings since its inception.

So far, the public-accessible articles I had found were glowing, heralding many of TNC's projects as altruistic and its founder, Devin Nakesh, as beneficent. I tapped my fingernail against the tabletop, frowning and wondering how I could find anything that wasn't propaganda. There was nothing to be found anywhere about Project Expansion, but of course there wouldn't be. TNC was determined the project would remain a secret until they decided to unveil it.

The whole experience had left a bad taste in my mouth but I didn't know why.

"Shhhh," one of the librarians said from the front desk.

I mouthed an apology at him and stopped tapping my finger. I closed the browser and got up from the slippery wooden chair which had probably served this community library for a half-century or longer.

A series of creaking and groaning noises filled my ears as the floor shook beneath my feet. I paused, unsure if I had imagined it or not. No, the floor was shifting.

The sound of the windows rattling drew my eyes up to the old warped panes. I met the librarian's gaze, both of us parodies of surprise.

There was a groaning sound from the floor and an old crack in the wood split further. Faintly, a couple of vehicle alarms could be heard from outside. A library patron rushed out, one hand rooting deeply in her pocket for her keys.

When the earthquake seemed to be over, I walked to the front desk.

"You okay?" I asked the librarian, a petite balding man in a neat wool vest of blue and green argyle.

"I do believe we just had a little quake," he said with an off-putting, high-pitched voice. He whipped a red paisley kerchief from his back pocket and dabbed it against his brow. More sweat oozed from his forehead. He took his glasses off, held them out, and peered through them as though able to predict that the next quake would not happen until both of us were long dead. He put them back on his face with trembling fingers. "Don't let it concern you."

"I won't." I smiled. "Thanks. Might want to check the pipes, though."

He lost his smile and paled as though it was not only a capital idea to check the pipes, but that they had most certainly ruptured and even now water was pouring over the boxes and boxes of books and magazines he had left to rot in the basement. He bustled away.

I headed for the front door. I had told the girls I'd meet them for lunch. I took out my phone and texted Targa to let her know I was on my way and asking if they were okay. I received a thumbs up reply. She texted that she was with Georjie and Saxony and that Saxony was on the phone with her mother being schooled on earthquake safety. I smiled at this and tucked my phone away.

I headed in the direction of the school on foot. Passing an empty playground, I was struck by how the swings were still swaying, the rusty chains expressing a moody symphony of squeaks.

The earth heaved under my feet again and a deep rumbling sound accompanied it. All of the hair on my body swept to attention at the sound. That thunder was *unnatural*.

I staggered and fought to right myself as the terrain tipped and swayed like the deck of a ship in a bad storm. Car alarms went off all around me in a dissonant cacophony of wails and blats.

The light changed and I thought the sun must have skated behind a cloud, but when I looked up, there were no clouds. The horizon to the north of Saltford was a pallid shade of gray. As I watched, eyes narrowing and heart pounding, the gray moved, leaching the blue out of the sky as it went. The gray was darkening, and increasing in size. Oddly, it seemed to be traveling low, almost through the city, rather than over it.

Glancing around, I noticed several people on the street, but no one in my immediate vicinity. As the ground rolled underneath me, I tore off my jacket and sweater, then staggered toward a small copse of trees to stash my things. I kicked off my shoes and left my jeans in a puddle on a pile of dry leaves. Phasing literally on the fly, I climbed into the air above Saltford on a falcon's wings.

As I wheeled north toward the gray, my *Hanta* vision narrowed on the mass of boiling shadow moving into Saltford. I strained against the wind to get closer. The storm was moving fast and erasing color as it came. The heat of my hunter's killer instinct ignited as I closed the gap, scanning the ground for someone, scanning the sky for the dark left-spinning double-helix that screamed *demon*.

A dark shape, with two sharp jutting columns suggestive of horns, moved toward the northeastern suburb of Saltford. It was blurry, like I was seeing it through frosted glass.

The caustic scent of evil burned my nose, endorsing the supernatural nature of the approaching creature, but the tell-tale spinning column was missing. There was nothing connecting this shadow-creature to the Æther.

I had not been an active *Hanta* for long, but I had never seen any intelligent animate being without a connection to the Æther; even silkworms had a thin glimmer of silk reaching up into the mysterious beyond.

What *was* this? It almost looked like a storm cloud moving across the landscape. If I didn't know better, I would think that was exactly it —a freak storm.

Far below, the wails of sirens, the screams of humans, and the creaks and groans of buildings were distant but increasing in both urgency and strength. Whatever this thing was, it was bringing destruction with it.

I dove and phased from a flesh falcon to a spirit bird, picking up speed as I passed from one realm to the other. But a strange thing occurred as I phased—the optics of the thing sharpened and then fuzzed out again.

What I saw mid-phase and between the realms lit my battle-rage. My whole *Hanta* being shuddered and blazed. It had been like peeking through the crack in a fence while walking by and catching a glimpse of the dog on the other side with its gleaming teeth bared and snapping.

I had a momentary glimpse of a thing with nuclear eyes and a bulging muscular frame tipped with horns. What was thunder momentarily became a slow, resonant laughter that filled me with horror.

But the view of this beast, once I completed the phase, went fuzzy and confused again, looking more storm than creature. Once again it sounded more like thunder than laughter.

I phased back into a flesh-and-blood falcon, looking through the crack between realms again.

The thing was now larger, closer, and had reared back on hind legs as it crashed into the city, massive limbs raised to strike. Its feet were cloven-hoofed, yet its arms were equipped with clawed hands.

Again, I lost the view as I completed my phase. Frustrated, I released a scream of fury. Trying to stop in the middle of a phase was like trying to run on marbles. I slipped from one realm to the other, unable to grasp anything and hold myself in the middle.

A trail of gray spread from the thing like a plague and a huge crack shot through the earth, opening the ground under an entire neighborhood. I watched in horror as the yawning mouth in the earth opened wide. Houses splintered and shifted, basements caved in. Street lights swayed, tilted, and fell, crushing parked cars. People ran screaming through the street, trying to escape the destruction.

Phasing again, I saw something in between that made my blood run cold. It flashed by in an instant but I saw enough to understand that the creature was *feeding*. The spinning columns connecting the people to the Æther were blurring *toward* it. Not only their helixes, but their very forms were blurring as well.

I could not wait. In spirit form I bolted for the dark mass, which already appeared to have doubled in size.

Hot righteous anger erupted as I reached, talons outstretched, to rip this demon from its place and drag it to the center of the Earth.

When I struck, a total and complete black closed over me. The air vacuumed from my lungs and from around my body. Pressing in on all sides was a substance like muck or soft clay. It felt as though I'd been swallowed by a bag of slime.

I tried to breathe and the muck went down my throat. I thrashed, hardly able to move in the heavy, cold, wet body of the beast. A muffled laughter filled my ears and vibrated around me. Fingers of panic fluttered around my heart, clutching at my mind until they closed fast. I was suffocating, blind, and deeply revolted by the feeling of being swallowed alive. The slime more than coated my feathers and filled my nostrils, it seeped into my pores and smothered me completely.

Desperately I thrashed and toiled, directionless and confounded. At the feeling of the slime pulling away from the tip of a wing, I strove in that direction. I *sludged* my way through this trap as my whole being screamed for air.

I burst from the muck, my mind woolly and body aching. The

ooze crawled across my body and wrung itself from my feathers reluctantly, as though it could only stray so far from its owner.

I shuddered as I finally came free of it. Bewildered, I spiraled around the creature, staying clear of every part of it, as it rained destruction on the world below me.

Saltford was under supernatural attack. Something had to be done, and who else was to do something about this but me? But what could I do? I'd already proven that I couldn't take this thing down the way I had the Oni in Japan. It was something different.

I needed help. I needed Yuudai.

Pointing my beak to the sky, I phased into a crane and headed for the white.

23

SAXONY

The sky to the north grew black with a strangely shaped thundercloud. Dark and angry as a bruise, it loomed over the city and blocked out the sun. The air grew cold and I pulled my jacket closed.

It seemed that suddenly, Saltford was skating on ice as it swayed under our feet and the earth moaned. The three of us staggered, eyes wide and focused on the dark cloud approaching, hands thrust out for balance. People began to scream and run as panic set in. Someone yelled something about the end of the world. Others dove under picnic tables or ran for their cars. A bunch of kids pelted for the school.

A series of heavy thudding sounds came from nearby as bricks and chunks of cement fell from the building and hit the ground near the school's foundation. Cracks appeared at its base, shooting up through the mortar. The whole building swayed, giving me vertigo. I squeezed my eyes shut to try and settle my stomach.

"Move!" Georjie screamed at a group of girls who were sitting and leaning up against the school, frozen with fear at the sudden chaos.

One of them got to her feet and yanked on her friend's arm.

Several bricks hit the ground next to them and the girls screamed, scrambling to get out of the way.

Georjie toed off her sneakers and thrust her hands out, her eyes illuminated with a bright light. Targa leapt out of her path and into me. The two of us got out of the way as we realized what Georjie was doing. We got behind her as wind picked up her blond hair and whipped it back.

I felt Targa grasp my hand hard as we watched a sapling shoot from the soil near the base of the school and become a full-grown tree in moments, while students scrambled off the grass in efforts to get away from falling debris. Bricks and stonework tumbled into the dense canopy, their fall arrested briefly. The debris trickled through the branches to land on the ground with heavy thuds.

"Georjie," I tried to say, but I was so astounded at what she'd just done and what was happening that it came out as a rasp.

She'd just exposed herself. Big time. But she'd saved several students from being flattened. I noticed at least one person standing off to the side, gaping at the tree which had appeared out of the school's foundations, holding their phone up and taking photos or videos.

"Oh, this is bad," I groaned, watching as another student joined the first, this one definitely filming both the tree and the approaching storm.

"Get out of here!" I yelled at them.

Cracks shot through the mortar of the school walls like the building was made of glass. Dust crumbled and drifted over the tree and the grass, turning the green to gray. Or was it the dust doing that? I squinted at the base of the school, watching the color leach out of everything. It wasn't the dust turning everything to gray...

A stampede of people came running through the parking lot, looking over their shoulders and screaming. Behind them, a fuming gray fog that was almost smoke, or smoke that was almost fog, swept across the city, swallowing buildings and cars and turning people into silhouettes stumbling through the haze.

I heard sounds of disgust and screams of terror, people yelling out names in panic, looking for one another. The strangest thing about this smoke was that it had *edges*. There were stark borders between the fog and the clear air around it.

A terrific crack filled the air and the sound of grinding rock and crumbling concrete drew my attention back to the school. The cracks were huge now, and wove through the side of the high school where Georjie's tree reached up from the earth and along the brick wall like a hand hoping to catch something.

"The whole building is coming down." Georjie's tone was not panicked, her voice not even loud. Maybe something about the wraith she'd fought in Ireland had taken the edge off strange events like this, but my heart was pounding like war-drums.

"Georjie, let's go!" My voice was husky and an awful crawling feeling was all over my face and arms, making my clothing feel heavy and caked in swamp guck.

The grinding noise increased and my eyes flew up to the second story of the high school. A section of the storm, moving independently from the main body, swung toward the school like a huge fist. Blue daylight flashed at me through gaps in the fog-smoke. I blinked and tried to refocus my eyes, unsure of what I was seeing.

"It's a thing," Targa whispered beside me, her hand gripping my shoulder. "It looks like a freak storm but it's something else, right? A... creature? Are you seeing what I'm seeing?"

I nodded and felt my inner fire bellow to life. What was this force? If it was a natural phenomenon, it was the strangest one I had ever seen. But strange things had happened before. I'd read about them in the news, like how spiders rained from the sky in Australia, or the sky turned bright red in Wales after a tropical storm blew metallic dust across the ocean.

I squinted, watching with disbelief, as a disembodied part of the storm crashed through the school. At first there seemed to be no effect. The 'fist' passed through the bricks and windows like a ghost. But moments later the school's walls swayed, leaned dangerously, and groaned like the building had a soul and it knew it was dying. More fat cracks threaded their way through the brickwork.

"Saxony." Targa tugged on my arm. With monumental effort, I tore my eyes from the ghostly fist and followed Targa's gaze.

Georjie had become the Wise. She looked the way she had in the photograph I had thought was photoshopped. The face was hers, the form was hers, but Georjie's expression was alight with a terrible and beautiful wrath.

Goosebumps swept up the back of my neck. I barely recognized my friend. Her eyes were white lights, her arms lifted and fingers flexed. Dirt covered her feet and disappeared up her pant legs.

The walls of the school gave way.

"There are students still inside!" I made to dart forward but Targa kept me back. "Let me help," I rasped.

"Wait!" Targa's hand squeezed, almost painfully. "What are you going to do? Light the whole thing on fire? She has a plan!"

I glanced at Georjie and her body seemed to surge with tension.

Trees and vines and surfeit of plants wound their way through the walls of the school, wrapping tendrils and green muscular arms around chunks of brick wall and crumbling cement. Huge vines as thick as tree trunks snaked around and through the building as kids crawled from the first-floor windows and ran from the doorways, dragging one another, helping each other escape. Like the tentacles of some subterranean kraken, the plants whipped and unfurled to thread themselves through the building, holding it up.

Georjie couldn't stop the school from crumbling, but she was slowing it enough to give the people inside a chance to escape.

My jaw sagged at the sight before us. A fractured building woven through with rich green plant-life—and Georjie's plant-life did not lose its color; if anything it seemed to pulse with an ethereal green light. Amazement held me still and my heart surged with pride.

Targa made a sound almost like laughter. "Now she's just showing off!"

A profusion of purple flowers the size of tractor tires burst open along several of the vines, along with large green leaves which thrust outward from thick stems and unfurled like verdant green umbrellas.

The whole network of plant reinforcement stretched and swayed as the school took the impact of the storm-beast.

There was an angry rumble from both the sky and the earth.

"Are those..." I squinted at the giant flowers festooning the school like oversized party decorations. "Are those morning glories? How is she..." I sniffed. Yes, the air had become fragrant with a floral scent.

Georjie turned toward us, her eyes once more limpid and sweet. A moue of disgust curled her lip.

"Go, let's go!" She wiped at her arms, trying to get rid of the slimy feeling.

"Georjie, kids have you on film," I cried as we took off running toward the nearest blue sky.

She didn't reply because a car came careering out of the parking lot of the convenience store across the street and jumped the curb as it barreled toward us. It sideswiped a picnic table in an effort to avoid us. Targa hit me full in the side as we dove out of the way.

I landed hard and all the air whooshed from my lungs. As I was gasping for air I got another good look at the storm-creature. Sucking oxygen and blinking at the view behind us, I thought I saw, just for a moment, the shape of shoulders, thick swinging arms, and a turning head topped with horns. It was like a shadow-giant moving down the street, its bulk swaying.

Then the image was gone, and if I didn't know better I would think I'd imagined it. Now it just seemed like a freak storm, sweeping across Saltford, moving fast and growing like a mushroom cloud.

I wheezed as I rolled to my knees and grabbed Georjie's arm to help her up.

"Go, go, go!" Targa was already on her feet and taking off.

She nearly yanked my arm from its socket as she hauled us up and away. Her pure strength shocked me, but I was too dazed by what was happening to process it properly. I felt as though Armageddon must have struck. Was the whole world under attack, or just Saltford?

As the storm passed near us, wind whipped our hair and lightning flashed angrily overhead.

"Ugh!" A profoundly disgusted sound came from Georjie.

My skin felt coated in something thick, cold, and slimy. I ran a hand along my arm and looked at it, but there was nothing to be seen. I shuddered and fought down a gag.

Targa, Georgie, and I ran for the nearest blue sky, more than half a block to the southeast. We raced toward the clean-looking air over the beach and the Atlantic, our skin still crawling.

Saltford had become a city bending and groaning under the weight of an apocalyptic event. My mind raced as I watched my hometown fall to pieces. What could we do? People scattered and ran through the streets, which became treacherous as they heaved. Cars swerved wildly across the blacktop as their drives tried to avoid people and other cars, sometimes succeeding, sometimes not. Alarms and sirens signaled a city in chaos and panic. And somewhere behind us came the frightening sounds of splintering wood and twisting metal.

People were getting injured, probably dying. Terror had taken the city.

My blood thundered hot and fast next to my eardrums. Something exploded with a series of popping sounds, like fireworks. I squinted through the gloom to see that it actually was a collection of fireworks in someone's garage, spewing colored sparks from the open door. The garage had a dangerous lean to it, as did the house behind it.

We reached the edges of the storm-beast and passed into sunlight. The feeling of muck crawling across my skin and being squeezed out of my hair and clothing was so bizarre that I hardly noticed the ground moving. It felt as though the invisible slime that covered us while we were in the shadows had to stay in the shadows, and as we moved toward fresh air it crawled across our bodies away from the sunshine.

I felt a shudder through the soles of my feet. The sound of heaving and ripping pavement could be heard behind us. But when the smell of actual smoke reached my nose, my head snapped up.

I slowed down and did a three-sixty, scanning for fire. The skin across the left side of my body tingled, and the fire inside roared to life.

"Saxony, look." Targa's voice pulled my attention to where she was pointing at the sky.

The shadow was growing larger and seemed to be twisting. The way the storm was moving gave me the vague impression of a golfer drawing back a club to swing. As the shape unwound, the sound of splitting earth and pavement was so loud that we clamped our hands over our ears. Thunder swelled to a nearly unbearable volume and the strangest lightning I had ever seen forked down from somewhere in the belly of the storm-beast.

Where it struck, fire leapt up, zooming down a block of post-war homes like they were kindling.

Rage ripped through me at the sight of Saltford homes burning. My fists clenched as I watched the storm-beast preparing another strike. Now this thing was using *my* element to attack my hometown?

Not on my watch.

I ran. Targa's and Georjie's voices were faint behind me. I pelted through a narrow alley between houses, vaulted a chain-link fence, crossed a park, and skirted a copse of trees before reaching the street that was on fire.

Baking air turned the world into a mirage. Fire belched from windows, fueled with supernatural energy. The heat was incredible, the speed with which the fire had spread was astonishing. Flames leaped from rooftop to rooftop. There were people in the streets frantically making phone calls–likely going unanswered. There were people in the burning houses, but it would take forever to search every home.

I had to put the fires out.

Running down a walkway between homes to the back alley, I lifted my hands and began to walk, suffocating the flames as I went. I wanted to run as I worked, but extinguishing these flames took time and energy. Everything about this fire felt unnatural, like they were being fed by a strange, invisible fuel. As though they were connected to the entity which had given birth to them, they resisted and fought to stay alive.

I walked, hands lifted, eyes glowing, smothering the strange supernatural flames until I reached the last building, almost at the ocean. The street was full of half-burnt and blackened homes. They spewed toxic smoke into the belly of the storm above, which now loomed over the entire city. My blood felt like lava in my veins. In the time that had elapsed since Georjie had held up the school, the storm-beast had quadrupled in size. Why was it *growing*?

My mouth went dry as the sounds of a city in panic, under siege, filled the air. How was this thing to be destroyed?

Two running figures appeared; faint forms in the dim light. Georjie and Targa. I became aware of the cold feeling of slime coating my skin. I moved toward them and a strip of sunlight along the rocky cove.

"The world has gone crazy," Georjie said with a cracked voice. "That thing is just getting bigger, like it's feeding off the frenzy or something."

A flash of light on the horizon to the east pulled my attention to the Atlantic. My brain seemed to seize up. Was it just me, or was the ocean climbing into the sky?

"What's that?" I pointed.

The girls followed my line of sight. Georjie's face expressed confusion but understanding passed over Targa's immediately.

"Tidal waves follow earthquakes," she said, shielding her eyes from the sun.

"Only earthquakes that happen underwater, though. Right?" I peered at my aquatic friend, dread looming in my belly. "Not when they happen on land."

"Who is to say that thing didn't shake the earth out there, too? It seems bent on destroying us." Targa gazed at the rapidly growing line of blue. "Either way, that thing is a tsunami and it's headed straight for Saltford."

24

AKIKO

Yuudai?

The silence was resolute, steadfast, and unyielding. My voice was more like a thought, one that seemed to glide and echo softly, like silk slipping across skin.

Yuudai, help me.

I had no sense of passing time. It could have been seconds or years before I received the answer.

Akiko? His voice was like a candle in the dark, glimmering and warm, a distant but distinct presence. *What is it, little Hanta?*

I am facing something new. It's nothing like the Oni I took down in Japan.

Tell me. Yuudai's voice deepened and his words came slowly.

Haltingly, and yet with a strange urgency which contrasted with the very nature of the Æther itself, I told him what I had seen. I described the way the thing appeared clearly only when I was mid-phase. I told him how I'd tried to get a grip on it with my talons and became swallowed by a cold and suffocating darkness that felt as though it would leach into my very soul.

I could sense Yuudai listening, thinking. When I had finished he had only one word for me.

Wait.

The Æther was nothing but peace again.

Silver streaks began to cross my vision. Suddenly and silently, Yuudai was there, tall and strong and beautiful. I was there, too, my human form bathed in white light. I looked down at my hands, my clothes, the ones I had been wearing last. Yuudai was dressed in a simple white button-up shirt and black jeans. His long black hair lay stark against his shirt as he looked down at me with a sad smile.

"You're here!" Relief flooded me and I reached up to hug him. My arms passed through him.

"Yes, and no," he said. "*Hanta* can use the Æther as a meeting place when the occasion calls for it, but we are not here in the flesh." He reached out to touch my cheek but I felt nothing.

I didn't have time to learn the mysteries of the Æther. "Will you help me take down this demon, Yuudai? Between the two of us..."

But he was shaking his head. "It's not a demon, Akiko."

"It's not?"

"Well." He made an expression of allowance. "It's not *just* a demon. It's an Archon. An evil spirit of the ancient world, high up in the demonic hierarchy. It's above *Hanta* like you and me."

"What do you mean, *above* us." I was outraged by this statement. How could an evil force like that be above us? We were creatures of the Æther, forces for good. Didn't that put this thing, this Archon, *below* us?

"I don't mean above in the sense that it's higher up, just that it's a stronger force than you and me, or any *Hanta*."

My lips parted but I was speechless. This was not the answer I was expecting from Yuudai. Frustration burbled over.

Yuudai could see it on my face. "Listen–"

"I don't have time to listen to you talk about how we can't defeat it. There has to be a way. People are dying, my city is being destroyed. I can't just do nothing!"

Yuudai began to fade as I pulled away from him.

"Wait!" He reached out a long arm and his face was earnest. "You do have time. The Æther is a sanctuary from time. All things work out the way they are meant to, whether you visit the Æther mid-event or not. When you go back, you'll go back to the *when* you are needed in."

I made an unhappy grunt, still smarting over the idea that this Archon could not be defeated.

"Listen to me, so you understand." Yuudai's form cleared again and the white retreated. "In the beginning, it was not like it is now. Myths and legends of all nations and cultures are based on something real, no matter how fantastical they seem. There was a mixing of gods with humans in those days, and their offspring were giants. The giants of old were evil, cannibalistic creatures, preying on humans before the great flood wiped them out. Even now, evidence of these giants is everywhere on Earth; it is there for people to see, if they only look upon it with an open mind."

"You mean, people see it but don't know what it is?"

He dipped his chin in partial agreement. "People see what their belief-system allows them to see. You see this creature and recognize it for what it is, but someone else might see it and their mind will tell them it's a storm." Yuudai's mouth quirked in a half-smile. "Neither perception is wrong. But I digress."

"Half gods," I said, reminding him where we were.

Yuudai nodded. "Because these giants were demi-gods, they were partially immortal. Though their fleshly bodies perished, their spirits remained trapped in the space between realms, never able to fully materialize in one or the other. There is no rest for them. They feed on chaos, death, and fear, just like any demon, but they need a great deal more of it to survive. They are cunning and manipulative."

"That's what this thing is? An old dead giant?" I shook my head with disgust. "He should have stayed asleep. Why is he awake now?"

Yuudai took a guess. "He's probably hungry."

"Hung..." I halted mid-speech, remembering how the spinning columns connecting people to the Æther had blurred in the Archon's direction. I shuddered. "Ugh."

"In the days of old, they were present where they had the most nourishment—during battles, gladiatorial events, plagues, the raiding and the pillaging of villages. As men have developed technologies, become more peaceful and educated and found ways to feed everyone, the events the Archons rely on for sustenance have become fewer and further between, so they've learned to work with humans to orchestrate these events."

I wrapped my arms around myself but the chill which had settled into my bones would not ease. "So, now?"

"Now." Yuudai looked sad. "They offer things like long life, talent, power, money, and fame to those who are willing to make deals with them. Those people are put into places of power and then begin forwarding a demonic agenda. When their plans are thwarted, as they sometimes are, the demons become desperate and hungry. The use what energy they have to manifest as much as they are able to. They become single-minded and primal, like their giant ancestors. All they want is a buffet of chaos and fear and death to become strong again. If this Archon is attacking Saltford, it is likely because there was a plan that went awry and Saltford was the nearest place it could feed."

"I understand all of that. But how do I kill it?"

"You can't, Akiko." Yuudai's eyes were full of sorrow. "Only an Archangel can kill an Archon."

"Well, how to I summon an Archangel then?" I cried out wretchedly.

"They either come, or they don't."

"That's it?" I felt sick.

"I'm sorry, little *Hanta*." Yuudai's face and body began to fade, swallowed by the white. "There is only one thing that is for certain, Akiko, and that is that love is the most powerful force in the universe." His voice became that distant candle, dimming now. "When all else fails, love does not."

25

SAXONY

Targa sprinted for the beach, her skin changing from dirty gray to bright white as sunlight bathed her. Already the distant wave had quadrupled in size and was growing fast.

"Targa!" Georjie called, her voice sounding as burnt out as mine.

This time it was me telling Georjie to wait, the way Targa had held me back from the school while Georjie did her work. "She can...she might..."

"Might what?" Georjie cried. She danced in place as though not sure whether to follow Targa or run away. "That thing is millions of gallons of water moving at high speed!"

"She can either stop it, or we're dead anyway," I replied, shielding my eyes from the sun as Targa's figure got smaller.

"I can't watch." Georjie covered her eyes but then peeked through her fingers. "What is she doing?"

"She's chasing the ocean," I murmured. As Targa ran down the beach, the water ran away from her. At first I thought it was Targa sending the water back and exposing the rocky floor of the Atlantic, then I realized the water was being sucked out to sea as though by a vacuum.

The hump of blue on the horizon had become a wall. The sound of rolling thunder, a stampede of giant horses with heavy hooves reached us. The din rose and rose.

Boats tied offshore dropped. Their hulls hit rock and they tipped over as the water was sucked from underneath them. Targa ran past them.

The coming wave would destroy half of Saltford and it was nearly here. Only seconds remained before it crashed over us.

Georjie and I reached for one another and I felt her hand close over mine and hold fast. I squeezed her back and thought of my family. My eyes misted up and blurred my vision but I brushed the moisture away. If I was going to die today, I wanted to go clear-eyed.

Targa was a small figure against the wall of blue when she stopped running. The thundering wave dwarfed her like one long skyscraper. Her back arched and her hands went up. Her hair was wild black ribbons in the wind. Her tiny fragile frame would be swallowed up in the next second.

Georjie's hand nearly broke mine and a sob tore from her throat.

There was a thunderous crashing sound like water striking solid rock. The wave came to an abrupt halt at the feet of the mermaid standing before it. The wave rocketed straight up into the sky as though it had come against a glass wall.

Georjie and I watched, mouths and eyes stretched wide, heads tilting back, necks craning, watching the wave stretch up and up and up and grow thin. Sunlight penetrated and the wall of water rapidly changed color as it spread against Targa's will. It morphed through dark gray blue through a million shades of blues and greens until it became clear and sparkled with the light coming through it. The effect was mesmerizing and beautiful.

The water reached its zenith and curled backward. As though arching over a barrel, it began to rain down into the ocean as a waterfall. Droplets caught the sun and became flashing diamonds before striking the water and dimpling the ocean's surface. The first spatters became a torrent of falling water behind the wall of the ascending wave. Vertigo swept through me and I put a hand on Georjie's shoulder to keep from swaying on my feet.

"Wow," Georjie whispered beside me.

All I could do was nod.

The tsunami was losing power; the cycle of climbing and falling water began to shrink. The water levels in Saltford's harbor began to climb.

Targa kicked off her shoes and dove headfirst into the wall, disappearing into the gray-blue. Whatever magic she'd used to stop the wave was released, and water flowed across the ocean floor, bubbling and churning, whipping up dirty froth. It picked up the boats which had been beached. Garbage and wreckage was tossed about, but the Atlantic calmed rapidly.

"Where did she go?" Georjie asked.

All I could do was shake my head.

26

PETRA

The sky to the south was a dark cloud punctuated by flashes of lightning. Knowing that it was some kind of nasty supernatural creature helped my eyes process what I was seeing. The storm looked like a blurry roiling shadow, a woolly prehistoric creature having a tantrum.

I had tried several vehicles at the field station without success. The newer vehicles were down from my EMP. Finally, I found an old Blazer they had used for snow removal. When I turned the key left in the ignition, its engine roared to life.

Even with my foot holding the gas pedal to the floorboard, I could not get faster than ninety kilometers per hour, and I was still hours away from Saltford. The road was a winding two-lane highway that seemed to meander over hill and dale like it had time to kill.

I let out another groan of frustration and clenched the steering wheel. There was a reason TNC had always used a helicopter.

I crested a hill, the Blazer chugging lazily. A helicopter whirred by, heading south along the coastline. Half expecting the TNC chopper, even though I'd destroyed their helicopters along with the rest of the station, I rolled down my window for a better look. The chopper was red—an emergency responder.

A van loomed in front of me, taillights red as it sat crooked in the road. I gasped and jammed my foot on the brake. The bucket on the front of the Blazer scraped against the asphalt as the truck came to a jolting halt.

At least the brakes were still in good order.

My heart thudded erratically at the sudden stop, then even more as desperation clawed its way up my throat. I got out of the Blazer to the sound of a few blasts of car horns ahead.

Beyond the van, a line of vehicles sat bumper to bumper along the highway all the way to Saltford.

"No." I stared at the jam in disbelief, panic rising. I got out of the Blazer and slammed the door.

"Been here for twenty minutes a'redy," said a voice from the nearby van. A man with a ball-cap perched high on his head hung out of the window, his arm dangling over the door.

"What's happened?" I asked him. "Do you know why we're not moving?"

"Nawp." He lifted the ball-cap and fluffed up the brown curls on his brow. He pointed a thick finger toward one of the people on their cell phone. "That feller there says a friend of his says a quake hit town this morning, two times, one right after t'other." He hammered a fist against his palm twice, hard and fast. "Earth's opened up in spots and everything, one across this here road so people can't cross. Nothin' to do but wait, or go back way round by Bellevue."

"Thanks." I started jogging.

"Got some extra beer in a cooler if you care to pass the time..."

His voice receded as I left the van behind me. If I couldn't drive to Saltford, I'd find the front of this jam and see if I couldn't hitch a ride or commandeer a vehicle. I set a pace along the shoulder, dodging angry travelers and those who were chill enough to lay back with their feet cocked up through an open window with the music going.

I passed by one lady, deep in the ditch, who was on her knees, hands folded in prayer. I understood how she felt. I could use a little help from a higher power right about now. It struck me, as my breathing grew labored, that I was supposed to be an Air Elemental.

That was how they'd categorized me. So why did I feel so heavy and slow? At this pace, I'd reach Saltford by Halloween. For all of my incredible abilities, I would arrive too late to help.

My thoughts went to the Elemental girls. I hoped they were where they needed to be. Frustration sank its hooks deep in my heart. This could not be. I *had* to get there. Now. I ran faster, but felt all the feebler for it.

A memory rushed to the forefront—a dream. I saw my own hand in front of my face, turning to sand and crumbling, breaking apart and flying on the wind. A rush of adrenalin accompanied the memory and a *stretching* feeling followed. I felt the wind passing through my body, the molecules of my frame spreading apart.

I felt *light*.

There was a sound like the rushing of white-water over rocks: suddenly I was free. I tried to laugh, but I no longer had a throat.

My body blew apart and became a million tiny particles of sand. I swirled into the air, picking up height and velocity. My clothing drifted to the ground, caught a gust of wind, and landed on someone's windshield. The car door opened and someone got out. They picked up my pants and looked at them, then looked up, confused. Their expression turned to awe at the sight of the sandstorm overhead. In seconds, they fell out of my view.

My vision expanded. Everything passed below me at a frightening pace. The crooked line of vehicles looked like toys... up to a bridge and across a river that had become unstable, one corner drooping dangerously into the chasm beneath it. As quickly as I registered this, it passed by and was gone. The terrain became a blur.

The black clouds over Saltford loomed. The storm sometimes appeared to have limbs—thick muscular ones lifting and smashing—and other times it was simply a mass of darkness. Booms of thunder rolled across the land and lightning flashed from the belly of the Archon.

Alarms grew loud, as did the creaking and groaning of buildings and the angry crashing of the Atlantic. Smoke billowed up and was swallowed in the body of the thing.

I curved inland and banked, gathering speed. Dead ahead was my target, an Archon raining destruction on my city with the Atlantic as its backdrop.

My name drifted out of my memory. All mortal trappings faded from consciousness.

I was the screaming of high wind. I was the tempest. My battlefield was the skies above the city, and the stakes were the city itself.

I bore down on the shadow of death with all the fury of the Euroklydon.

27

AKIKO

I plummeted from the Æther, crying out with disappointment. My stork's wings shrank and became those of a falcon. The white faded and a view of Saltford bled into my vision like watercolors seeping into fabric. The city was suffocated by smoke and the fury of the Archon. Electricity crackled from its body as the amorphous shape seemed to inhale and grow larger.

It fed on chaos, fear, and death...

Love never fails? How was I supposed to fight this thing with love? The very idea seemed ridiculous.

I phased and landed on the beach in a run on human legs, slowing down to a halt to gather my breath. I turned as the sound of a screaming wind reached my ears. My jaw dropped.

A second storm, made of sand, blocked out the sky to the northwest and curved as though riding high on the track at a velodrome. Its particles were separate from one another, yet clearly formed one confederate being.

A face with a great yawning jaw formed in the sand and then disappeared as quickly as it had come. Fingers formed to reach and then dissolve. There was something familiar about that face.

"Petra?" I whispered, blinking up at the strangeness unfolding before me. I looked at her. I looked at the Archon, then back at the sandstorm again. She was a titanic force on a collision course with the Archon.

She was far away but moving fast, bearing down on the Archon with the fury of a tempest.

The Archon seemed to twist to look, and paused.

When the sandstorm barreled into the Archon, the sound was unlike anything I had ever heard before. There was the scream of a gale, high-pitched and with an edge that made me cringe. I clapped my hands over my ears as the wind whipped my hair about my head in a frenzy. The scream transformed into a thunderous roar, then multiple roars in different pitches overlapping one another. One of the roars sounded like a bellow of pain.

The sandstorm's energy gathered into a tight projectile just before puncturing the Archon's bulk as a lance, shooting through the Archon and out the other side before breaking into two, curving around and barreling through again like twin turbines.

The Archon staggered and the destruction of Saltford ceased as Petra drove it back toward the Atlantic. What commenced was a titanic wrestling match between the Archon and the tempest, and the sounds of supernatural thunder filled the skies over the city and the waters of its harbors.

I clenched my fists as I watched Petra push the Archon out over the ocean. It seemed that some of the sands passed through the Archon without any effect at all, while others raked and blasted it, tearing through its black smoky hide and making it stumble and fight to right itself. My eyes leaked moisture from the resulting winds.

I took to the sky in the form of a falcon once again, and through the briefest window in mid-phase, I caught a clearer view of a huge horned beast, bulging with unnatural strength, topped with long, wicked horns. Its body writhed and its clawed fists swung at the storm that dared to face it. I caught a glimpse of the damage the Euroklydon was inflicting on its form; cracks opened up on the Archon's black hide, a lurid red simmering beneath.

And then my view was gone and the beast once more became blurry and without definition.

My *Hanta* vision then told me another story. A small form in the heaving ocean just beyond the harbor drew my attention. It was Targa. Her connection to the Æther spun strong and white. Two more Ætheric connections drew my eye to where Saxony and Georjayna were on the beach, watching the Euroklydon and the Archon battle over the water.

The Archon seemed to sway and then push back toward Saltford, its dark shape leaning into the storm as though trying to shove a boulder up a hill. The Archon gave a jerking heave and a small shipping vessel seemed to come from nowhere; flying toward the beach, tumbling and turning toward Saxony.

I screamed out a warning cry. Saxony's hands flew up, illuminated with flames, as Georjayna barreled toward her and knocked her aside. The boat exploded on the beach with a blast of broken boards and parts; the girls huddled with their hands over the heads.

The Archon advanced again on Saltford, with the Euroklydon whirling and screaming her fury around it. The surprise of her attack had won her the first round, but it seemed she could merely slow the beast down, perhaps injure it, not stop it. The Archon was pushing back toward land, step by agonizing step.

I wheeled over Saltford, observing the havoc the beast had wreaked upon my city. Cracks in the earth had opened up like great gashes. Fires raged in patches, feeding off the winds. Smoke swirled and plumed, filling the sky with toxic fumes.

The Archon advanced slowly; the Euroklydon was losing. It crossed the beach, then it crossed Atlantic Avenue. Another crack split open under the city, and more houses slumped and tilted.

Emotion clogged my throat.

Saxony and Georjayna, red and blond hair whipping in the wind, came together, talking and gesturing. Targa came running up the beach, wet and half-naked with her shirt slapping around her thighs. She threw her arms around them and they held one another. Their heads bent together, and gesturing, they seemed to be shouting words over the noise of the storm.

Then, as one, they broke apart and scattered along the beach. Targa ran into the water, bracing herself waist-deep in the churning Atlantic.

Georjie ran across Atlantic Avenue and planted her bare feet in the soil.

Saxony ran furthest, up the beach to where huge boulders had been collected and made a kind of break. She climbed up on the rocks and skipped over them, stopping on a large flat one several meters into the water. As she turned to face the Archon, her eyes were lit like lanterns. Her fists ignited with blue-white flame. Streaks of fire reached into the air. Her arms had become twin flame-throwers.

Thunder crashed as the Archon turned toward the source of the flame.

At the Archon's back, a cliff suddenly jutted up from the Earth. The burnt wrecks of houses splintered and fell back out of view as the earth made a gaping mouth fixing to swallow the Archon whole. From the wall of soil, thick roots like tentacles reached for the Archon, wrapping around and through its bulk. The terrain arched over the beast's head and crashed down over it, swallowing it. A dust cloud obscured everything, filling the air with particles of dirt.

Two massive fists rose from the Atlantic and crashed over everything. The water swallowed the dust and churned over the shores and part of Atlantic Avenue where the Archon had been.

As the water swirled away and the smoke and fire from Saxony's flames dwindled, I phased into spirit.

My heart dropped.

The Archon surged upward through the soil and water and rose back into the sky, unaffected. Thunder rolled like wicked laughter and those horrible nuclear eyes found the tiny frames of its attackers. The sands of the Euroklydon swirled overhead, banking for another attack.

It was no use. It would not be put down. Those wicked horns lowered as the beast dropped to all fours, targeting Saxony as she stood on the rock, eyes still blazing, fists still flaming. She lifted her hands and slowly beckoned it. My heart swelled with pride.

Targa disappeared under the water and reappeared at the base of the rock where Saxony stood. Georjie ran across the beach and stood with her feet in the sand in front of Saxony and Targa. The three of them faced the Archon, tense, waiting. The ocean surged as Targa's blue eyes blazed righteous anger. Georjie's eyes were white and blazing, while Saxony's glowed red.

My heart filled with love for them. They would fight to the death, this was apparent. This was also something I could not allow.

When all else fails, love does not.

I wheeled fast and tight, heading out over the Atlantic with Saltford at my back. Picking up speed, I wheeled again, shooting straight toward the Archon which was still advancing on my friends.

Its horns rose against the sky as it reared back on hind legs, lifting massive, blurry claws.

Aiming for the region of the heart, where the Euroklydon had opened a smoldering red gash in its smoky hide, I passed over my friends' heads. Pinning my wings tight to my body, I arrowed for a target I knew was there but couldn't see.

A fraction of a second before impact, I phased.

28

SAXONY

A starburst of lightning flashed in the sky. Shards of light exploded from the central point of the storm-beast. I blinked and shielded my eyes, wincing at the pain in them as the light sliced through my vision and seemed to pierce my brain with a lance.

While I blinked at the sky, the scene over Saltford suddenly and drastically changed.

The storm-beast had vanished. The sky was a beautiful crystalline blue, save for the smoke from fires and the dust from disturbed earth hanging in low clouds over Atlantic Avenue.

The sounds of alarms filled the air, and a few small figures could be seen moving in the streets.

The tempest which had made war with the storm-beast looked momentarily lost. Losing power, the sands swirled and shifted in the skies, as though searching for its target. It was beautiful to behold, like a flock of starlings flying together against the clear canvas of blue.

"What...what just happened?" Targa reached up to help me down off the rock.

We waded out of the Atlantic and met Georjie on the beach.

"Did you see the falcon?" Georjie asked, throwing her arms around Targa and me and squeezing us hard.

"What falcon?" Targa asked, her voice sharp. She pulled back and looked from Georjie to me. Only now did her face truly telegraph fear. Not once during the whole horrific attack had Targa looked as frightened as she did now.

"I thought I'd imagined it," I rasped, rubbing a hand across my nose.

"*What* falcon?" Targa's voice cracked.

I looked at Targa and put a hand over the wet hair at the nape of her neck. "It was there for only a moment, and then...the flash of light."

"No," Targa whispered. A fat tear rolled down one cheek, followed by another and another and then her eyes were streaming endlessly. "No. She didn't."

"She'll be all right." Georjie put her hands on either side of Targa's face, wiping away the tears that just kept coming. "She's a *Hanta*. She fights demons, that's what she does. She'll show up, you'll see. She said she takes them deep underground, that's gotta take a bit of time. Don't you think?" Georjie wrapped her arms around Targa and looked at me over Targa's black hair, pleading for agreement.

I nodded. "She'll be back. Just give her a minute."

I wrapped my arms around Georjie and Targa and took a breath. I felt Targa shiver so I let my fire heat my body up, warming her until steam rose from her shirt and her hair. She relaxed against my warmth.

I found that my throat had closed up and I thought there was a good possibility it would never open again. I searched the skies and ground for Akiko, hoping for another glimpse of the brave little falcon. My heartbeat slowed to heavy, aching thuds.

The water had begun to settle. The shores of the Atlantic were full of garbage—broken fishing boats, fishing gear, ropes and nets, and random bits of trash which swept in and out of the ocean. The water was a murky brown and capped with dirty foam.

"Guys..." Georjie pulled away from our hug and drew our attention from the water to the sky. She took a step back. "Whoa."

The swirling sand funneled together and was coming straight for us. I could have sworn for a moment I saw a face in the shifting particles—a familiar face.

"It's..." I began.

The sand arrowed for the beach and came together. As though filling a hollow glass sculpture, legs formed of the sand, which grew into a pelvis and a torso.

As her arms congealed and her head topped the sand-figurine now walking across the wrecked beach toward us, I somehow found her name. "It's Petra."

She became flesh in full color, naked and bone dry save for her bare feet as a wave swept over them. Her dark hair was wild and flew around in a breeze and then settled over her brown shoulders. She was a vision straight out of poetry as she closed the distance between us, her expression calm.

"Of course that was you," Georjie said on an exhale. "Tempest. Euroklydon."

"You're frightening," I said, my voice hoarse. The words sounded distant to my ears, like someone else had said them. And my eyes went from Petra to the skies, still searching, still waiting for the return of a certain avian creature. Any moment now, Akiko would phase into flesh on the beach and join us.

"Are you guys okay?" Petra bent and grabbed a torn yellow raincoat from the random garbage on the beach. She made a face of disgust as she pulled the wet plastic coat over her bare torso and zipped it up. "I don't know what happened. One second that thing was there and then, boom, it just vanished!"

The sound of alarms and sirens and shouting voices had only increased and carried on the breeze. But the beach was empty except for us.

Taking the idea from Petra, Georjie went and picked up a piece of canvas. She held it out to Targa. "Cover up, hon. There are people with cell phones around. I'm already freaked out about the attention we're going to get when the worst of this passes."

"You were recorded?" Petra asked.

I nodded. "Pretty sure Georjie was. When the storm first started."

"That was no storm." Petra's face grew thunderous. "It was pure evil. Nakesh made the proverbial deal with the devil, if you know what I mean."

Targa, Georjie, and I gaped at her in shock.

"How do you know that?" Targa asked, half-heartedly holding the shred of canvas around herself. "I mean, we know it was evil, but how do you know Mr. Nakesh made a deal with that thing?"

"Because I unleashed it by accident when I confronted him." Petra's mouth was a flat line. "There is no more Field Station Eleven, by the way. No more Project Expansion."

"I don't care about the project anymore. Today, there was almost no more Saltford," I said. "I need to find my family."

"I don't even know where to start. I need to call my mom." Targa looked around, bewildered. "I lost my cell in the water."

Georjie nodded. "You can use mine. I should call Mom, too. And then see if there's anything left of our house."

"And you?" I asked Petra.

"There's someone I need to find, just down that way," Petra replied as we began moving across the wrecked beach toward the city. "Where's Akiko, by the way? Was she with you?"

Georjie, Targa, and I shared a look of worry.

"We don't know where she is, but there's a pretty good chance that she took down that thing all by herself."

Petra's eyebrows spiked upward. "Seriously? What is she? I've been dying to ask," Petra said. "TNC said they didn't want her and I've been confused by that ever since."

"*Akuna Hanta*," Targa said. "A hunter of demons."

Petra took this in and then started laughing.

Targa and I shared a bemused look.

"A demon hunter? Really?" Petra said through her laughter.

"Why is that funny?" Georjie asked as we skirted the mess of dirt and wreckage covering Atlantic Avenue.

"Nakesh made a deal with an ancient demonic force and then tried to hire three Elementals to help him execute his evil plan. Three Elementals, who happened to be best friends with a demon hunter." She continued laughing. "Now *that* is poetic justice."

The rest of us didn't find it quite so funny because our demon hunter was still missing.

"I don't get how building domes for people to live in is an evil plan," Georjie said. "It might have been a crackpot idea, but it still seemed like their hearts were in the right place."

Petra lost her smile. "I have a friend who I'm hoping will be able to explain it to me, too. But you'll have to trust me for now, TNC's intentions were not altruistic. That reminds me, Georjayna, the plants from the prototype may need your attention. I took the dome down."

Georjayna nodded distractedly. "Okay."

We walked together in silence for a while, listening to a city in shock and ruminating.

Petra spoke up again. "How important is it to keep your identities a secret?"

"Very," I said. "Extremely."

I thought of how much Basil had impressed upon me that no one but my family, he, and the other students at Arcturus know what I was. I had already spilled the beans to my friends, which he wasn't going to be happy about. Now the world was going to know and probably have video evidence very shortly uploaded to the web once the people who took the recordings got their bearings. It might have been done already.

"It's imperative." Targa had an edge to her voice.

"Hey!" A voice pulled our attention down the beach to where a man was running toward us, waving. He had a cut on his forehead and part of one pantleg was burnt. The skin of his shin was red and blistered, but it seemed by his expression that he wasn't in any pain.

We stopped walking to watch him approach.

"I've been looking for you," he said to me, panting as he stopped just a few feet away. He bent over and gasped for air. "You're the fire lady. What you did..." He straightened, catching his breath. He shook his head in wonderment. "I always thought there had to be people like you out there. Pyromancers, you know."

I opened my mouth but didn't know what to say.

"She's not a pyromancer," said Targa, but the sound of her voice made me turn and gape at her. Her voice had become layered and musical, like violins that seemed to come from everywhere. "She's just a teenager who goes to Saltford High."

"Not a pyromancer..." The man's face went soft and expressionless, his eyes vacant, as he repeated after her.

"Saltford was hit by an earthquake and a freak storm today, nothing more." Targa continued speaking in that incredible voice.

Georjie, Petra, and I shared looks of amazement.

"There was nothing supernatural about what went on," she continued.

"Nothing supernatural..."

By the time she was done with him, the man seemed to be confused about why he was on the beach. He murmured something about needing to find his dog before wandering off at a stagger which then became a jog.

"Are you going to do that to everyone in Saltford who thinks they saw something cray-cray?" I asked Targa. "'Cause that could be tricky."

Targa shook her head and let out a defeated sigh. "I don't know. There's going to be fallout from this. My mom is going to freak out if anyone caught me on tape."

"They wouldn't have caught you in mermaid form, surely," I suggested, putting an arm around Targa's shoulders. "You were underwater where no one could see you."

"And what about stopping the wave?"

"Hey at least you didn't have fins while you're doing it." I gave her a reassuring squeeze but I understand how she felt. I had thrown a lot of fire around, and someone had almost certainly caught Georjie lacing vines through the school. Pretty much every student had a mobile phone with a video camera on them at all times.

"Would you like me to send out an EMP?" Petra asked.

"EM-" Georjie began, puzzled.

"Electromagnetic pulse," she explained.

"You can do that?"

"Of course she can," I added with a laugh. "Girl can turn into a sandstorm and make force-fields. An EMP is a cakewalk."

"What would an EMP do?" Targa stepped gingerly around a bunch of broken glass on the road.

"Fry all the electronics in the city, all the cell phones, laptops, computers..."

"Emergency vehicles, hospital machines," Georjie added. The sound of sirens from the city took over when no one said anything right away. "Maybe now isn't the best time to cut off communication and handicap the emergency teams."

"Tempting, though." Targa gave a nervous laugh.

"Listen," Petra said, stopping us at the intersection of Atlantic and Grace. "I have a friend who is an amazing hacker. He's the whole reason TNC's evil plan was stalled. If something turns up on the internet that you're not happy with, I'm sure he'll be able to take it down. Two things are going to work in your favor in this situation." She held up one finger. "First, do you have any idea how much fake video there is online claiming to have caught a superhuman on tape? Anyone who has access to a computer and some mediocre CG skills can make something that's pretty convincing. You can claim it was faked and most people would believe you."

"And the second thing?" I prompted, not overly comforted by the first.

Another finger joined the first. "People are going to be so freaked out by the storm itself, I can't imagine a handful of kids seeing your powers at work are going to trump it."

She put down her hand and let this all think in.

"Why don't you just wait and see what happens." Petra shifted inside her rain jacket again. "Between Jesse's skill and Targa's voice, I bet we can put it down well enough until it all blows over."

It was the only plan we had that didn't involve crippling the city at a time when it needed all the functioning electronics and communication lines that still worked, so we agreed.

Petra headed off in the direction of a residential area, while Targa, Georjie, and I agreed to stick together. We began to walk west, the direction of my home. We kept looking over our shoulders toward the ocean, expectant of Akiko's return.

29

SAXONY

Saltford was brought to its knees, but it didn't lose its head. Schools were repurposed into temporary shelters for those who had lost their homes. Except for Saltford High, which would need to be completely rebuilt because that damage was permanent. Georjie had removed all of the vines holding up the rubble of the school once darkness had fallen, but not before news crews got photos of the incredible sight.

Amazingly, the death toll was only seven, and one petite Asian girl was still unaccounted for. Injuries, on the other hand, were in the thousands. It seemed almost everyone in Saltford had at least a cut or a scrape. There was a lot of smoke inhalation, a lot of broken bones, and the burn unit was almost full with victims of the fires. Remarkably, many of these injured people recovered fully and quickly subsequent to a visit from a certain blond volunteer.

Nothing had publicly surfaced about three superhuman girls working together to save Saltford, but I was sure it was only a matter of time.

The storm was being touted as Petra had suggested it would be—a freak occurrence of nature, and this was what my parents and RJ all believed as well. I didn't see much point in setting them straight. Jack, however, practically locked me in his room until I told him the whole story, including the offer from TNC, since I couldn't hide anything from him anyway.

I called Basil to let him know my trip to England to attend Arcturus would be delayed while I helped clean up my neighborhood and helped friends who were impacted by the quake to rebuild.

The Sutherland home and my home escaped unscathed, but Targa's trailer had been swallowed up along with many of the trailers in her park. She stayed with Georjie until Mira got home and the two of them checked into a hotel while they decided what to do. My money was on them going back to Poland right away rather than having Targa finish school in Saltford. Our high school was a pile of rubble, so she'd have to relocate anyway, and why stay in a place where people knew her face and someone might confront her about what had happened during the storm?

Liz came home right away to be with Georjie, and to her credit, she put all of her work on hold to help the clean-up efforts.

It was going to take a while to rebuild. There were entire neighborhoods with gorges running through them which would have to be cleaned up and stabilized and decisions made about what to do with the property.

As the days passed, though, my heart grew heavier and heavier. Akiko had still not turned up, and not having any idea what happened to her was weighing us down like rocks.

About a week after the attack, Georjie texted Targa and me with an SOS to meet at her place with a characteristically cryptic message: *I received a package in the mail. You guys have to see this.*

Georjie ushered us into her front foyer and closed the door. She had a fat envelope in her hand.

"Come on. I'll make you guys a coffee," she said, sprinting up the stairs.

Targa and I shared a look as we kicked off our shoes and followed her up to the kitchen. Georjie made us cappuccinos and we sat at the table together. Georjie slid the envelope across to me.

"Open it."

Georjie's address had been messily scrawled on the front of the envelope, but the handwriting was unfamiliar and barely readable.

"There's no return address."

Georjie shook her head. "No. But it's from Petra."

I took the envelope and pulled out a thick wad of folded paper. I opened it up and stared at the documents with confusion.

"How do you know?" Targa peered over my shoulder.

"Petra and I went to take care of the plants at the dome site," Georjie explained. "She said she'd be sending something."

It dawned on me after flipping through a few pages what I was looking at. "These are deeds!"

"Deeds to what?" Targa took some of the pages and read them, brows pinched.

I looked up at Georjie, my jaw slack. "To TNC's dome properties. Petra's friend must have dug these up."

Georjie was nodding. "Look at the names. Recognize any of them?"

I scanned over several before running into one I recognized, then another, and another. "They're all famous people. Rich people, politicians, movie stars."

"Only rich and famous people," Georjie emphasized. "You might not know all of those names, but I can guarantee you that if you start looking them up, you'll find they're all affluent and powerful. Elite families with old money. Relations of world leaders, including presidential families."

"So they never had any intention of offering property inside the domes to middle-class or poor people? They never earmarked anything for charity?"

"Nope. Petra's brilliant computer guy pulled up blueprints and zoning documents. There is nothing to support that they ever planned to give anything to poorer people, or even regular people. It was all offered only to rich and powerful people. And it gets worse."

"There is so much here," I said, sifting through the pages, "it'll take forever to make sense of it."

"Worse?" Targa asked, pushing her coffee aside and spreading out some of the documents. "How does it get worse?"

"The domes were never conceived as permanent places to live, the way TNC wanted us to think. They were conceived as more like the world's fanciest bomb shelters." Georjie nodded at the stack of paper. "There's a letter from Petra at the back. It's messy, looks like she wrote it in a hurry, but she explains what's inside and said that we need to destroy all of this evidence when we're done with it."

"I'll say," I muttered.

"That thing, the creature, it wasn't the only one. It was just the *closest* one. TNC was planning a huge catastrophe for every major continent, and it was all to feed the Archons. She said that about every seventy-five years or so, the Archons need to feast. The small-time stuff that happens isn't enough for them. The last one was World War II and the Holocaust."

"It's been seventy-three years since World War II," Targa said. "So, what? It was time? And this was their plan?" She shuddered visibly. "It's beyond ghastly, it's incomprehensible."

"A plague for North America, a nuke for Asia, poisonous rain for Europe," Georjie listed them off on her fingers. "But they wanted to offer rich and important people a way to be protected while the outside world imploded. If their plan went so far as to decimate the planet, they'd have people to rebuild the population with. Hence, the domes."

"I can't even believe the plot was this big," I sputtered. "This is insane. This is a level of evil there are no words for."

"That's what Petra and Akiko stopped from happening," Georjie added, quietly.

"Where is Petra now?"

"Read for yourself." Georjie slid a handwritten page toward Targa and me.

I read aloud.

Dear Elementals,

I said I would try and explain the domes better, well, this is the best we can do at the moment. What I've sent you is a jumbled mess of documents, and I'm sorry I'm not there to make better sense of it. But I have faith you'll see the full picture and I know you'll agree that the most urgent thing right now is to kill this monster while it's crippled. Devin Nakesh is gone, so it's possible TNC's deal with the Archons is off, but we don't know for sure. We don't know if TNC is still trying to manufacture domes on other continents right now or not, but it doesn't matter. They won't succeed. TNC will not survive to execute another project, not as long as I have wind in my lungs. I promise you that.

"That's it?" I turned it over, looking for more.

"It's all she had time for, I guess."

"It's enough." Targa shuddered. "I don't know about you guys but I've had enough of sinister plots and freak demonic storms and big corporations with lots of money and power. I'm about ready to run and hide in the ocean."

"Or Poland," Georjie said with a smile. She began gathering the documents and shoving them back in the envelope. "If you guys don't object, I'm going to burn these."

We didn't.

Georjie went to a cupboard and got a large metal bowl. She beckoned us outside on the second level porch and set the bowl on the stone table. She put the papers in the bowl and looked at me.

I reached out a finger and touched the nearest page, igniting the whole thing. We each took a seat and watched the papers burn and the smoke drift up into a clean evening sky.

"Why us?" Targa murmured, her eyes on the flame as it began to die down.

"Why us what?" I asked, crossing my arms and leaning on the table.

"Why are we Elementals? In all the craziness that has taken place since the night of our sleepover, we haven't had two seconds of peace to really talk about it."

Georjie chuckled. "It's true. I was about to speculate when Petra knocked on the door and interrupted us. Remember?"

It did come to my memory. "You said you had a theory about it."

"Feels wrong to share it without Akiko here, though," Targa said.

"I had a kind of vision of the future when I was in Ireland," Georjie said. "I didn't tell you guys about it before because…" She paused. "Because I could see you," she looked at me and her eyes cut to Targa, "and you. But…"

"You couldn't see Akiko." The hairs on my forearms stood at attention.

Georjie nodded and looked miserable.

"It's not your fault. No one knew what was coming." I said these comforting words to Georjie, but my stomach felt like stone. It was confirmation that Akiko really was gone.

"Akiko said herself that she didn't think she was one of us," Targa said, her voice just above a whisper.

"She'll always be one of us," I said, my throat tightening.

"Of course," Georjie said, "Akiko is family. But she's not an Elemental, she's something else, something not so earthly."

"So what's your theory then?" Targa's eyes looked almost black in the dying light. They shone as they looked at Georjie, expectant.

"When I got home from Ireland, I went out into my backyard and took off my shoes."

"If anyone had ever told me I'd see you walk barefoot through dirt I would have laughed in their face," I said with a smile. "Oh, how things change."

"Yeah." Targa chuckled.

Georjie smiled. "Have you guys ever heard of ley lines?"

I shook my head and Targa said she hadn't either.

"My Aunt Faith first told me about them. She said they are energetically rich lines running through the earth like a grid. Ley lines connect places with supernatural significance. The places in the grid where the ley lines meet are, as you can imagine, very rich with supernatural energy. And the ley lines move; they're not always in the same place. When I take off my shoes and stand with my feet in the dirt, I can see them."

Targa and I shared an impressed glance. "Really?" I leaned forward. "What do they look like?"

"Like a stripe of bright light."

"The way your eyes look when you're the Wise," Targa added.

Georjie nodded. "Saltford sits at the intersection of three of these lines. In fact, our high school sits right where they cross."

I dropped my chin with surprise. "Three?"

We went silent and listened to the crickets chirp for a moment.

"So, what do you think that means?" I asked.

"With no one to explain it to me, I have to guess," Georjie said. "But I think it means Gaia, if you want to use the term, has chosen us to be a benevolent force against forces like this." She jerked her chin at the cinders in the bowl. "Maybe this is nature's way of fighting back?"

"Sat," Targa said.

"What?" Georjie and I looked at her, confused.

"You said *sits* at the intersection of three ley lines. But our high school doesn't exist anymore."

"Maybe that's a good thing," I said holding up my hands. "Don't shoot me, but my little brother has some funky powers too, and maybe Gaia wasn't sure where to stop. I don't fancy someone like Nick Hiller or Pat Ulley getting supernatural powers, do you?"

Georjie and Targa laughed at the idea of two of the biggest bullies in school becoming supernaturals.

Georjie leaned forward. "They say that after high school, friends grow apart and real life begins." She looked at me. "You're going to go to Arcturus and who knows who you'll meet and what you'll learn." She shifted her gaze to Targa. "If I can read you right, I'm guessing you're going to be on a plane to Poland pretty soon."

Targa didn't deny it.

Georjie reached out a hand and clasped one of mine and one of Targa's, bringing them together and putting her other hand over the top.

"I promise, that no matter where life takes us, no matter how far apart we might travel, that if you ever need me, I'll come running. You don't have to promise me the same, I would never put that kind of pressure on you, but I want you to know that everything I am loves everything you are, and always will."

It surprised me to discover I had tears pouring down my face, and neither Targa's nor Georjie's cheeks were dry either. I squeezed my friends' hands.

"Me too," I sniffed. "I can't say it as eloquently as that. But I love you both. When you need me, you call me. I'll move heaven and earth to be there."

Targa's eyes were shining and water was streaming from her eyes unbidden. "I also promise this."

EPILOGUE

AKIKO

A LONG SWORD lit with blue flames stood point down in a block of white marble. The landscape was a white backdrop of nothingness. I was in the Æther, but I couldn't remember getting here. I looked down at myself, my hands. I was whole, and dressed in jeans and a white and blue plaid shirt. It was an outfit I knew well and in fact it was the last outfit I could remember wearing. I looked up at the flaming sword again, then looked behind myself for someone or something that might clue me in to what was happening.

"Yuudai?" My voice echoed into infinity.

Slowly, my friend materialized from the white.

"Akiko," he began, but stopped when he saw the flaming sword. His face became still. "So, you won then."

"Won?"

"You defeated the Archon."

I gasped and staggered backward as the memory hit me. It came flooding out of the white and all around me, filling my memory suddenly like a brilliant liquid.

I'm dead. I should be dead. Is this death?

"Why are you here?" was the question that came out of my mouth.

"You called me, Akiko," Yuudai answered with a smile, his black hair swayed gently against his shoulders, moving from the heat of the sword.

"Why am *I* here?" Yes, that was a better question.

"To take this up, I presume." Yuudai gestured to the sword. "After all, it's got your name on it."

I stared at the sword, seeing no name anywhere. I walked forward, and the blazing blue fire from the sword was both hot and cold against my face. I had *sensation*. It was the only thing I could feel, in fact. My eyes dropped the length of it to the white marble where glyphs were engraved into the stone. I squinted at them and they seemed to swim and change and form a word I could read. My own name.

"I don't understand, Yuudai. Help me make sense of this, please." My fingers curled in and out and I found myself positively *yearning* to take the sword in my hand.

He chuckled softly. "I should think it self-explanatory, but if you need it spelled out, I can do that. Little *Hanta* willingly gave up her life in the ultimate act of love."

"So I *did* die then?"

"It's what you thought was going to happen," he went on, "otherwise you would not see this beautiful flaming weapon in front of you. But *Hanta* don't die. They ascend."

"Asc-" I stopped. "What am I now then? An archangel or something?"

Yuudai put a finger to his lips and smiled. "Drop the *arch*, I think, but I'm no expert."

I let out a long breath and the blue flames leapt and danced toward me, calling to me. "What happens when I touch it?"

"We'll say goodbye, I should think. You'll be going where I can't follow." He spread his hands. "The rest is a mystery."

"Can I ever be human again?" I looked at him. "Will I ever see my friends again?"

I was already grasping for their names, which seemed to be fading from my memory the way water evaporates from cloth.

"You were never human to begin with, Akiko."

"Wait!" There were faces swimming in my mind, faces I loved but faces that were already fading. "I don't want to forget!"

I sucked in a breath, clutching at the memories of my human experience. I was losing them. And fast.

Desperately, I called out to the man with the black hair who was also fading into the white. "Tell them I love them!" Tell them..."

He was gone. There was nothing but me and the blue sword and being drawn toward it like a magnet. The sword was irresistible.

I moved forward on a strong, confident stride with nothing else in my mind but the sword.

My sword.

I wrapped my hands around the flaming blue handle, pulling it free from the marble. The blue flames engulfed my hand, my arm, my body, filling me, changing me.

I am Malachi, the sword whispered to my mind. *Welcome, Angel.*

<<<<>>>>

WHAT TO READ NEXT…

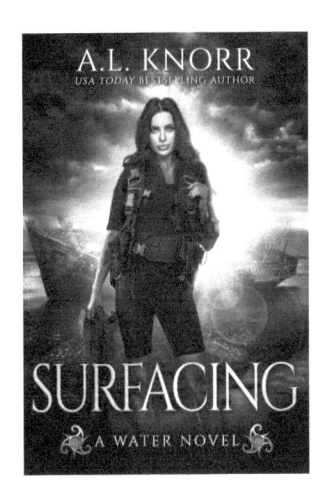

Surfacing ties together Returning and Born of Water and chronicles Mira's struggles as a single mom and how she joined the all-male salvage team. Don't miss it! Order your copy on Amazon

ACKNOWLEDGMENTS

A huge thank you to Teresa Hull and Nicola Aquino for their sharp eyes and even sharper questions. Thank you to my VIP Reader's for their never ending support and encouragement (and defence against trolls). Thank you to my family and friends for having my back and standing with me when things are hard. Thank you to YOU, dear reader for having enough faith in me to pick this book up and make it to the end of the Elemental Origins Series!

Does this book signal the end of these characters' stories? Not at all! Even now I am working on *Surfacing*, a story that links *Returning* to *Born of Water*. I also have more stories percolating for Saxony, Targa, and Georjayna. I hope you'll join them on their adventures!

If you enjoyed this story, or any of my work, please take the time to pen a review on Amazon, they help authors like me even more than you know! Positive reviews make a title more visible so other readers who might like them can find them more easily.

Thank you again for spending some of your reading time with me. Now it's back to the keyboard!

Warm hugs,
Abby

ABOUT THE AUTHOR

A.L. Knorr is a rocketing Canadian author with more than 116,500 copies of her books downloaded in her first year of publishing. A nature enthusiast who loves shipwrecks, nautical history, and well-written fantasy, Abby dreamed of being a writer since she understood what a story was. She has plans to expand the Elemental stories, especially focusing on mermaid stories in 2018. Join Abby and other readers in her private VIP Reader Lounge group on Facebook, or sign up for a free copy of *Returning, Episode I* on her website at www.alknorrbooks.com.